STORIES SUBVERSIVE: THROUGH THE FIELD WITH GLOVES OFF

STORIES SUBVERSIVE: THROUGH THE FIELD WITH GLOVES OFF

Short Fiction by Nellie L. McClung

CANADIAN
SHORT
STORY
LIBRARY
No. 20

Edited and
with an introduction by
Marilyn I. Davis

University of Ottawa Press

Canadian Short Story Library
John Moss, General Editor

© University of Ottawa Press, 1996
Printed and bound in Canada
ISBN 0-7766-0424-4

Introduction © Marilyn I. Davis.
All stories are reproduced by permission of the McClung
Estate.

Canadian Cataloguing in Publication Data
Main entry under title:
McClung, Nellie L., 1873–1951
    Stories subversive: through the field with gloves off:
short fiction

(The Canadian short story library; no. 20)
Includes bibliographical references.
ISBN 0-7766-0424-4

I. Davis, Marilyn I., 1930- II. Title. III. Series.

PS8525.C52S86 1996   C813'.52   C96-900917-8
PR9199.3.M4237S86 1996

University of Ottawa Press gratefully acknowledges the support
extended to its publishing programme by the Canada Council, the
Department of Canadian Heritage, and the University of Ottawa.

Series design concept: Miriam Bloom
Cover photo courtesy of B.C. Archives and Records Service
(Cat. No. 84316)
Book design: Marie Tappin

Distributed in the U.K. by Cardiff Academic Press Ltd., St. Fagans Road,
Fairwater, Cardiff CF5 3AE

CONTENTS

Introduction

Nellie Letitia McClung (1873–1951) was an extremely popular author in her time. It was through her recitation tours in southern Manitoba and Ontario that many Canadians first came to know her.[1] McClung's recitals of passages from her first two novels—*Sowing Seeds in Danny* (1908) and its sequel, *The Second Chance* (1910)—did much to introduce both westerners and easterners to her fiction.

Newspaper accounts in both Manitoba and Ontario praised her graceful manner, her clear enunciation—every syllable could be heard in the furthest corner of the churches and halls where she read—and her sparkling eyes, which "combine with a naturally strong and attractive personality to hold her audiences simply spell-bound." She provoked roars of laughter and gentle tears, and particularly appealed to her audiences for her natural manner: she "lacks the less fascinating mannerisms of the average elocutionist . . . [and] she makes the scenes seem to be taken from somewhere around one's own home, and the characters are very real. . . ." McClung was greeted by capacity crowds wherever she went and invariably "took her audiences by storm." She received so many requests from audiences in Ontario on her first tour that she was persuaded to return a year later (1911). In Toronto alone, the public demanded that she give at least five recitals in 1910.[2]

McClung's first novel, *Sowing Seeds in Danny*, was a Canadian bestseller that has continued to charm readers through numerous reprints, the latest in 1965. Her short story "The Neutral Fuse," which is included in this selection, secured honourable mention in *O'Brien's Best Short Stories* (1925), "an honour accorded only two or three Canadian writers in the past."[3] The McClung short story "Flowing Gold," which first appeared in the Toronto *Star Weekly* in early January 1931, was given a "very clever radio adaptation by Edgar Stone," director of the University of Toronto's Hart House Theatre. It was dramatized on the Toronto radio station CFRB. The same adaptation was staged by the Hart House Players on 15 January 1931 and again one week later.[4] McClung's Canadian publisher had advised her, in late 1905, to submit short stories to "magazines, or large weeklies, American as well as Canadian, in order to get your name known to the public. Then you would have a prepared constituency of readers . . ."[5] for a first novel. Soon she began to receive numerous requests for short stories from American magazines like the *Ladies' Home Journal*, the *Delineator* (where Theodore Dreiser held sway),[6] *The American Magazine*, and the *Woman's Home Companion*. In Canada, periodicals such as *Canadian Magazine*, *Saturday Night*, and *Canadian Home Journal* vied for her short stories. McClung's became a household name in both countries. Theodore Dreiser wrote to her American publisher: "I hope you will let me have more of her work. . . ."[7] In Canada, M.O. Hammond of the Toronto *Globe* shrewdly advertised that he had secured a McClung short story: "It is one of the best short stories published in recent years . . . you realize at once why publishers are so eager for control of her manuscripts."[8]

Since those days, mainstream literary critics— mainly male critics—have almost consistently belittled and dismissed McClung's fiction as sentimental, melodramatic, and romanticized "rural idylls" when, in fact, the *essential* thrust of her writing is antiromantic.[9] Her work is filled with irony and satire—sometimes gently spoofing, sometimes biting—especially when it evokes the harsher realities of women's lives during the early days of the opening of the West: "winter-killed souls," she calls these spirit-broken women.[10] Certainly no author writing in the first quarter of this century could entirely escape such Victorian literary influences as optimism. Clara Thomas, for one, has countered the masculine tendency to debase McClung's work, by reading her fiction as "realism written in the romantic mode."[11]

McClung, in this respect, was often criticized for her happy endings. She knew very well that "this world in which we find ourselves . . . is a bad world in some ways and

a very sad world some times," and some of her short stories
reflect this perspective, particularly those with rural settings.
Still, her writer's creed convinced her that authors can help
a troubled world "by telling the truth. Unreal writing does
no good, and although I am not fond of sordid ugliness, I
prefer being dragged through the sewers of reality, to reading something unrelated to life." When sordid details in fiction were purposeful McClung accepted them. When they
appeared merely as "cheap sensationalism" she rejected
them. "I think a writer should above all things portray life,"
she asserted. Therefore, "because there are more decent
people than the other kind, it is keeping nearer to the truth
to portray those who go right, rather than of those who go
wrong." Hence her many happy endings.[12]

McClung's rejection of despair was born of her
childhood pioneer experiences in the West. She lived
through family tragedies—and near tragedies—and things
appeared hopeless until obstacles were seemingly miracu-
lously overcome. Prosperity and disaster alternated from
year to year, the vagaries of the prairie climate bringing one
year drought, failed crops, and financial adversity, the next
year the opposite. When McClung was older she recognized
the drab, barren, treadmill existence of some of her neigh-
bours, the never-ending emptiness of their lives. Even as a
child of eight as she and her family trekked westward with
optimism to God's promised land, she came face to face
with the despair of some would-be pioneers who had given
up and straggled backward, falling away from the Mooneys'
determined forward march. McClung's optimism was born,
too, of her religious upbringing, which taught her that to
maintain hope in the face of apparently unendurable hard-
ship was a better response than to give in to pessimism and
defeat. The western pioneer who lacked hope had little
chance of surviving. Optimism was also a trait of McClung's
ebullient personality; she searched always for the better
qualities in the people she met and in the human condition,
learned, perhaps, from her most beloved author, Charles
Dickens. Optimism, for McClung, was not an acquired

Victorian literary affectation. Her work, in this respect, reflects not only her own experience but the experience of others in her environment, who knew that a positive outlook could sustain one, whereas pessimism was pointless and defeatist.

Similarly, because she frequently used her fiction as a vehicle for her feminist ideas—to oppose those laws and tools of social conditioning that oppressed women of her day—McClung has been labelled a didactic moralizer whose "crusading spirit led her often to present what she saw in the forms of the Methodist and temperance literature of the day." [13]

Perhaps one should point out, regarding the term *didacticism*, that the standard authorities on literary terminology have for many years held that "all literary art exists to communicate something," that the term "is often used contemptuously, but if all didactic writing were destroyed all literatures would be greatly impoverished." "Didacticism," the authorities add, "is an acceptable aspect of literature unless it becomes deplorably self-righteous in tone." [14]

McClung was too intelligently broad-minded, too humane and compassionate, and far too honest and down-to-earth to write in a self-righteous manner. The closest she comes to doing so is in the short story "The Grim Fact of Sisterhood," which is reprinted in this representative selection of McClung's short fiction. As one of the leading first-wave feminists of her day, she approached fiction from the modern sociologist's perspective, analyzing social institutions and social conditioning in her lifelong fight to emancipate women from the oppression of patriarchal society.

McClung set out to write fiction with two purposes in mind. On the one hand, she sought "to brighten the spirits of rural people in the West"—"my people," she affectionately called them—"whose lives were burdened by drudgery in the early pioneer days. To this end she employed considerable humour, a trait which was a natural part of her disposition." [15] Her engaging sense of humour is best reflected in this selection of McClung short stories by "The Live Wire,"

"The Elusive Vote," and "Banking in London." On the other hand, she was acutely aware of the "winter-killed" souls of many rural women, who were severely oppressed not only by the trials and privations of their primitive existence, but by the ways in which their husbands marginalized women by treating them as chattels and as second-class citizens. Women and children have rights, McClung argued, that are not given credence in male-dominated society. She used her fiction as a vehicle to make both men and women aware of the undue restrictions on women and the anti-female laws and attitudes of the day. Today's feminists would call this *consciousness-raising*, and they would relegate the contemptuous term *didactic* to the dustbin.

One brief example of humour combined with feminist consciousness-raising can be found in McClung's third novel, *Painted Fires* (1925). A young girl innocently reports to her church youth group:

> "Our washerwoman's sister killed her man up at Gimli." Her employer goes to visit the convict to see if she won't repent and feel sorry. The convict says indeed she is sorry, "sorry she had not killed him years ago . . . God had been good to her and let her find the axe just as she was getting the worst of it."[16]

The employer comes home "all shaken up"; indeed the passage is meant to shake the book's readers up, and force them to re-think their values. Our modern judicial system is still struggling with the issue of convicting battered women who, when they can take no more, kill their husbands. Prison or probation?

In another passage McClung comments with her usual caustic irony, about the case of a woman who is viciously hit over the head with a chair by a husband who disagrees with her: "Such crude methods of dealing with women can only be safely used inside the hallowed precincts of matrimony,"[17] where married women were considered objects by their husbands, though not always with such disastrous results.

Too many people, Nellie McClung once said, "walk through the field with gloves on,"[18] something male critics commonly accuse McClung herself of doing. One is forced to wonder whether they have actually read her work, let alone given it close textual analysis. Let us scan the issues that crop up in McClung's fiction:

> wife and child battering; verbal and emotional abuse (of wives by their husbands); alcoholism (with the damage it inflicts on families); unnecessary squalor; prairie madness caused by a severe sense of isolation and loneliness; vote fixing; racial prejudice with its resultant irrational hatred; injustice; illegitimacy and single motherhood; loss of faith in a beneficent God because of unendurable hardships; the greedy hoarding of money as an end in itself; female suffrage and antiquated laws against women; lives of quiet desperation because of helpless bondage to the narrow confines of the kitchen; constant debilitating pregnancies for want of legalized birth control; deprivations of many kinds—mental, moral, physical; murder of abusive parents carried out by children; useless and unnecessary rural death for want of medical attention; the empty, good-for-nothing lives of some of the middle class; social affectations and class consciousness; the need for day care centres; and the non-assimilation of natives who want to be rooted in their own culture.[19]

Many of these were taboo topics in McClung's day, so she may be considered not only a courageous writer, but one well in advance of her time.

Exposing such harsh realities is scarcely a characteristic of romanticism, a kind of writing that today is seen as reflecting "a psychological desire to escape from unpleasant realities."[20] "Yet at least one student of McClung dismisses her work partly because of its lack of relevance to our age!"[21] Many of the above issues are openly addressed today by crisis hotlines or shelters for battered women and children. It is impossible, then, to agree with critics that McClung is *merely* writing romantic rural idylls, or that her writing failed to grasp social issues—issues which even modern male critics appear insensitive to, in spite of changed attitudes. Randi Warne, from her theological perspective, has also exposed some of McClung's realistic responses, correctly arguing that they were a consequence of the novelist's "Christian Social Activism."[22] In effect, as a recent critic of early Canadian literature has argued,

> Too much Canadian literary criticism in the past has been based upon a shockingly incomplete knowledge of its subject. If we are to get beyond the clichés of Victorian response, it is important to find out more about what [an early Canadian] writer *actually wrote* and the conditions under which she had to work.[23]

It is particularly bewildering that modern Canadian literary critics—both male and female—have not examined McClung's short stories. Many of these contain her best writing, and they frequently lie in direct contradiction to the most common criticisms levelled against her work. This fact merely compounds the case against authors like McClung whose fiction has been underrated, dismissed, or neglected. With the growth of Women's Studies programmes in the last fifteen to twenty years, feminist literary critics have been attempting to recover and revalue the work of the great number of women writers "in the female tradition, from decade to decade, rather than from Great Woman to Great Woman." It is not adequate, the above critic believes, to be satisfied with analyzing the work of Austen, the Brontës, Eliot, and Woolf. "As we recreate the chain of writers in this tradition, the patterns of influence and response from one generation to the next, we can also begin to challenge the periodicity of orthodox literary history, and its enshrined canons of achievement."[24] Another feminist critic affirms: ". . . as newly re-issued and out-of-print texts reveal, and from the careful textual feminist analyses that accompany their resurrection, subversive stories seem to characterize female texts."[25] Indeed, McClung herself complained:

> Women have felt, have lived, have enjoyed and suffered, but few of them have expressed it in words. Men have told us what we think, what we dream, what we aspire to, what we like and dislike, what we ought to be, what we are and what we are not! What we would like to be, and never can be![26]

The complacent attitude of male authors, she added, reflects that "sex-prejudice is not dead."[27]

As does much modern feminist fiction, McClung's novels and short stories "radically question assumptions about the limits of women's experience, and bring into question the masculine portrayal of what they think women's experience is or ought to be."[28] "They reveal the struggles women face growing up female in a world where women are victimized and devalued."[29] By "voicing the voiceless,"[30] as she herself put it, much of McClung's writing "enacts protest as well as articulating it" and, adds Mary Jacobus, McClung's subversive writing contains the power "to destabilize the ground on which we stand,"[31] and not pay tribute to the status quo. In the feminist endeavour to uncover and recover a history of the consciousness of women, particularly in the Canadian context, McClung's fiction should play no small part. Some of the stories in this selection of her short fiction address such issues, and reflect the conclusion "that the re-educating of the literary imagination is the major task of the new feminist theory."[32]

To this end, the remainder of this introduction will be divided into two sections. The first will offer a biographical outline, revealing McClung's development as a beloved but outspoken advocate for women's rights. She took this path in spite of attempts by her conservative Scottish mother to repress the natural exuberance of her talkative, outgoing youngest daughter and to turn her into a prim and proper Victorian maiden: a shrinking violet who would hold no opinions of her own, and who would live in the shadow of the male members of the family, serving their needs much as a servant does his master. This section will also follow McClung's development as a writer, from tentative beginnings writing amusing stories for her children and their friends to her emergence as one of Canada's most popular authors.

The second section will comment on some of the themes and stylistic touches in the McClung stories that follow, which effectively serve her narrative purpose: whether for pure humour, for feminist consciousness-raising, or to make the reader aware of the attitudes and feelings of the women of her era who otherwise would have remained voiceless. McClung was sensitive and responsive to the condition "of the common people everywhere—the man who sits beside you at the lunch counter, the woman who writes letters in the rest room [women's lounge], the people who stand in line buying railway tickets. They all have at least one story"—a real, down-to-earth story, of everyday life. It was among such common people that McClung would seek realistic material for her fiction. On one occasion, for example, "I helped a woman to wash her dishes one night in a country hotel, and she told me in five minutes a story which I will write some day. . . . There it was—a whole story, and a sad one."[33]

Such responsiveness to the tribulations of the ordinary person expands our awareness of the consciousness of women in the early days of this century, during the opening of the Canadian West. Such stories have an important place in the recovery of our national past, and in the development of an awareness of our national, as well as personal, identity.

◦∽◦

Nellie Letitia (Mooney) McClung was born in 1873, the last of six children, on a small pioneer farm about a mile south of Chatsworth, in Grey County, Ontario.[34] Young Nellie Mooney adored her elderly father, John Mooney, because of his delightful Irish wit and humour, which offset her dour mother's stern, Scottish Presbyterian heritage. Letitia Mooney's strict Calvinism was also countered by her husband's more relaxed Methodism. Letitia consistently sought to repress the spirit of her lively youngest daughter, and force it to conform to the strictest Victorian ideals of what constituted a proper lady: seen but not heard. Nellie's more amiable father, however, was inclined to indulge his youngest daughter; he was more like a loveable grandfather than a stern Victorian parent. As a child, Nellie Mooney was a natural mimic, and her father playfully encouraged this talent. As an adult, her allegiance to the Irish character, rather than the Scottish, stood her in good stead when, as a public speaker on issues such as women's suffrage, she couched the logic of her arguments in humour, which rocked her male audiences with laughter and made her arguments stick in their minds.

In the 1860s and 1870s, in Grey County, however, the Mooneys were largely subsistence farmers. The land was stony and hard to cultivate, and 150 acres held little promise for Nellie's three brothers, who saw only a limited future as hired hands for other farmers. By the late 1870s the myth of the Golden West was in full flower, inspired by Butler's *Great Lone Land* (1872) and the glowing reports that appeared almost daily in the "Latest from Manitoba" column in the Toronto *Globe*. Nellie's eldest brother, Will, was determined to go, with or without the family, so the decision was made. Will preceded the Mooneys and staked claims for himself, his father, and his brother George in the newly opened Souris Valley area of south-central Manitoba. Nellie Mooney, aged eight, followed with the rest of her family in 1880. It was not until she was sixty-two that McClung graphically recorded the excitement and rigours of their trek west and the pioneer life they lived, in the memorable first volume of her autobiography, *Clearing in the West: My Own Story* (1935),[35] which ends with her marriage to Wes McClung, son of the Methodist minister in whose home Nellie boarded while teaching school in southern Manitoba.

From her teen years Nellie Mooney had resolved to be a writer. When she looked about her she saw too many rural people who lived drab, monotonous lives, stunted by the endless round of chores in a pioneer environment where farm families were isolated from other human beings. Increasingly Nellie wished to "lift the burden" from these downtrodden people with their treadmill existence. She also dreamed of fame as a great author "and send my tho'ts [sic] to the millions and sway the minds of many," as her favourite author, Dickens, had done. At first, marriage seemed incompatible with her goal of being a writer, and she struggled between her love for Wes McClung and her ambition to become an author. Wes, however, assured her she need not forego her ambition if they married, and so, she reasoned, "I knew I could be happy with Wes. We did not always agree but he was a fair fighter, and I knew I would rather fight with him than agree with anyone else."

Five children followed fairly quickly, four boys and a girl, and McClung expressed her creativity by making up stories to tell her children and their friends. When she was working on her first novel in the early 1900s, she asked her American publisher if he could find a paying source for a group of as yet unidentified children's stories, but nothing seems to have come of this. Such fiction as "A Short Tale of a Rabbit" and "The Ungrateful Pigeons" was published in her first volume of short stories, *The Black Creek Stopping-House* (1912).[36] As for the young Pearlie Watson in her first novel, *Sowing Seeds in Danny* (1908), many a critic argued that such realistic children were much needed in an era when the reprehensible Elsie Dinsmore books held sway with the sentimental heroine constantly awash in tears. McClung's children vowed they preferred their mother's stories over all others, and no wonder, for there is a charming and humorous realism about McClung's fictional children— who were, she said, based on close observation of her own children. Her narratives written for Methodist and Presbyterian Sunday School papers at this time—one of the few outlets for budding authors—were every bit as delightful.

They differed radically from the stuffy, sermonizing stories of her fellow writers, whose children were merely stilted, miniature adults. Although she was one of the most popular Canadian writers of her day, McClung never did become the "great" writer she wanted to be. She is, however, a *significant* Canadian writer, and should not be ignored. When she did indeed "sway the minds of many," it was through her public life as a prominent first-wave feminist activist and social reformer.

McClung's feminist reform activities began over the issue of women's suffrage. Did women have the right to be treated as full human beings and citizens, by having the same voting rights as men? Social tradition said no. Such traditionalist, conservative-minded men, according to McClung, merely reflected the "sex prejudice" and "sex jealousy" extant in a male-dominated society. Women, on the other hand, had begun to ask themselves whether they should not have a say in determining the nature of the society in which they lived and raised their children. To do so, they needed female empowerment, by means of voting rights. In McClung's day, however, women were considered inferior to men. Being less physically strong, the argument went, women were less intelligent too, with minds not fit to grapple with the subtleties of politics. Yet at the same time gentlemen placed women on a pedestal of sensitivity and purity, from which they should not descend to dirty their hands in political matters that were sometimes corrupt. At any rate, if "nice" women had the vote, some men argued, they would be loathe to use it in the hurly-burly at the public polls. If women voted, they might disagree with their husbands at election time, leading to the break-up of the family; and when women went out to vote, they would be throwing their children into the hands of lower-class servant-girls—indeed, if gentlewomen had the vote, they might try to secure it for these same servant-girls! As McClung quickly pointed out, if the male voting lists were determined by class and, say, whether a man had a criminal past, "there would be a strange alteration in the voting list!" Male and female supporters of women's suffrage were asking for the vote *on the same basis under which men had the vote*, and they were asking for it as a *civil right*, not as a privilege. In a world where a woman's sole function was perceived as a biological one—as wife and mother—it was thought her influence was best exerted indirectly in supporting and obeying her husband and raising her children ("the hand that rocks the cradle rules the world"). For women to step outside their traditional narrow confines—what today's feminist would call kept barefoot, pregnant, and in the kitchen—was seen by some men as causing the break-up of civilization.

In Manitoba, McClung became the unofficial leader in the suffrage battle against the pompously self-righteous Conservative premier, Sir Rodmond Roblin, who subscribed to every nineteenth-century myth and cliché about the natural limitations of women. When the Manitoba Liberals put women's suffrage on their political platform, every Liberal candidate wanted McClung as a speaker because of her oratorical power and her skill in couching the logic of her arguments in humour, and not least because of her witty responses to hecklers. On one occasion a man called out, "In Colorado, where women have the vote, a woman stuffed a ballot box. What does the lady say about that?" "Well," she quipped, "we women can't have lived with men all this time and not picked up some of their little ways!" As a result, wherever McClung appeared she was met with standing-room only crowds and "a perfect storm of cheering and applause." On 28 January 1916 the women of Manitoba became the first in Canada to win the provincial vote and the right to hold office. The other western provinces and Ontario soon followed. Years later McClung recalled with zest that it was "a bonny fight," "a knock-down and drag-out fight" that brought together rural and urban women, and women of all social classes.

During these years McClung published her first two novels and her first collection of short stories, *The Black Creek Stopping-House* (1912). During the war years, she published two collections of essays, the more memorable *In*

Times Like These (1915), largely concerned with the women's suffrage issue, and the sometimes moving *Next of Kin* (1917), influenced by the fact that her eldest son, Jack, was a soldier serving in the centre of the European war. It was not until 1921, in her third Pearlie Watson novel, *Purple Springs*, that she introduced the suffrage issue, along with other women's issues of her day and ours.

McClung fought two other major battles for women's rights. She joined the fight, led by her Edmonton friend, Judge Emily Murphy, for the right of women to be appointed to the Senate, and she herself spearheaded the fight for the ordination of theologically qualified women in the United Church of Canada. In the former case, Murphy learned that five interested persons could request an interpretation of the British North America Act. Murphy brought in McClung and three other prominent Alberta feminists: Irene Parlby, Louise McKinney, and Henrietta Muir Edwards. They first appealed to the Supreme Court of Canada, whose decision was an unqualified no. Had the Fathers of Confederation meant for women to sit in the Senate, they argued, they would have referred to Senators and Senatresses! The "Famous Five," as they later became known, then took their case to the Judicial Committee of the Privy Council in England, at that time the final arbiter of interpretations of the British North America Act. On 18 October 1929 the lord chancellor, Lord Sankey, read his judgement in full, as opposed to presenting the usual summary, perhaps because the decision would have tremendous influence on the public position of women throughout the British Empire. The Judicial Committee took a liberal interpretation, overturning the negative decision of the Supreme Court of Canada. The women of Canada were jubilant over this victory, although McClung had had little use for the Senate, because she opposed patronage appointments and because the "moribund" old Senators had rejected the Canadian women's appeal for the old-age pension in 1926. If only women could get enough seats in the Senate, she thought they could push through more humane legislation.

The battle for the ordination of women in the newly formed United Church of Canada (1925) took much longer, and McClung, as usual, was in the forefront of the fray in spite of the fact that for some time she had been critical of the institutional church. In McClung's view the male-dominated church held women "in mild contempt," always spoke of women "in bulk" as if they were not individuals, claimed "to understand women better than they understood themselves," and gave "a masculine interpretation of religion." The Protestant religion lost much, she argued, "when it lost the idea of the motherhood of God," a feminist theological concept we now think of as modern. In this matter, as in so many others, McClung was ahead of her time. She pointed out, too, that "the church has contributed a share in the subjection of women," from the marriage service through the refusal to grant women positions of power in the church. For her, "the church preached resignation when it should have sounded the note of rebellion" concerning women's battles to be recognized as both human beings and citizens. With memorable sarcasm and her habit of reducing the argument to the absurd, which so delighted her audiences, McClung wryly proclaimed, "Now, with the Senate doors open, there are only the two *great* institutions that will not accept women on equal terms: the church and the beer parlours." In 1936, the Saskatchewan Conference laid down the gauntlet. Either ordain Lydia Gruchy, who was theologically qualified and who had managed a three-point rural charge very well for eleven years, they said, or we will do it ourselves. The diehards in the church capitulated. The fight had taken ten long years.

Other highlights of McClung's life were her appointment, in September 1921, to the Ecumenical Methodist Conference in London, England, where, according to newspaper accounts, she stirred up the otherwise sedate assembly with her "daring words." She was a member of the Alberta Legislative Assembly from 1921–1926, and in 1936 she was the only woman appointed to the board of governors of the newly reorganized Canadian Broadcasting Corporation. In the fall of 1938 she was one of Canada's representatives to the League of Nations in Geneva, Switzerland.

During her years in the Alberta Legislature, McClung found the time to write her last—and her best—novel, *Painted Fires* (1925), about the difficulties facing a Finnish immigrant girl, Helmi Milander, whose romanticized, get-rich-quick idealism about the new world is false: a "painted" illusion, not a "realistic" image of life. Her expectation of an Edenic life of ease and glamour is progressively undermined, first by her pseudo-friend, Eva, who betrays Helmi by sending her to an opium den—Helmi thinking she is getting medicine for the addicted Eva. The justice system, the reform school (ironically called "the Girls' Friendly Home"), even her husband, fail Helmi in her times of need, but the strength of her character leads her to triumph over those forces of a patriarchal society that hinder her progress. She is one of McClung's many strong female characters who are antidotes to the tearfully sentimental Victorian heroine; Helmi, like McClung's earlier Pearlie Watson, is "scornful of the tears of lovelorn maidens" and can "stand alone, reason, lead, instruct, command." They are self-determining "rebels" against the passive, self-sacrificing Victorian ideal.[37]

Throughout her feminist career, however, McClung also fought for less spectacular women's rights, such as better working conditions in urban sweatshops for women supporting families but shamelessly exploited by employers. She supported the cause of married women who did not need to work outside the home, but wanted to, when married women were expected to be exclusively homemakers. Indeed, McClung went so far as to advocate women's economic independence from men, a circumstance her own writing skills afforded her vis-à-vis her husband, Wes. She saw this arrangement as beneficial to both partners. She fought for an amendment to the Homestead Act, which would permit women, on an equal footing with men, to be granted free land in the opening West, and for a Dower Law, which would protect married women from losing a homestead they had maintained alongside their husbands.

She sought better housing for poor, urban immigrants, and improved medical care for women on isolated farms, involving a system of rural nurses and hospitals. In fact, McClung supported universal Medicare as we know it today. "It should be as freely available as police and fire protection," she said. With like-minded women, McClung fought for equal pay for women and men doing equal or comparable work; for the freedom of women to choose any career they wished, even if it was seen as a male preserve; for mothers' pensions; for old-age pensions; for prison reform. These campaigns may not have received the publicity that her three major battles for women's rights did, but they were equally important to the ordinary women for whom McClung constantly sought fair play in an insensitive, male-dominated society content with the status quo. Many of these issues find their way into McClung's sixteen novels, short stories, and other books.

Nellie Letitia (Mooney) McClung would have been a remarkable woman in any age, but in the repressive, patriarchal society of her day she was the leading women's rights activist and social reformer, and she changed the face of Canada. One writer, at the time of her death in 1951, referred to Nellie McClung as the "unofficial 'No. 1 Woman' of Canada."[38]

~

McClung has laid claim to four books of short stories: *The Black Creek Stopping-House* (1912), *All We Like Sheep* (1921), *Be Good to Yourself* (1930), and *Flowers for the Living* (1931). In fact only the first two of the four contain what we understand today as developed short stories. The latter two are largely collections of sketches from half a page to three pages long. The sketch has attractive qualities of its own, of course, but the selection of McClung's short stories offered in the pages that follow is more memorable and representative of her style and her varied themes.

The reader will find that all the stories that follow share common characteristics of McClung's style. The first sentence of every McClung story grabs the reader's attention with its immediacy and economy of words, and effectively plunges the reader right into the tale. Descriptions of nature are brief, concrete, sensuous, authoritative, used for specific effect, and physically situate the reader in the author's western environment generally, and within each story specifically. The reader always has a graphic sense of place whether outdoors, inside an English bank, or in a squalid prairie cabin. The descriptive details, too, are carefully chosen to convey the mood and personality of the characters. Indeed we readily visualize her characters even when there is little, if any, physical detail offered, for their characters and personalities are conveyed vividly through their distinctive speech idiom and the attitudes they express in response to the various situations in which they find themselves.

Many of McClung's stories exhibit a broad range of humour: of the absurd, tongue-in-cheek, situational, ironic, understatement, intentional bathos, and a great deal of satire. McClung's playful antipathy to the romance mode, which runs like a leitmotif throughout her novels, is at times evident in her short fiction. There is some spoofing of romance, for example, in "The Elusive Vote," with the melodramatic race to get John Thomas Green to the voting booth before it closes only to have him deliberately spoil his ballot. Pearlie Watson's romantic games of pretend in "The Live Wire," with their melodramatic catastrophes marked by her rote-learned temperance lessons in the Band of Hope, are delightfully spoofed. On the other hand McClung's criticism of the superficial and empty-headed women of the artsy-craftsy set in "You Never Can Tell," who romanticize—in a rather cruel way—the life of the plain, down-to-earth Mrs. Dawson, has more bite. Similarly stories with tragic endings like "The Return Ticket" and "The Grim Fact of Sisterhood" are distressingly bleak and heart-breaking. "Carried Forward" and the "Neutral Fuse" narrowly avoid grim despair. The suffering in these stories depicts that sadness in the world which McClung also affirmed, and balances the cheerfulness that critics have too exclusively attributed to her work. Nevertheless, McClung claimed to have "no art in writing—except that I have a good memory and am a close observer,"[39] and indeed her work shows little consciousness of the craft. Essentially she was a good storyteller who had resolved that "when I wrote I would write of the people who do the work of the world and I would write it from their side of the fence and not from the external angle of the casual visitor."[40] Like any good writer, McClung wrote about what she knew, which is one reason her stories are so real to us.

The fiction of McClung's era has been criticized for avoiding "Indian and Métis characters [who are] rare and . . . usually degenerate creatures destined for a merciful extinction," and furthermore that this type of writing "generally gives the impression that nothing happened until the white settlers arrived."[41] McClung's "Babette" and "Red and White" are exceptions. In the latter story, both Rosie Starblanket and her son Johnny recall native life before the white man arrived: wolves howling about the camp in the wilderness, stories of Indian mythology and of Johnny's ancestors and their ways, big game hunts, and inter-tribal warfare. Rosie tries to keep these tales alive for her son, who has recently returned from four years in a white mission school in Brandon and is now living between two worlds: neither white nor Indian. In this way Rosie tries to compensate for the white man's robbery of her son's native culture and environment. Rosie's stories bring her own spirit alive, a spirit long stifled by "good for nothing" whites toward whom she feels smouldering resentment for their domineering, patronizing ways and their attempt to "take everything." In "Red and White," McClung depicts white men, not natives, as the degenerates.

McClung's story records a few stereotypes about natives shared by the majority of her readers in the 1920s, and the positive attitude toward the mission boarding schools, with their "rigid discipline," has certainly fallen into disrepute today. Her view that they were kindly places existing solely for the benefit of native children is at variance with the story's lesson that natives should be free to speak their own language and live according to their own cultural preferences, and McClung seems unaware of the contradiction. Still, the tale's essentially non-assimilationist stance is truly remarkable for the 1920s. In "Babette," however, McClung readily embraces the notion of assimilation of the Métis into white society. At the same time, she quashes the Anglo-Saxon sense of cultural superiority, by having Babette give George Shaw a deserving comeuppance at the story's end. Implicitly the tale challenges the common view that northern Europeans—particularly the British—were necessarily the superior immigrants. The same case is made in "O, Canada!"

McClung also manages to get a satirical jab in at the typical anti-feminist who was arbitrarily opposed to the vote for women. In "Red and White," Brown, a degenerate Member of Parliament for Winnipeg, visits the summer resort where Johnny and Rosie Starblanket still live. He tries to seduce his waitress, Minnie Hardcastle, who is Johnny's native girlfriend and, as it turns out, ironically, Brown's natural child. Minnie reacts haughtily to Brown's oily, insinuating manner, which puts him in a rage. Brown likes the old-fashioned kind of woman: servile, frivolous, empty-headed, and hungry for the outrageous flattery Brown uses to manipulate passive women for his own ends. He has no understanding of Minnie's inherent dignity, self-esteem, and independence of mind. The fact that women—even "these mongrel half-breeds," as he puts it—should demand the right to vote, refusing to admit their natural inferiority to men like him, enrages Brown even further. As a half-breed female, Minnie Hardcastle has *two* counts against her in the eyes of the anti-suffragist. Brown's was a common masculine attitude that McClung encountered again and again in her campaign for women's suffrage.

McClung's "The Way of the West" confronts the problem of an old face—Old World traditions—forcing itself on a new land with a new cultural reality. Here, the

fiery anti-American, anti-Catholic Orangeman, Thomas
Shouldice, like the too-English housekeeper, Mrs. Mauvers,
in "Carried Forward," and the haughty Mrs. E.P. Smith,
formerly of Prince Edward Island, in "The Grim Fact of
Sisterhood," has formed his inflexible attitude from cultural
imperialists from the East who would impose their views on
the developing West. McClung presents these views as negative forces for alienation and disharmony in a new land
where compromise and adaptation are required.

McClung believed it was "the task of the writer to
interpret the country"—a task that is not foreign to modern
Canadian authors. She would have agreed with Archibald
MacMechan and Robert Kroetsch that "in a sense we
haven't got an identity until somebody tells our story. The
fiction makes us real."[42] In *Painted Fires* (1925), for example,
a church Canadian Girls in Training project is to introduce
an immigrant girl into the group. The leader, Miss Rogers,
comments that foreign girls are essentially like us even if
they dress or wear their hair differently. " 'I guess every one
would want to be born British if they could,' said Hattie
complacently." Miss Rogers disagrees. She is American born
and bred, and, like everyone else, likes her own country best.

> But we are making a new country here in Canada,
> and we will love it best of all because we are making
> it. We are making paths and laying down founda-
> tions, and that is what makes life here so interest-
> ing. Now the Finn girl [Helmi Milander] . . . is a
> Canadian from choice . . . so let us consider her a
> true Canadian.[43]

McClung never looked to central Canada or
England for the roots of western Canadian culture, except
perhaps in the matter of hygiene and nutrition for Eastern
European peasant immigrants. In "The Way of the West,"
then, McClung supplied her solution to the challenge of
new land meeting old culture, by the spirit of brotherhood:
"Where could such a scene as this be enacted," she concludes,
"a Twelfth of July celebration where a Roman Catholic

priest was the principal speaker, where the company dispersed with the singing of 'God Save the King,' led by an American band?" "Nowhere," she answers, "but in the Northwest of Canada" where disparate groups of immigrants are intent on building a distinctively Canadian nation.

McClung was severely attacked in the Toronto *Sentinel*—the organ of the Orange Order—for her "crude ideas concerning the ideals of Orangemen," whose professed concern was the preservation of the civil and religious liberties of both Catholics and Protestants. The *Sentinel* alleged that McClung's "The Way of the West" was "offensive," "prejudiced," and "insulting," for no Catholic priest "could be the hero of an Orangemen's story." "For this ridiculous story," the editorial asserted, "Mrs. McClung deserves a medal from the Vatican." Ironically, the *Sentinel*'s editor appears to have been completely unaware that he was contradicting his own arguments for religious liberty. McClung responded to the article by distinguishing between the Orange Order's principles and its practices. The former she respected, the latter she condemned, for "they remind us (Protestant and Catholic alike) of some things that we should try to forget—the old hatreds, bloodshed and bitterness." For McClung, "new times demand new methods."[44] "God," she said, "reveals himself in many ways." Religion she likened to a bridge, and she firmly held that "it is a sin to lay our axe to the arch of another man's bridge."[45] In defiance of the Orange Order, McClung continued to use this tale in her recitals in the West and in Ontario.

"The Runaway Grandmother" resurrects the slovenly bachelor George Shaw from the pages of "Babette." He is prosperous now, but realizes he needs a housekeeper and runs the risk of placing another advertisement for one in the wake of a series of failed domestic arrangements. One Irish woman had seemed ideal until "one day she went to Millford, and came home in a state of wild exhilaration, with more of the same in a large black bottle." Knowing the terrible toll alcohol abuse took in the opening up of the Canadian West,[46] McClung rarely gave way to humour where drunkenness was involved, but here, as in "The Live Wire," she had fun with it. The essential lesson, however, is that if vigorous elderly persons like Mrs. Harris are put out to pasture when they're used to being active, independent, and in control of their lives, then psychologically they are made to feel useless, dispirited, and lacking in self-worth. Those who succumb to this deprivation of wholeness give up and die an early death. Grandma Harris, however, fights this social convention, runs away, and hires out as housekeeper-companion to George Shaw, thus keeping both mind and body busy and vital. McClung frequently expressed the idea that work came close to being a social panacea, and recorded this idea in a theologically unortho-dox way in a poem that ends:

> Perhaps the snake was wise
> And what we call the "Fall" might well be called the
>   "Rise."
> The only creatures that can live at ease
> Day after day and not be hurt are these:
> The long-haired Persian and the Pekinese![47]

In "The Return Ticket," on the other hand, the problem of alcohol is a cause of serious ill health in a loving wife and McClung, though sympathetic, is not amused. Being a very compassionate woman, she always blamed the liquor business, which grew fat on the tears of women and children, rather than those alcoholics who succumbed to its lure. In this story, Annie's husband, Dave, often disappeared for weeks at a time on drunken binges, " 'and her not know-ing where he was or how he would come home! He worried her always'." Annie's silence about Dave's drunkenness, and her naïve sense that she could reform him, merely served to facilitate his addiction, in today's terms, and, "if recent research on the families of alcoholics is to be trusted, McClung is accurately describing a common phenomenon in alcoholic families."[48] After treatment at the famous Mayo Clinic in the United States, and standing a good chance of recovery, Annie just gives up in spiritless defeat when she receives no encouraging letter from her husband, who is off on one of his drunken binges. The return ticket, unnecessarily bought in advance, is for the return of her body in a coffin, a situation she despairingly anticipates. McClung has artfully laid the mood for this sad story in her early paragraphs set in the forlorn Emerson railway station: the red lantern gleaming "like an evil eye"; "the one barred lantern whose bright little gleam of light reminded one uncomfortably of a small, live mouse in a cage, caught and doomed. . . ." At times one senses more craft in the story-teller than McClung would admit to.

The unhappy ending of "The Return Ticket," as with "The Grim Fact of Sisterhood," is rare in McClung's fiction. Hence, her particular description of what constitutes a happy ending:

> By happy ending I mean that a gleam of hope must shine through the darkness some place. I see no good in a book that teaches that life is a hopeless mess . . . Error and sorrow and failure are our portion in life I know, yet no more than joy and achievement and happiness, and it is the work of the writer to portray them in true proportion, and even if the sorrowful predominates one thought must prevail, that life is . . . not wasted, not utterly wasted.[49]

At times, however, McClung was compelled to write of "winter-killed" souls like Annie's where the human spirit has been crushed.

Three of her short stories, "The Live Wire," "The Elusive Vote," and "Banking in London," are as close to pure comedy as McClung could get. Here she rivals Stephen Leacock, Canada's best-known humourist. "The Live Wire" was expanded to form part of McClung's first novel. Like many of the chapters, it stands on its own, for, as she remarked about *Sowing Seeds in Danny*, it was put together "like lengths of a stove pipe." This story introduces the "engaging little gamin"[50] named Pearlie Watson, who would win the hearts of both American and Canadian readers with her Irish brogue (which McClung learned from her Irish father) and her amusingly romantic imagination, which McClung spoofs. Pearlie develops, throughout the Watson trilogy, from a charming child of twelve into a young feminist schoolteacher, not unlike McClung herself, who fights for women's suffrage even in the face of hostility. Unlike the passive Victorian heroine, Pearlie Watson "is her own person and requires no parent to provide identity." She is a child "with force of character,"[51] a strong will, and a strong ego that knows its worth.

The touches of political humour that lace "The Live Wire" positively scintillate in "The Elusive Vote," beginning with the statement that the focal character, John Thomas Green, is a "great and glorious argument for woman suffrage." Green is slow-witted and totally uninterested in politics, and he votes for whomever he is told to vote for. Yet intelligent women, informed about the political issues of the day (Reciprocity), were denied the right to vote. The humour of the piece lies in the machinations of the two parties to secure Green's vote: to make sure he votes "right." Both Grit and Conservative party members are presented by McClung as comic figures, full of manipulative guile as indeed was the brainless James Ducker in "The Live Wire." The politicians' comeuppance at the end of both stories is a prime example of McClung's broad humour.

It is difficult not to relate "Banking in London" to Stephen Leacock's earlier "My Financial Career," which appeared in his popular first book, *Literary Lapses* (1910). Leacock was as ardent an anti-feminist as McClung was a feminist. "Non-traditional" women like McClung were for Leacock "the sign of social disintegration," for they refused to recognize their natural "inferiority" to men, were "incompetent" and "utterly unscrupulous," and fancied themselves capable of reasoning and of pursuing careers— illogically expecting salaries equal to those of men in the same profession.[52] The bashful, insecure would-be depositor of Leacock's narrative is countered by McClung's independent-minded and self-confident—if frustrated—female depositor. Far from being the wilting female rattled by the gravity of the masculine world of banking, McClung's focal character mercilessly satirizes the pompous British bank manager for his patronizing manner and his absurd demands—an attitude that this writer can assure the reader still exists in English bankers today, and is every bit as frustrating as it was for McClung in 1921 when she was a delegate to an International Methodist Convention in London, England. One can only assume that the narrator in "Banking in London"—as in "The Return Ticket"—is McClung herself. Leacock's character makes a fool of himself; McClung's makes a fool of the bank manager. One might read Leacock's and McClung's stories as companion pieces of typical Canadian humour: benign and nonsensical.

"Carried Forward" is one of McClung's most memorable stories and is typical of her feminist crusades against the social and legal injustices perpetrated against women and children. This is a feminist story of consciousness-raising: the deliberate education of women in those conditions that oppress them. Such fiction is protest fiction. It is also subversive, for it seeks to undermine the status quo. Much of McClung's fiction, in fact, must be assessed as feminist social activism; otherwise it remains *un*interpreted or *mis*interpreted. In this story, the portrait of Annie Berry above her coffin is youthful, vital, and confident, in sharp contrast to the faded, worn-out face in the coffin. It is the face of a thirty-year-old woman who for years had been "dragging around half dead" from overwork and excessive childbearing, who always had "a baby in her arms and another on the way." It is the face of a woman who had no control over her own body. As Annie's mother cynically sums it up, it is " 'a great plan, and a great world for men.'" The implication is that birth control should be legalized, for when the story was written (and until as late as 1969) it fell under the Canadian criminal code as an "obscenity." Indeed the term "birth control" was coined only in 1914. Although "organized groups to foster [birth control] did not appear until the 1920s," and although it was a taboo topic, commercially made contraceptives were readily available under-the-counter in both urban and rural pharmacies.[53] McClung implies in the story that Luke Berry should have made use of contraceptives. McClung's husband was a pharmacist, and she would have been well aware of their availability.

As for being overworked, it is a fact that farm wives in the pioneer West bore a very heavy burden. Though Luke Berry, a prosperous farmer, has all the hired help he wants, he fails to get domestic help for his wife and seven children, the oldest of whom is twelve. Annie Berry is free labour, and Luke mourns her loss as he would the loss of one of his workhorses—which in fact he treats with greater kindness. Certainly feminists of the day "challenged the allocation of economic priorities which gave the barn precedence over the house . . . Again and again they lectured farm women that their labour is a commodity with real value and that it was not true economy to save everything but themselves."[54] When Annie tries to raise such issues, Luke simply shuts her out with his silence and walks away from her problems. "The essential crime in the story, we come to realize, has been the husband's inexorable strangulation, over the years, of [Annie Berry's] spirit and personality. . . ."[55] In such a patriarchal world, the woman, her "sense of self effaced, [becomes] unable to acknowledge, let alone assert, [her] own [or her children's] needs." Luke Berry "maintains power over his wife through enforced isolation and silence, which contributes to her self-doubts" and her passive self-effacement.[56] Between the Berrys is a "failure of communication . . . which is quite timeless—or, as some would prefer to put it, surprisingly modern."[57] Hence the lesson of the story, which is Annie Berry's sad legacy to her little daughter, Hilda: " 'Learn to speak out, Hilda, when you feel something ought to be said. . . . Don't let anyone make you feel so frightened that you cannot speak'." To speak out is to fight on behalf of wronged womanhood and against various forms of gender abuse: mental, moral, physical, social, psychological.

Stories like "Carried Forward" are women's fiction for male as well as female readers. Such women's fiction had moved in the direction of "female realism, a broad, socially informed exploration of the daily lives and values of women within the family and the community." It provides " 'women's view of life, woman's experience'."[58] McClung anticipated more books written by women, "from a new angle, and a new method of reasoning, and surprizing [sic] may be the conclusions reached."[59] She would scarcely be surprised by the large number of Canadian women authors writing today, or by what they have to say about the female consciousness and the female experience, understood from a woman's point of view. Many of the stories by Ethel Wilson, Alice Munro, Margaret Laurence, and Margaret Atwood, to name but a few Canadian women novelists, fulfil McClung's prophecy. Indeed Margaret Laurence recognized that "it is still enormously difficult for a woman to have both a marriage and a family, and a (writing) profession. I often become angry when I think of this injustice. . . ." Perhaps this is why "Nellie McClung has long been a heroine of mine."[60]

Critical reappraisal of the work of a literary heroine such as Nellie L. McClung, who can inspire one of our best modern women authors, is long overdue, as is re-publication of the best of her long-neglected work. William Arthur Deacon, Canadian literary critic and man of letters wrote to McClung in 1948, only three years before her death, that writers like her bore the brunt and the pressure of being pioneer novelists in the early days of this century when it was a meagre vocation in Canada.[61] Though their writing is sometimes rough by modern standards, they paved the way for modern Canadian writers like Margaret Laurence. Clara Thomas has observed parallels between the work of McClung and Laurence, her sister western novelist, though she points out that what "shouts" in McClung's fiction is more subtly dealt with in Laurence's finely crafted fiction. Yet what Thomas says of Laurence can be said of McClung: each recorded the "truth to women's experience" as each discovered it in her respective era.[62] Where male norms tend to differ from those of women and tend to be far removed from the realities of women's lives, outspoken voices such as McClung's and Laurence's must not be lost in the history of women's consciousness. Knowing about the experience of women in McClung's day may serve to enrich our knowledge of women's experience in our own.

∽

Notes

1   Mary Hallett and Marilyn Davis, *Firing the Heather: The Life and Times of Nellie McClung* (Saskatoon: Fifth House Publishers, 1993), 228.

2   Ibid., 95–99.

3   *The Authors' Bulletin* (November 1926), 28.

4   Provincial Archives of British Columbia [PABC], McClung Papers, vol. 22(1), various telegrams from George Mitford to Nellie Letitia McClung [NLM], all dated January 1931.

5   PABC, McClung Papers, vol. 1(7), letter, from William Briggs to NLM, 13 July 1905.

6   L.M. Montgomery was ecstatic when she was published in a "first-class" magazine like the *Delineator*. See *The Selected Journals of L.M. Montgomery—Volume 1: 1889–1910*, eds. Mary Rubio and Elizabeth Waterston (Toronto: Oxford University Press, 1985), 270.

7   PABC, McClung Papers, vol. 10(2), letter from Dreiser to Henry W. Lanier at Doubleday, American publisher of *Sowing Seeds in Danny* (5 May 1908).

8   Ibid., vol. 30, newspaper clipping from the Toronto *Globe*, (Saturday (?), November [likely 1910]).

9   Hallett and Davis, *Firing the Heather*, 238ff. Dick Harrison, in *Unnamed Country: The Struggle for a Canadian*

Prairie Fiction (Edmonton: Hurtig Press, 1970), 87, though a critic of McClung's novels, makes a telling point when he observes: "What remains of permanent value in Nellie McClung's writings is the tone of pragmatic anti-romance which *occasionally* wins out over the sentimentality that mars much of her work" (emphasis added). Had Harrison followed up on this insight, he would have discovered that McClung's mind was *essentially* anti-romantic, and that much of her fiction reflects this.

10 Hallett and Davis, *Firing the Heather*, 238ff.

11 Clara Thomas, in a conversation with the author.

12 Hallett and Davis, *Firing the Heather*, 252.

13 Garden Roper et al., "Writers of Fiction, 1880–1920," in *Literary History of Canada*, ed. Carl F. Klinck (Toronto: University of Toronto Press, 1965; rev. 1978), 330.

14 See "Didacticism," in William Flint Thrall and Addison Hibberd, *A Handbook to Literature* (New York: Odyssey Press, 1960).

15 Hallett and Davis, *Firing the Heather*, 228.

16 Ibid., 257–258.

17 NLM, *Painted Fires* (Toronto: Thomas Allen, 1925), 3–8.

18 Hallett and Davis, *Firing the Heather*, 267.

19 Ibid.

20 See "Romanticism," in Thrall and Hibbard, *A Handbook to Literature*.

21 Eric Callum Thompson, "The Prairie Novel in Canada: A Study in Changing Form and Perception," Ph.D. dissertation, University of New Brunswick, 1972.

22 Randi R. Warne, *Literature as Pulpit: The Christian Social Activism of Nellie L. McClung* (Waterloo, Ont.: Wilfrid Laurier University Press, 1992).

23 Michael A. Peterman and Carl Ballstadt, eds., *Forest and Other Gleanings: The Fugitive Writings of Catharine Parr Traill* (Ottawa: University of Ottawa Press, 1995), 2 (italics added).

24 Elaine Showalter, "Towards a Feminist Poetics," in *Women Writing and Writing About Women*, ed. Mary Jacobus (London: Harper and Row, 1979), 34–35.

25 Lorna Irvine, *Sub/Version: Canadian Fiction by Women* (Toronto: ECW Press, 1986), 5.

26 Hallett and Davis, *Firing the Heather*, 253.

27 PABC, McClung Papers, vol. 23(3), typescript, "Speak Up! Ladies!" n.d.

28 Gillian Beer, "Beyond Determinism: George Eliot and Virginia Woolf," in *Women Writing and Writing About Women*, ed. Jacobus, 18–19.

29 Melody Graulich, "Violence Against Women: Power Dynamics in Literature of the Western Family," in *The Women's West*, eds. Susan Armitage and Elizabeth Jameson (Norman: University of Oklahoma Press, 1987), 113.

30 See Misao Dean, "Voicing the Voiceless: Language and Genre in Nellie McClung's Fiction and Her Autobiography," *Atlantis* XV (Autumn 1989): 65–75.

31 Mary Jacobus, "The Difference in View," in *Women Writing and Writing About Women*, ed. Jacobus, 17–19.

32 Irvine, *Sub/Version*, 269.

33 PABC, McClung Papers, vol. 24(3), NLM, typescript, "The Writer's Creed" (ca. 1909).

34 The following paragraphs, unless otherwise indicated, are summarized and paraphrased from Hallett and Davis, *Firing the Heather*.

35 NLM, *Clearing in the West: My Own Story*, with an intro. by Veronica Strong-Boag (Toronto: Thomas Allen,

1935, 1976). This, and particularly the less accurate, less complete, second volume of McClung's autobiography, *The Stream Runs Fast* (Toronto: Thomas Allen, 1945), must be read with some degree of caution as at times the novelist's art is given more play than a strict autobiography affords.

36 See Marilyn I. Davis, "Fiction of a Feminist: Nellie McClung's Work for Children," in *Canadian Children's Literature*, no. 62 (1991).

37 Elaine Showalter, *A Literature of Their Own: British Women Novelists from Brontë to Lessing* (Princeton, N.J.: Princeton University Press, 1976), 100, 123, 181.

38 PABC, McClung Papers, unidentified clipping, an editorial; reprinted courtesy of *The Family Herald and Weekly Star*, 1951.

39 PABC, McClung Papers, vol. 24(3), typescript [ca. 1909].

40 NLM, *Clearing in the West*, 226.

41 Harrison, *Unnamed Country*, 80.

42 PABC, McClung Papers, vol. 17, newspaper clipping, "Western Writers Guests at Reception Here," Ottawa *Journal* (18 November 1937); see also Robert Kroetsch, quoted in Eli Mandel, "Romance and Realism in Western Canadian Fiction," in *Prairie Perspectives No. 2*, eds. A.W. Rasporich and H.C. Classen (Toronto: Holt, Rinehart & Winston, 1937), 198.

43 NLM, *Painted Fires*, 40.

44 PABC, McClung Papers, vol. 23.

45 NLM, "What Life Has Taught Me," *Onward* (30 December 1951).

46 See James Gray, *Booze: The Impact of Whiskey on the Canadian West* (Toronto: Macmillan, 1972).

47 PABC, McClung Papers, vol. 22(3).

48　Warne, *Literature as Pulpit*, 29.

49　Hallett and Davis, *Firing the Heather*, 100–101.

50　Edward McCourt, *The Canadian West in Fiction* (Toronto: Ryerson Press, 1949), 73.

51　Nina Baym, *Women's Fiction: A Guide to Novels By and About Women in America, 1820–1970* (Ithaca, N.Y.: Cornell University Press, 1978), 168.

52　Warne, *Literature as Pulpit*, 105–114.

53　"Birth Control," in *The Canadian Encyclopedia* (Edmonton: Hurtig Press, 1985).

54　Marilyn Barber, "Help for Farm Homes: The Campaign to End Housework Drudgery in Rural Saskatchewan in the 1920's," *Scientia Canadensis* IX (June 1985): 7–8.

55　Annette Kolodny, "A Map for Rereading: Gender and the Interpretation of Literary Texts," in *The New Feminist Criticism*, ed. Elaine Showalter (New York: Pantheon Books, 1985), 56–57.

56　Graulich, "Violence Against Women," in *The Women's West*, eds. Armitage and Jameson, 120.

57　Inga-stina Ewbank, "Ibsen and the Language of Women," in *Women Writing and Writing About Women*, ed. Jacobus, 127.

58　Elaine Showalter, *A Literature of Their Own*, 28, 33.

59　PABC, McClung Papers, vol. 23(3), typescript, "Speak Up! Ladies!" n.d.

60　Margaret Laurence, *Dance on the Earth: A Memoir* (Toronto: McClelland and Stewart, 1987), 136.

61　Thomas Fisher Rare Book Library, University of Toronto, William Arthur Deacon Papers, letter from Deacon to NLM, 14 January 1948.

62 Clara Thomas, "Women Writers and the New Land," in *The New Land: Studies in a Literary Theme*, eds. Richard Chadbourne and Hallvard Dahlie (Waterloo, Ont.: University of Waterloo Press, 1978), and *All My Sisters: Essays on the Work of Canadian Women Authors* (Ottawa: Tecumseh, 1994).

The Live Wire

"Who is this young gentleman or lady?" Dr. Clay asked of Pearlie Watson one day when he met her wheeling a baby carriage with an abnormally fat baby in it.

"This is the Czar of all the Rooshias," Pearl answered gravely, "and I'm his body-guard."

The doctor's face showed no surprise as he stepped back to get a better look at the czar, who began to squirm at the delay.

"See the green plush on his kerridge," Pearl said proudly, "and every stitch he has on is hand-made, and was did for him, too, and he's fed every three hours, rain or shine, hit or miss."

"Think of that!" the doctor exclaimed with emphasis, "and yet some people tell us that the Czar has a hard time of it."

Pearl drew a step nearer, moving the carriage up and down rapidly to appease the wrath of the czar, who was expressing his disapproval in a very lumpy cry.

"I'm just 'tendin' ye know, about im bein' the Czar," she said confidentially. "Ye see, I mind him every day, and that's the way I play. Maudie Ducker said one day I never had no time to play cos we wuz so pore, and that started me. It's a lovely game."

The doctor nodded. He knew something of " 'tendin' games" too.

"I have to taste everythin' he eats, for fear of Paris green," Pearlie went on, speaking now in the loud official tone of the body-guard. "I have to stand between him and the howlin' mob thirstin' for his gore."

"He seems to howl more than the mob," the doctor said, smiling.

"He's afraid we're plottin'," Pearl whispered. "Can't trust no one. He ain't howlin'. That's his natcheral voice when he's talkin' Rooshan. He don't know one English word, only 'Goo'! But he'll say that every time. See now. How is um precious luvvy-duvvy? See the pitty man, pull um baby toofin!"

At which the czar, secure in his toothlessness, rippled his fat face into dimples, and triumphantly brought forth a whole succession of "goos."

"Ain't he a peach?" Pearlie said with pride. "Some kids won't show off worth a cent when ye want them to, but he'll say 'goo' if you even nudge him. His mother thinks 'goo' is awful childish, and she is at him all the time to say 'Daddy-dinger,' but he never lets on he hears her. Say, doctor"— Pearlie's face was troubled—"what do you think of his looks? Just between ourselves. Hasn't he a fine little nub of a nose? Do you see anything about him to make his mother cry?"

The doctor looked critically at the czar, who returned his gaze with stolid indifference.

"I never saw a more perfect nub on any nose," he answered honestly. "He's a fine big boy, and his mother should be proud of him."

"There now, what did I tell you!" Pearlie cried delightedly, nodding her head at an imaginary audience.

"That's what I always say to his mother, but she's so tuk up with pictures of pretty kids with big eyes and curly hair, she don't seem to be able to get used to him. She never says his nose is a pug, but she says it's 'different,' and his voice is not what she wanted. He cries lumpy, I know, but his goos are all right. The kid in the book she is readin' could say 'Daddy-dinger' before he was as old as the Czar is, and it's awful hard on her. You see, he can't pat-a-cake, or this-little-pig-went-to-market, or wave a bye-bye or nuthin'. I never told her what Danny could do when he was this age. But I'm workin' hard to get him to say 'Daddy-dinger.' She has her heart set on that. Well, I must go on now."

The doctor lifted his hat, and the imperial carriage rolled on.

She had gone a short distance when she remembered something:

"I'll let you know when he says it, doc!" she shouted.

"All right, don't forget," he smiled back.

When Pearlie turned the next corner she met Maudie Ducker. Maudie Ducker had on a new plaid dress with velvet trimming, and Maudie knew it.

"Is that your Sunday dress?" she asked Pearl, looking critically at Pearlie's faded little brown winsey.

"My, no!" Pearlie answered cheerfully. "This is just my morning dress. I wear my blue satting in the afternoon, and on Sundays, my purple velvet with the watter-plait, and basque-yoke of tartaric plaid, garnished with lace. Yours is a nice little plain dress. That stuff fades though; ma lined a quilt for the boys' bed with it and it faded gray."

Maudie Ducker was a "perfect little lady." Her mother often said so. Maudie could not bear to sit near a child in school who had on a dirty pinafore or ragged clothes, and the number of days that she could wear a pinafore without its showing one trace of stain was simply wonderful! Maudie had two dolls which she never played with. They were propped up against the legs of the parlour table. Maudie could play the "Java March" and "Mary's Pet Waltz" on the piano. She always spoke in a hushed vox tremulo, and never played any rough games. She could not bear to touch a baby, because it might put a sticky little finger on her pinafore. All of which goes to show what a perfect little lady she was.

When Maudie made inquiries of Pearl Watson as to her Sabbath-day attire, her motives were more kindly than Pearl thought. Maudie's mother was giving her a party. Hitherto the guests upon such occasions had been selected with great care, and with respect to social standing, and blue china, and correct enunciation. This time they were selected with greater care, but with respect to their fathers' politics. All Conservatives' and undecided voters' children were included. The fight-to-a-finish-for-the-grand-old-party Reformers were tabooed.

Algernon Evans, otherwise known as the Czar of all the Rooshias, only son of J. H. Evans, editor of the Millford *Mercury*, could not be overlooked. Hence the reason for asking Pearl Watson, his body-guard.

Millford had two weekly newspapers—one Conservative in its tendencies and the other one Reform. Between them there existed a feud, long standing, unquenchable, constant. It went with the printing press, the subscription list, and the goodwill of the former owner, when the paper changed hands.

The feud was discernible in the local news as well as in the editorials. In the Reform paper, which was edited at the time of which we write by a Tipperary man named McSorley, you might read of a distressing accident which befell one Simon Henry (also a Reformer), while that great and good man was abroad upon an errand of mercy, trying to induce a drunken man to go quietly to his home and family. Mr. Henry was eulogised for his kind act, and regret was expressed that Mr. Henry should have met with such rough usage while endeavoring to hold out a helping hand to one unfortunate enough to be held in the demon chains of intemperance.

In the Conservative paper the following appeared:

> We regret to hear that Simon Henry, secretary of the Young Liberal Club, got mixed up in a drunken brawl last evening and as a result will be confined to his house for a few days. We trust his injuries are not serious, as his services are indispensable to his party in the coming campaigns.

Reports of concerts, weddings, even deaths, were tinged with partyism. When Daniel Grover, grand old Conservative war-horse, was gathered to his fathers at the ripe age of eighty-seven years, the Reform paper said that Mr. Grover's death was not entirely un-expected, as his health had been failing for some time, the deceased having passed his seventieth birthday.

McSorley, the Liberal editor, being an Irishman, was not without humor, but Evans, the other one, revelled in it. He was like the little boys who stick pins in frogs, not that they bear the frogs any ill-will, but for the fun of seeing them jump. He would sit half the night over his political editorials, smiling grimly to himself, and when he threw himself back in his chair and laughed like a boy, the knife was turned in someone!

One day Mr. James Ducker, lately retired farmer, sometimes insurance agent, read in the Winnipeg *Telegram* that his friend the Honorable Thomas Snider had chaperoned an Elk party to St. Paul. Mr. Ducker had but a hazy idea of the duties of a chaperon, but he liked the sound of it, and it set him thinking. He remembered when Tom Snider had entered politics with a decayed reputation, a large whiskey bill, and about $2.20 in cash. Now he rode in a private car, and had a suite of rooms at the Empire, and the papers often spoke of him as "mine host" Snider. Mr. Ducker turned over the paper and read that the genial Thomas had replied in a very happy manner to a toast at the Elks' banquet. Whereupon Mr. Ducker became wrapped in deep thought, and during this passive period he distinctly heard his country's call! The call came in these words: "If Tom Snider can do it, why not me?"

The idea took hold of him. He began to brush his hair artfully over the bald spot. He made strange faces at his mirror, wondering which side of his face would be the best to have photographed for his handbills. He saw himself like Cincinnatus of old called from the plough to the Senate, but he told himself there could not have been as good a thing in it then as there is now, or Cincinnatus would not have come back to the steers.

Mr. Ducker's social qualities developed amazingly. He courted his neighbors assiduously, sending presents from his garden, stopping to have protracted conversations with men whom he had known but slightly before. Every man whose name was on the voters' list began to have a new significance for him.

There was a man whom he feared—that was Evans, editor of the Conservative paper. Sometimes when his fancy painted for him a gay and alluring picture of carrying "the proud old Conservative banner that has suffered defeat, but, thank God! never disgrace in the face of the foe" (quotation from speech Mr. Ducker had prepared), sometimes he would in the midst of the most glowing and glorious passages inadvertently think of Evans, and it gave him gooseflesh. Mr. Ducker had lived in and around Millford for some time. So had Evans, and Evans had a most treacherous memory. You could not depend on him to forget anything!

When Evans was friendly with him, Mr. Ducker's hopes ran high, but when he caught Evans looking at him with that boyish smile of his, twinkling in his eyes, the vision of chaperoning an Elk party to St. Paul became very shadowy indeed.

Mr. Ducker tried diplomacy. He withdrew his insurance advertisement from McSorley's paper, and doubled his space in Evans's, paying in advance. He watched the trains for visitors and reported them to Evans. He wrote breezy little local briefs in his own light cow-like way for Evans's paper.

But Mr. Ducker's journalistic fervor received a serious set back one day. He rushed into the *Mercury* office just as the paper went to press with the news that old Mrs. Williamson had at last winged her somewhat delayed flight. Evans thanked him with some cordiality for letting him know in time to make a note of it, and asked him to go around to Mrs. Williamson's home and find out a few facts for the obituary.

Mr. Ducker did so with great cheerfulness, rather out of keeping with the nature of his visit. He felt that his way was growing brighter. When he reached the old lady's home he was received with all courtesy by her slow-spoken son. Mr. Ducker bristled with importance as he made known his errand, in a neat speech, in which official dignity and sympathy were artistically blended. "The young may die, but the old must die," he reminded Mr. Williamson as he produced his pencil and tablet. Mr. Williamson gave a detailed account of his mother's early life, marriages, first and second, and located all her children with painstaking accuracy. "Left to mourn her loss," Mr. Ducker wrote.

"And the cause of her death?" Mr. Ducker inquired gently, "general breaking down of the system, I suppose?" with his pencil poised in the air.

Mr. Williamson knit his shaggy brows.

"Well, I wouldn't say too much about mother's death if I were you. Stick to her birth, and the date she joined the church, and her marriages—they're sure. But mother's death is a little uncertain, just yet."

A toothless chuckle came from the adjoining room. Mrs. Williamson had been an interested listener to the conversation.

"Order my coffin, Ducker, on your way down, but never mind the flowers, they might not keep," she shrilled after him as he beat a hasty retreat.

When Mr. Ducker, crestfallen and humiliated, re-entered the *Mercury* office a few moments later, he was watched by two twinkling Irish eyes, that danced with unholy merriment at that good man's discomfiture. They belonged to Ignatius Benedicto McSorley, the editor of the other paper.

But Mrs. Ducker was hopeful. A friend of hers in Winnipeg had already a house in view for them, and Mrs. Ducker had decided the church they would attend when the session opened, and what day she would have, and many other important things that it is well to have one's mind made up on and not leave to the last. Maudie Ducker had been taken into the secret, and began to feel sorry for the other little girls whose papas were contented to let them live always in such a pokey little place as Millford. Maudie also began to dream dreams of sweeping in upon the Millford people in flowing robes and waving plumes and sparkling diamonds, in a gorgeous red automobile. Wilford Ducker, only son of the Ducker family, was not taken into the secret. He was too young, his mother said, to understand the change.

The nomination day was drawing near, which had something to do with the date of Maudie Ducker's party. Mrs. Ducker told Maudie they must invite the czar and Pearl Watson, though, of course, she did not say the czar. She said Algernon Evans and that little Watson girl.

Maudie, being a perfect little lady, objected to Pearl Watson on account of her scanty wardrobe, and to the czar's moist little hands; but Mrs. Ducker, knowing that the czar's father was their long suit, stood firm.

Mr. Ducker had said to her that very morning, rubbing his hands, and speaking in the conspirator's voice: "We must leave no stone unturned. This is the time of seedsowing, my dear. We must pull every wire."

The czar was a wire, therefore they proceeded to pull him. They did not know he was a live wire until later.

Pearl Watson's delight at being asked to a real party knew no bounds. Maudie need not have worried about Pearl's appearing at the feast without the festal robe. The dress that Camilla had made for her was just waiting for such an occasion to air its loveliness. Anything that was needed to complete her toilet was supplied by her kind-hearted mistress, the czar's mother.

But Mrs. Evans stood looking wistfully after her only son as Pearl wheeled him gaily down the walk. He was beautifully dressed in the finest of mull and valenciennes; his carriage was the loveliest they could buy; Pearl in her neat hat and dress was a little nurse girl to be proud of. But Mrs. Evans's pretty face was troubled. She was thinking of the pretty baby pictures in the magazines, and Algernon was so—different! And his nose was—strange, too, and she had massaged it so carefully, too, and when, oh when, would he say "Daddy-dinger"!

But Algernon was not envious of any other baby's beauty that afternoon, nor worried about his nose either as he bumped up and down in his carriage in glad good humor, and delivered full-sized gurgling "goos" at every person he met, even throwing them along the street in the prodigality of his heart, as he waved his fat hands and thumped his heavy little heels.

Pearl held her head high and was very much the bodyguard as she lifted the weighty ruler to the ground. Mrs. Ducker ran down the steps and kissed the czar ostentatiously, pouring out such a volume of admiring and endearing epithets that Pearl stood in bewilderment, wondering why she had never heard of this before. Mrs. Ducker carried the czar into the house, Pearl following with one eye shut, which was her way of expressing perplexity.

Two little girls in very fluffy short skirts sat demurely in the hammock, keeping their dresses clean and wondering if there would be ice-cream. Within doors Maudie worried out the "Java March" on the piano, to a dozen or more patient little listeners. On the lawn several little girls played croquet. There were no boys at the party. Wilford was going to have the boys—that is, the Conservative boys—the next day. Mrs. Ducker did not believe in co-education. Boys are so rough, except Wilford. He had been so carefully brought up, he was not rough at all. He stood awkwardly by the gate watching the girls play croquet. He had been left without a station at his own request. Patsey Watson rode by on a dray wagon, dirty and jolly. Wilford called to him furtively, but Patsey was busy holding on and did not hear him. Wilford sighed heavily. Down at the tracks a freight train shunted and shuddered. Not a boy was in sight. He knew why. The farmers were loading cattle cars.

Pearl went around to the side lawn where the girls were playing croquet, holding the czar's hand tightly.

"What are you playin'?" she asked.

They told her.

"Can you play it?" Mildred Bates asked.

"I guess I can," Pearl said modestly. "But I'm always too busy for games like that!"

"Maudie Ducker says you never play," Mildred Bates said with pity in her voice.

"Maudie Ducker is way off there," Pearl answered with dignity. "I have more fun in one day than Maudie Ducker'll ever have if she lives to be as old as Melchesidick, and it's not this frowsy standin'-round-doin'-nothin' that you kids call fun either."

"Tell us about it, Pearl," they shouted eagerly. Pearl's stories had a charm.

"Well," Pearl began, "ye know I wash Mrs. Evans's dishes every day, and lovely ones they are, too, all pink and gold with dinky little ivy leaves crawlin' out over the edges of the cups. I play I am at the seashore and the tide is comin' in o'er and o'er the sand and 'round and 'round the land, far as eye can see—that's out of a book. I put all the dishes into the big dish pan, and I pertend the tide is risin' on them, though it's just me pourin' on the water. The cups are the boys and the saucers are the girls, the plates are the fathers and mothers and the butter chips are the babies. Then I rush in to save them, but not until they cry 'Lord save us, we perish!' Of course, I yell it for them, good and loud too—people don't just squawk at a time like that—it often scares Mrs. Evans even yet. I save the babies first. I slush them around to clean them, but they never notice that, and I stand them up high and dry in the drip-pan. Then I go in after the girls, and they quiet down the babies in the drip-pan; and then the mothers I bring out, and the boys and the fathers. Sometimes some of the men make a dash out before the women, but you bet I lay them back in a hurry. Then I set the ocean back on the stove, and I rub the babies to get their blood circlin' again, and I get them all put to bed on the second shelf and they soon forget they were so near death's door."

Maudie Ducker had finished the "Java March" and "Mary's Pet Waltz," and had joined the interested group on the lawn and now stood listening in dull wonder.

"I rub them all and shine them well," Pearl went on, "and get them all packed off home into the china cupboard, every man jack o' them singin' 'Are we yet alive and see each other's face.' Mrs. Evans sings it for them when she's there."

"Then I get the vegetable dishes and bowls and silverware and all that, and that's an excursion, and they're all drunk, not a sober man on board. They sing 'Sooper up old boys,' 'We won't go home till mornin'' and all that, and crash! a cry burst from every soul on board. They have struck upon a rock and are going down! Water pours in at the gunnel (that's just me with more water and soap, you

STORIES SUBVERSIVE

know), but I ain't sorry for them, for they're all old enough to know that 'wine is a mocker, strong drink is ragin', and whosoever is deceived thereby is not wise.' But when the crash comes and the swellin' waters burst in they get sober pret' quick and come rushin' up on deck with pale faces to see what's wrong, and I've often seen a big bowl whirl 'round and 'round kind o' dizzy and say 'woe is me!' and sink to the bottom. Mrs. Evans told me that. Anyway I do save them at last, when they see what whiskey is doin' for them. I rub them all up and send them home. The steel knives—they're the worst of all. But though they're black and stained with sin, they're still our brothers, and so we give them the gold cure—that's the bath-brick, and they make a fresh start.

"When I sweep the floor I pertend I'm the army of the Lord that comes to clear the way from dust and sin, and let the King of Glory in. Under the stove the hordes of sin are awful thick. They love darkness rather than light, because their deeds are evil! But I say the 'sword of the Lord and of Gideon!' and let them have it! Sometimes I pertend I'm the woman that lost the piece of silver and I sweep the house diligently till I find it, and once Mrs. Evans did put ten cents in a corner just for fun for me, and I never know when she's goin' to do something like that."

Here Maudie Ducker, who had been listening with growing wonder, interrupted Pearl with the cry of "Oh, here's pa and Mr. Evans. They're going to take our pictures!"

The little girls were immediately roused out of the spell that Pearlie's story had put upon them, and began to group themselves under the trees, arranging their little skirts and frills.

The czar had toddled on his uncertain little fat legs around to the back door, for he had caught sight of a red head which he knew and liked very much. It belonged to Mary McSorley, the eldest of the McSorley family, who had brought over to Mrs. Ducker the extra two quarts of milk which Mrs. Ducker had ordered for the occasion.

Mary sat on the back step until Mrs. Ducker should find time to empty her pitcher. Mary was strictly an outsider. Mary's father was a Reformer. He ran the opposition paper to *dear* Mr. Evans. Mary was never well dressed, partly accounted for by the fact that the angels had visited the McSorley home so often. Therefore, for these reasons, Mary sat on the back step, a rank outsider.

The czar, who knew nothing of these things, began to "goo" as soon as he saw her. Mary reached out her arms. The czar stumbled into them and Mary fell to kissing his bald head. She felt more at home with a baby in her arms.

It was at this unfortunate moment that Mr. Ducker and Mr. Evans came around to the rear of the house. Mr. Evans was beginning to think rather more favorably of Mr. Ducker, as the prospective Conservative member. He might do all right—there are plenty worse—he has no brains—but that does not matter. What need has a man of brains when he goes into politics? Brainy men make the trouble. The Grits made that mistake once, elected a brainy man, and they have had no peace since.

Mr. Ducker had adroitly drawn the conversation to a general discussion of children. He knew that Mr. Evans's weak point was his little son Algernon.

"That's a clever-looking little chap of yours, Evans," he remarked carelessly as they came up the street. (Mr. Ducker had never seen the czar closely.) "My wife was just saying the other day that he has a wonderful forehead for a little fellow."

"He has," the other man said, smiling, not at all displeased. "It runs clear down to his neck!"

"He can hardly help being clever if there's anything in heredity," Mr. Ducker went on with infinite tact, feeling his rainbow dreams of responding to toasts at Elk banquets drawing nearer and nearer.

Then the Evil Genius of the House of Ducker awoke from his slumber, sat up and took notice! The house that the friend in Winnipeg had selected for them fell into irreparable ruins! Poor Maudie's automobile vanished at a touch! The rosy dreams of Cincinnatus, and of carrying the grand old Conservative banner in the face of the foe turned to clay and ashes!

They turned the corner, and came upon Mary McSorley who sat on the back step with the czar in her arms. Mary's head was hidden as she kissed the czar's fat neck, and in the general babel of voices, within and without, she did not hear them coming.

"Speaking about heredity," Mr. Ducker said suavely, speaking in a low voice, and looking at whom he supposed to be the latest McSorley, "it looks as if there must be something in it over there. Isn't that McSorley over again? Low forehead, pug nose, bull-dog tendencies." Mr. Ducker was something of a phrenologist, and went blithely on to his own destruction.

"Now the girl is rather pleasant looking, and some of the others are not bad at all. But this one is surely a regular little Mickey. I believe a person would be safe in saying that he would not grow up a Presbyterian." Mr. Evans was the worshipful Grand Master of the Loyal Orange Lodge, and well up in the Black, and this remark Mr. Ducker thought he would appreciate.

"McSorley will never be dead while this little fellow lives," Mr. Ducker laughed merrily, rubbing his hands.

The czar looked up and saw his father. Perhaps he understood what had been said, and saw the hurt in his father's face and longed to heal him of it; perhaps the time had come when he should forever break the goo-goo bonds that had lain upon his speech. He wriggled off Mary's knees, and toddling uncertainly across the grass with a mighty mental conflict in his pudgy little face, held out his dimpled arms with a glad cry of "Daddy-dinger"!

That evening while Mrs. Ducker and Maudie were busy fanning Mr. Ducker and putting wet towels on his head, Mr. Evans sat down to write.

"Some more of that tiresome election stuff, John," his pretty little wife said in disappointment, as she proudly rocked the emancipated czar to sleep.

"Yes, dear, it is election stuff, but it is not a bit tiresome," he answered smiling, as he kissed her tenderly. Several times during the evening, and into the night, she heard him laugh his happy boyish laugh.

James Ducker did not get the nomination.

∽

"The Live Wire" was published in *The Canadian Magazine* (June 1906) and *The Woman's Home Companion* (October 1908); subsequently became a chapter in McClung's first novel, *Sowing Seeds in Danny* (Toronto: William Briggs, 1908), 87–116. Recently reproduced in *New Women: Short Stories by Canadian Women* (Ottawa: University of Ottawa Press, 1991), 246–256.

STORIES SUBVERSIVE

BABETTE

If George Shaw had been a Christian Scientist on the morning of the twentieth of October, he would have said that he had too much mortal mind. But he was a Methodist, and one who had departed from his first love, so he merely said that he felt like the very devil.

The rain fell dismally from the gray sky, dripped with steady insistence on the leaky roof of the shanty, and made dirty puddles on the floor. For three days and three nights the downpour had fallen, and still the gray sky hung heavy with moisture.

"Just what we need," growled Shaw ironically, as he looked out of the little fly-specked window on the dull gray morning. The grain stood in water-soaked shocks, its golden color almost gone. Beside the dripping straw-stack, the old black-and-white cow stood, humped and dejected, but with a look of resignation on her honest Holstein face. She shook the rainwater out of her ears as he looked, and again huddled closer to the straw-stack.

With a shiver, Shaw turned from the window and proceeded to light a fire in the little rust-red stove. Ashes littered the floor. A sooty pot with a few black potatoes, boiled yesterday in their skins, stood on the back covers. Dirty dishes littered the table. He filled the rusty iron tea-kettle from a yellow tin water-pail that stood on a raisin-box in a corner, and then made a circuitous route to the bread-box, avoiding the drops that fell with dismal precision from the roof.

He found the bread-box empty, and only then remembered that this was bread-day when Henri, the half-breed boy, would bring him the week's supply. But as Henri, after the manner of his leisurely kind, never appeared before noon, there was nothing for it but to breakfast on the soda-biscuits left from last week's baking. He set the box on the table, thereby disturbing two bright-eyed little mice who had also discovered the depletion of the larder.

Next he threw a handful of black tea into the teapot, filled it up with water and set it on the stove to draw—this was only Friday, and Sunday was the day for emptying the tea-leaves—and that was all.

While he drank the bitter black tea and ate the mouse-nibbled soda-biscuits he was surprised to hear footsteps approaching, and still more surprised when Henri appeared at the door with the bread-sack slung over his shoulder.

"Come in, come in, Henri!" exclaimed Shaw. "What has struck you this morning?"

Henri grinned as he laid down the gunny-sack, and Shaw noticed that his face bore the marks of recent and mighty conflict with soap and water.

"What's struck you, Henri?" Shaw repeated, his wonder growing as he noticed further details of the boy's toilet. "Have you experienced a change of heart?"

"No change heart," said Henri. "Change shirt, change socks, change everyt'ing. No change heart. Babette, she is home. Come on de car from de Vinnipeg. Babette wan beeg swell!"

"You don't say!" exclaimed Shaw, setting down his big white cup with its tracery of tea-stains. "You dressed up because your sister was coming home, did you?"

"Non!" said Henri in disgust, "dress up 'cause Babette say I got to. Babette say I wan dirty young peeg— Bah!"

"Good for Babette," laughed Shaw. "She certainly has you down fine, Henri."

Henri's eyes narrowed into slits.

"Babette say you leev lak wan dog," he remarked, watching Shaw furtively.

The white man flushed.

"Babette talks too much, I think," he answered with sudden dignity.

"Babette is wan beeg swell," repeated Henri, proudly. "Babette clean her teet' wan, two, t'ree tam every day. She wash her ear. She sweep, scrub, clean all tam. Mais oui, you should but see Babette. She is good peopl'."

"She certainly has tidied you up some, Henri."

"I mus' go now," said the lad. "Babette she say not stay long. She go at dad to-day. Clean him. Dad say he be dam'. Babette say we see."

"Say, Henri!" Shaw called after the boy. "Is Babette going to stay at home now?"

Henri stuck his head in the doorway.

"Mabee she stay," he said. "Mabee she marry you, if she want. Babette good peopl', Babette wan beeg swell," and Henri nodded his head to impress on his listener the advantages of such a union.

Shaw laughed again as the boy shut the door, and went on with his breakfast. The bread that Henri had brought was white and fine, and Shaw caught himself wondering if Babette had baked it. He remembered Babette quite well, although he had not seen her for four years. Then she had been a slim brown girl, barefooted and bareheaded, picking potatoes in the field, and dressed principally in a gunny-sack.

That was when he had first come to Manitoba and taken his homestead on the Souris river. The half-breed family were his nearest neighbors, but he had seen no more of Babette for she had gone to Winnipeg that winter with a family from Treesbank, presumably to school.

All morning the rain fell and dripped disconsolately into the little shanty where Shaw sat and smoked and watched the mice play around the empty pack-boxes. At noon a light wind sprang up, and the heavy clouds that so long had covered the face of the sky, rose, parted and rolled majestically away to the horizon. The sun, so long hidden, burst forth into full splendor, and the drenched fields steamed under its rays.

Shaw swallowed a hasty dinner and set off to the oatfield to open up the shocks, fearing that the wet heat would start the oats to growing under the delusion that it was spring. The trees flung down showers of big drops as he brushed through the big bluff that sheltered his oat-field on the north, and the fallen leaves gave out a sweet, wistful fragrance. In the maples the blue-jays chattered riotously, and from far away over the Brandon Hills came the honk of the wild geese. He looked up at the sound and saw their ragged, V-shaped flock making all speed southward as if they had already delayed too long.

From the field he looked down into the valley of the Souris. In the hollows the warm mist still lingered, and the birds sang as joyously as though the winter were over and gone, and tomorrow the crocuses would blossom. The river, widened out over the flat, glinted and flashed through the trees like a matrix stone, and once he saw a long-legged crane wading.

All afternoon Shaw worked away in the field in glad content. The soft Indian summer air was sweet as a caress, and stirred him into a responsive mood, and when the sun went down in a blaze of splendor, turning to crimson and gold the murky purple of the clouds that lay like dim-seen mountains on the horizon and touching the windows of a distant farm-house with flame, he leaned on his fork and watched with reminiscent eyes, thinking of his English home.

When he turned toward the shack, his thoughts darkened with the darkening landscape. The vision of his own dismal little shanty with its dirt and cheerlessness dismayed him. He knew just how it would look when he opened the door, the buzzing flies, the muddy floor, the racing mice— yes, Babette was right, he did live like a dog.

Reluctantly he swung the door wide, with an ache of homelessness on him. Then he started back with an exclamation of wonder.

There was a merry fire in the polished stove, and a delightful odor of fried ham greeted him. The tea-kettle gurgled and bubbled. A kettle of white, mealy potatoes stood on the back of the stove. The floor was scrubbed, his bed was made, there was a gay red cushion on his chair— Shaw stood bewildered in the doorway.

"Babette!" he ejaculated. "It must have been Babette. By George! that girl is making love to me."

As he looked around and saw new wonders, he gasped again. A clean towel hung beside the little looking-glass; the wash-basin that had long been lost was reposing on the little box that served as washstand, suggestively full of clean water; and the comb that had been missing since last Sunday lay beside it.

The supper was laid for two, a snowy-white flour-sack taking the place of a table-cloth. When Shaw sat down and noticed the other plate opposite his own, he was filled with apprehension. Was Babette going to swoop down on him and claim him as her own? He shivered, remembering the gunny-sack. Any girl that would undertake to clean up the old man could do anything, and besides, Henri said she would marry him if she wanted to.

That settled it. He locked the door.

The ham and eggs were deliciously fried, the potatoes were so clean and white they looked strange to him, and the comfortable meal was so welcome to the tired man that he forgot his fears and ate. Not until his appetite was appeased did he notice the other improvements—the clean window, the polished lamp-chimneys, the roll of papers and pile of magazines beside his bed.

"O Babette, Babette!" he said, laughing to himself. "You do know how to press your suit. I wish I could forget the old man and the gunny-sack, but I can't, and I'll be hanged if I know what to make of it all."

Just then he noticed a piece of paper sticking out from under the unused plate. He snatched it up curiously, and read:

"Dear Mister Pshaw! No I don't want you. Thank you all the same. I cleaned up your shantey to let you see how it feals to live like white folks. I have a gentleman frend in Winnipeg he wears clene collars and can alwas find his combe no more at present.

Babette Morin."

When he had finished reading, he sat for a few minutes, thinking deeply. Then he slowly unlocked the door.

⌒

"Babette" was published in *Canada-West* (November 1907): 49–52.

The Way of the West

Thomas Shouldice was displeased, sorely, bitterly displeased; in fact, he was downright mad, and, being an Irish Orangeman, this means that he was ready to fight. You can imagine just how bitterly Mr. Shouldice was incensed when you hear that the Fourth of July had been celebrated with flourish of flags and blare of trumpets right under his very nose—in Canada—in British dominions!

The First of July, the day that should have been given up to "doin's," including the race for the greased pig, the three-legged race, and a ploughing match, had passed into obscurity, without so much as a pie-social; and it had rained that day, too, in torrents, just as if Nature herself did not care enough about the First to try to keep it dry.

The Fourth came in a glorious day, all sunshine and blue sky, with birds singing in every poplar bluff, and it was given such a celebration as Thomas had never seen since the "Twelfth" had been held in Souris. The American settlers who had been pouring into the Souris valley had—without so much as asking leave from the Government at Ottawa, the school trustees, or the oldest settler, who was Thomas himself—gone ahead and celebrated. Every American family had brought their own flagpole, in "joints," with them, and on the Fourth immense banners of stars and stripes spread their folds in triumph on the breeze.

The celebration was held in a large grove just across the road from Thomas Shouldice's little house; and to his inflamed patriotism, every firecracker that split the air, every cheer that rent the heavens, every blare of their smashing band music, seemed a direct challenge to King Edward himself, God bless him!

Mr. Shouldice worked all day at his haymeadow, just to show them! He worked hard, too, never deigning a glance at their "carryings on," just to let them know that he did not care two cents for their Fourth of July.

His first thought was to feign indifference, but when he saw the Wilsons, the Wrays, the Henrys, Canadian-bred and born, driving over to the enemy's camp, with their Sunday clothes on and big boxes of provisions on the "doggery" of their buckboards, his indifference fled and was replaced by profanity. It comforted him a little when he reflected that not an Orangeman had gone. They were loyal sons and true, every one of them. These other ignorant Canadians might forget what they owed to the old Flag, but the Orangeman—never.

Thomas's rage against the Yankees was intensified when he saw Father O'Flynn walking across the plover slough. Then he was sure that the Americans and Catholics were in league against the British.

A mighty thought was conceived that day in the brain of Thomas Shouldice, late Worshipful Master of the Carleton Place Loyal Orange Lodge No. 23. They would celebrate the Twelfth, so they would; he'd like to see who would stop them. Someone would stand up for the flag that had braved a thousand years of battle and the breeze. He blew his nose noisily on his red handkerchief when he thought of this.

They would celebrate the Twelfth! They would "walk." He would gather up "the boys" and get someone to make a speech. They would get a fifer from Brandon. It was the fife that could stir the heart in you! And the fifer would play "The Protestant Boys" and "Rise, Sons of William, Rise!" Anyone that tried to stop him would get a shirt full of sore bones!

Thomas went home full of the plan to get back at the invaders! Rummaging through his trunks, he found, carefully wrapped with chewing tobacco and ground cedar, to keep the moths away, the regalia that he had worn, proudly and defiantly, once in Montreal, when the crowd that obstructed the triumphal march of the Orange Young Britons had to be dispersed by the "militia." It was a glorious day, and one to be remembered with pride, for there had been shots fired and heads smashed.

His man, a guileless young Englishman, came in from mowing, gaily whistling the refrain the Yankee band had been playing at intervals all afternoon. It was "Dixie Land," and at first Thomas did not notice it. Rousing at last to the sinister significance of the tune, he ordered its cessation, in rosy-hued terms, and commended all such Yankee tunes and those that whistled them to that region where popular rumor has it that pots boil with or without watching.

Thomas Shouldice had lived by himself for a number of years. It was supposed that he had a wife living somewhere in "the States," which term to many Canadians indicates a shadowy region where bad boys, unfaithful wives, and absconding embezzlers find refuge and dwell in dim security.

Thomas's devotion to the Orange Order was nothing short of a passion. He believed that but for its institution and perpetuation Protestant blood would flow like water. He always spoke of the "Stuarts" in an undertone, as if he were afraid they might even yet come back and make "rough house" for King Edward.

There were only two Catholic families in the neighborhood, and peaceable, friendly people they were, too; but Thomas believed they should be intimidated to prevent trouble. "The old spite is in them," he told himself, "and nothing will show them where they stand like a 'walk'."

The next day Thomas left his haying and rounded up the faithful. There were seven members of the order in the community, all of whom were willing to stand for their country's honor. There was James Shewfelt, who was a drummer, and could play the tunes without the fife at all. There was John Barker, who did a musical turn in the form of a twenty-three-verse ballad beginning:

> "When Popery did flourish in
>   Dear Ireland o'er the sea,
> There came a man from Amsterdam
>   To set ould Ireland free!
> To set ould Ireland free, boys,
>   To set ould Ireland free,—
> There came a man from Amsterdam
>   To set ould Ireland free!"

GEORGIAN COLLEGE BOOKSTORE
825 MEMORIAL AVE.
ORILLIA, ON L3V 6S2
PH:(705)325-2740 FAX:(705)325-3690
HTTP://GEORGIANC.ON.CA
GST #R118937283

SALES   002 002 0B00128547
CASHIER: PAR   07/16/08 13:15

01 RAMPOLLA / POCKET GUIDE T
   101010 10187944   1 T   15.25

                  Subtotal   15.25
          GST 5% SALES TAX   0.76

     Items   1   Total   16.01

CASH   20.00

            Change Due   3.99

THANK YOU FOR SHOPPING AT THE
GEORGIAN COLLEGE BOOKSTORE
PLEASE RETAIN THIS RECEIPT FOR REFUND
AND/OR WARRANTY REQUIREMENTS

GEORGIAN
YOUR COLLEGE · YOUR FUTURE

THE BOOKSTORE

Bookstores & Computer Store
Barrie   Orillia   Owen Sound

Hours of Operation:

Barrie:	Monday to Thursday	7:45 a.m. to 7:30 p.m.
	Friday	7:45 a.m. to 4:30 p.m.
	May through August	7:45 a.m. to 4:30 p.m. daily
	BITS & BYTES	
	Monday to Friday	8:30 a.m. to 4:15 p.m.
	May through August	9:30 a.m. to 3:30 p.m.
Orillia:	Monday to Friday	8:45 a.m. to 4 p.m.
Owen Sound:	Monday to Thursday	8:30 a.m. to 4 p.m.
	Friday	8:30 a.m. to 1 p.m.

ALL REFUNDS REQUIRE ORIGINAL CASH REGISTER RECEIPTS WITHIN 10 WORKING DAYS OF PURCHASE; REFUND WILL BE ISSUED FOR ORIGINAL TENDER ONLY, NO EXCEPTIONS.

TEXTBOOKS
To be eligible for return, books must be in NEW CONDITION, unused, unmarked, undamaged. The slightest damage can make a book non-returnable. Do not write your name in your book. **IMPORTANT:** If original wrapping is broken, shrink wrapped book sets, or books containing tapes or software are NON-REFUNDABLE, unless defective. This policy has been set by the Publishers not the Bookstore.
EXCEPTIONS: SPECIAL ORDERS, CUSTOM PUBLICATIONS; these are FINAL SALE.

COMPUTER STORE: GC STUDENT SOFTWARE TITLES AND SPECIAL ORDERS ARE FINAL SALE ITEMS. All APPLE products are final sale items and any warranty issues must be resolved directly with Apple. Excluding Apple products, defective hardware returned within 10 business days may be exchanged for the same product.

NON-RETURNABLE ITEMS: Sale items, diskettes, food items, personalized items, and items marked FINAL SALE, custom jackets and rings.

Barrie Campus Bookstore: Phone (705) 722-1570; Fax (705) 722-5141
Bits & Bytes computer store: (705) 722-5178 http://bitsnbytes.georgianc.on.ca/
Orillia: (705) 325-2740, ext 3013   **Owen Sound:** (519) 376-0840, ext. 2093
www.georgianc.on.ca/bookstore

GEORGIAN

There was William Breeze, who was a little hard of hearing, but loyal to the core. He had seven boys in his family, so there was still hope for the nation. There was Patrick Mooney, who should have been wearing the other color if there is anything in name. There was John Burns, who had been an engineer but, having lost a foot, had taken to farming. He was the farthest advanced in the order next to Thomas Shouldice, having served a term as District Grand Master, and was well up in the Grand Black Chapter. These would form the nucleus of the procession. The seven little Breezes would be admitted to the ranks if their mother could find suitable decoration for them. Of course, the weather was warm and the subject of clothing was not so serious as it might have been.

Thomas drove nineteen miles to the nearest town to get a speaker and a fifer. The fifer was found, and, quite fortunately, was open for engagement. The speaker was not so easily secured. Thomas went to the Methodist missionary. The missionary was quite a young man and had the reputation of being an orator. He listened gravely while his visitor unfolded his plan.

"I'll tell you what to do, Mr. Shouldice," he said, smiling, when the other had finished the recital of his country's wrongs. "Get Father O'Flynn; he'll make you a speech that will do you all good."

Thomas was too astonished for words. "But he's a Papist!" he sputtered at last.

"Oh, pshaw! Oh, pshaw! Mr. Shouldice," the young man exclaimed, "there's no division of creed west of Winnipeg. The little priest does all my sick visiting north of the river, and I do his on the south. He's a good preacher, and the finest man at a deathbed I ever saw."

"This is not a deathbed, though, as it happens," Thomas replied with dignity.

The young minister threw back his head and laughed uproariously. "Can't tell that until it is over—I've been at a few Orange walks down East, you know—took part in one myself once."

"Did you walk?" Thomas asked, brightening.

"No, I ran," the minister said, smiling.

"I thought you said you took part," Thomas snorted, with displeasure.

"So I did, but mine was a minor part. I stood behind the fence and helped the Brennan boys and Patrick Costigan to peg at them!"

"Are ye a Protestant at all?" Thomas roared at him, now thoroughly angry.

"Yes, I am," the minister said, slowly, "and I am something better still; I am a Christian and a Canadian. Are you?"

Thomas beat a hasty retreat.

The Presbyterian minister was away from home, and the English Church minister—who was also a young man lately arrived—said he would go gladly.

The Twelfth of July was a beautiful day, clear, sparkling, and cloudless. Little wayward breezes frolicked up and down the banks of Moose Creek and rasped the surface of its placid pools, swollen still from the heavy rains of the "First." In the glittering sunshine the prairie lay a riot of color; the first wild roses now had faded to a pastel pink, but on every bush there were plenty of new ones, deeply crimson and odorous. Across the creek from Thomas Shouldice's little house, Indian pipes and columbine reddened the edge of the poplar grove, from the lowest branches of which morning-glories, white and pink and purple, hung in graceful profusion.

Before noon a wagon filled with people came thundering down the trail. As they came nearer, Thomas was astonished to see that it was an American family from the Chippen Hill district.

"Picnic in these parts, ain't there?" the driver asked.

Thomas was in a genial mood, occasioned by the day and the weather.

"Orange walk and picnic!" he replied, waving his hand toward the bluff, where a few of the faithful were constructing a triumphal arch.

"Something like a cake-walk, is it?" the man asked, looking puzzled.

Mr. Shouldice stared at him incredulously.

"Did ye never hear of Orangemen down yer way?" he said.

"Never did, pard," the man answered. "We've peanut men, and apple women, and banana men, but we've never heard much about orange men. But we're right glad to come over and help the show along. Do you want any money for the races?"

"We didn't count on havin' races; we're havin' speeches and some singin'."

The Yankee laughed good-humoredly.

"Well, friend, I pass there; but mother here is a WCTU-er from away back. She'll knock the spots off the liquor business in fifteen minutes, if you'd like anything in that line."

His wife interposed in her easy, drawling tones: "Now, Abe, you best shet up and drive along. The kids are all hungry and want their dinners."

"We'll see you later, partner," said the man as they drove away.

Thomas Shouldice was mystified. "These Americans are a queer bunch," he thought. "They're ignorant as all get out, but gosh! they're friendly."

Over the hill to the south came other wagons filled with jolly picnickers, who soon had their pots boiling over quickly constructed tripods.

Thomas, who went over to welcome them, found that nearly all of them were the very Americans whose unholy zeal for their own national holiday had so embittered his heart eight days before.

They were full of enquiries as to the meaning of an Orange walk. Thomas tried to explain, but, having only inflamed Twelfth of July oratory for the source of his information, he found himself rather at a loss. But the Americans gathered that it was something he used to do "down East," and they were sympathetic at once.

"That's right, you bet," one gray-haired man with a young face exclaimed, getting rid of a bulky chew of tobacco that had slightly impeded his utterance. "There's nothin' like keepin' up old institootions."

By two o'clock fully one hundred people had gathered.

Thomas was radiant. "Every wan is here now except that old Papist, O'Flynn," he whispered to the drummer. "I hope he'll come, too, so I do. It'll be a bitter pill for him to swallow."

The drummer did not share the wish. He was thinking, uneasily, of the time two years ago—the winter of the deep snow—when he and his family had been quarantined with smallpox, and of how Father O'Flynn had come miles out of his way every week on his snowshoes to hand in a roll of newspapers he had gathered up, no one knows where, and a bag of candies for the little ones. He was thinking of how welcome the priest's little round face had been to them all those long, tedious six weeks, and how cheery his voice sounded as he shouted, "Are ye needin' anything, Jimmy, avick? All right, I'll be back on Thursda', God willin'. Don't be frettin', now, man alive! Everybody has to have the smallpox. Sure, yer shaming the Catholics this year, Jimmy, keeping Lent so well." The drummer was decidedly uneasy.

There is an old saying about speaking of angels in which some people still believe. Just at this moment Father O'Flynn came slowly over the hill.

Father O'Flynn was a typical little Irish priest, good-natured, witty, emotional. Nearly every family north of the river had some cause for loving the little man. He was a tireless walker, making the round of his parish every week, no matter what the weather. He had a little house built for him the year before at the Forks of the Assiniboine, where he had planted a garden, set out plants and flowers, and made it a little bower of beauty; but he had lived in it only one summer, for an impecunious English couple, who needed a roof to cover them rather urgently, had taken possession of it during his absence, and the kind-hearted father could not bring himself to ask them to vacate. When his friends remonstrated with him, he turned the conversation by telling them of another and a better Man of who it was written that He "had no where to lay His head."

STORIES SUBVERSIVE

Father O'Flynn was greeted with delight, by the younger ones especially. The seven little Breezes were very demonstrative, and Thomas Shouldice resolved to warn their father against the priest's malign influence. He recalled a sentence or two from "Maria Monk," which said something like this: "Give us a child until he is ten years old, and let us teach him our doctrine, and he's ours for evermore."

"Oh, they're deep ones, them Jesuits!"

Father O'Flynn was just in time for the "walk."

"Do you know what an Orange walk is, Father?" one of the American women asked, really looking for information.

"Yes, daughter, yes," the little priest answered, a shadow coming into his merry gray eyes. He gave her an evasive reply, and then murmured to himself, as he picked a handful of orange lilies: "It is an institution of the Evil One to sow discord between brothers."

The walk began.

First came the fife and drum, skirling out an Orange tune, at which the little priest winced visibly. Then followed Thomas Shouldice, in the guise of King William. He was mounted on his own old, spavined gray mare, that had performed this honorable office many times in her youth. But now she seemed lacking in the pride that befits the part. Thomas himself was gay with ribbons and a short red coat, whose gilt braid was sadly tarnished. One of the Yankees had kindly loaned a mottled buggy-robe for the saddle-cloth.

Behind Thomas marched the twenty-three-verse soloist and the other faithful few, followed by the seven Breeze boys, gay with yellow streamers made from the wrapping of a ham.

The Yankees grouped about were sorry to see so few in the procession. They had brought along three or four of their band instruments to furnish music if it were needed. As the end of the procession passed them, two of the smaller boys swung in behind the last two Breezes.

It was an inspiration. Instantly the whole company stepped into line—two by two, men, women, and children, waving their bunches of lilies!

Thomas, from his point of vantage, could see the whole company following his lead, and his heart swelled with pride. Under the arch the procession swept, stepping to the music, the significance of which most of the company did not even guess at—good-natured, neighborly, filled with the spirit of the West, that ever seeks to help along.

Everyone, even Father O'Flynn, was happier than James Shewfelt, the drummer.

The fifer paused, preparatory to changing the tune. It was the drummer's opportunity. "Onward, Christian Soldiers," he sang, tapping the rhythm on the drum. The fifer caught the strain. Not a voice was silent, and unconsciously hand clasped hand, and the soft afternoon air reverberated with the swelling cadence:

> "We are not divided,
> All one body we."

When the verse was done the fifer led off into another and another. The little priest's face glowed with pleasure. "It is the Spirit of the Lord," he whispered to himself, as he marched to the rhythm, his hand closely held by the smallest Breeze boy, whose yellow streamers and profuse decoration of orange lilies were at strange variance with his companion's priestly robes. But on this day nothing was at variance. The spirit of the West was upon them, unifying, mellowing, harmonizing all conflicting emotions—the spirit of the West that calls on men everywhere to be brothers and lend a hand.

The Church of England minister did make a speech, but not the one he had intended. Instead of denominationalism, he spoke of brotherhood; instead of religious intolerance, he spoke of religious liberty; instead of the Prince of Orange, who crossed the Boyne to give religious freedom to Ireland, he told of the Prince of Peace, who died on the cross to save the souls of men of every nation and kindred and tribe.

In the hush that followed, Father O'Flynn stepped forward and said he thanked the brother who had planned this meeting; he was glad, he said, for such an opportunity for friends and neighbors to meet; he spoke of the glorious heritage that all had in this great new country, and how all must stand together as brothers. All prejudices of race and creed and doctrine die before the wonderful power of loving service. "The West," he said, "is the home of loving hearts and neighborly kindness, where all men's good is each man's care. For myself," he went on, "I have but one wish, and that is to be the servant of all, to be the ambassador of Him who went about doing good, and to teach the people to love honor and virtue, and each other." Then, raising his hands, he led the company in that prayer that comes ever to the lips of man when all other prayers seem vain—that prayer that we can all fall back on in our sore need:

> "Our Father, who art in heaven,
> Hallowed be Thy name,
> Thy Kingdom come."

Two hours later a tired but happy and united company sat down to supper on the grass. At the head of the table sat Thomas Shouldice, radiating good-will. A huge white pitcher of steaming golden coffee was in his hand. He poured a cup of it brimming full, and handed it to the little priest, who sat near him.

"Have some coffee, Father?" he said.

Where could such a scene as this be enacted—a Twelfth of July celebration where a Roman Catholic priest was the principal speaker, where the company dispersed with the singing of "God Save the King," led by an American band?

Nowhere, but in the Northwest of Canada, that illimitable land, with its great sunlit spaces, where the west wind, bearing on its bosom the spices of a million flowers, woos the heart of a man with a magic spell and makes him kind and neighborly and brotherly!

ᗧ

"The Way of the West," originally titled "July the First, Fourth, and Twelfph," was published in *The Globe* (Toronto: n.d.) and *The Black Creek Stopping-House, and Other Stories* (Toronto: William Briggs, 1912, 1919), 209–224.

The Return Ticket

n the station at Emerson, the boundary town, we were waiting for the Soo train, which comes at an early hour in the morning. It was a bitterly cold, dark, winter morning; the wires overhead sang dismally in the wind, and even the cheer of the big coal fire that glowed in the rusty stove was dampened by the incessant mourning of the storm.

Along the walls, on the benches, sat the trackmen, in their sheepskin coats and fur caps, with earlaps tied tightly down. They were tired and sleepy, and sat in every conceivable attitude expressive of sleepiness and fatigue. A red lantern, like an evil eye, gleamed from one dark corner; in the middle of the floor were several green lamps turned low, and over against the wall hung one barred lantern whose bright little gleam of light reminded one uncomfortably of a small, live mouse in a cage, caught and doomed, but undaunted still. The telegraph instruments clicked at intervals. Two men, wrapped in overcoats, stood beside the stove and talked in low tones about the way real estate was increasing in value in Winnipeg.

The door opened and a big fellow, another snow shoveller, came in hurriedly, letting in a burst of flying snow that sizzled on the hot stove. It did not rouse the sleepers from the bench; neither did the new-comer's remark that it was a "deuce of a night" bring forth any argument—we were one on that point.

The train was late; the night agent told us that when he came out to shovel in more coal—"she" was delayed by the storm.

I leaned back and tried to be comfortable. After all, I thought, it might easily be worse. I was going home after a pleasant visit. I had many agreeable things to think of, and still I kept thinking to myself that it was not a cheerful night. The clock, of course, indicated that it was morning, but the deep black that looked in through the frosted windows, the heavy shadows in the room, which the flickering lanterns only seemed to emphasize, were all of the night, and bore no relation to the morning.

The train came at last with a roar that drowned the voice of the storm. The sleepers on the bench sprang up like one man, seized their lanterns, and we all rushed out together. The long coach that I entered was filled with tired sleepy-looking people, who had been sitting up all night. They were curled up uncomfortably, making a brave attempt to rest, all except one little old lady, who sat upright, looking out into the black night. When the official came to ask the passengers where they were going, I heard her tell him that she was a Canadian, and she had been "down in the States with Annie, and now she was bringing Annie home," and as she said this she pointed significantly ahead to the baggage car.

There was something about the old lady that appealed to me. I went over to her when the official had gone out. No, she wasn't tired, she said; she "had been up a good many nights, and been worried some, but the night before last she had had a real good sleep."

She was quite willing to talk; the long black night had made her glad of companionship.

"I took Annie to Rochester, down in Minnesota, to see the doctors there—the Mayos—did you ever hear of the Mayos? Well, Dr. Smale, at Rose Valley, said they were her only hope. Annie had been ailin' for years, and Dr. Smale had done all he could for her. Dr. Moore, our old doctor, wouldn't hear of it; he said an operation would kill her, but Annie was set on going. I heard Annie say to him that she'd rather die than live sick, and she would go to Rochester. Dave Johnston—Annie's man, that is—he drinks, you know—"

The old lady's voice fell and her tired old face seemed to take on deeper lines of trouble as she sat silent with her own sad thoughts. I expressed my sorrow.

"Yes, Annie had her own troubles, poor girl," she said at last, "and she was a good girl, Annie was, and she deserved something better. She was a tender-hearted girl, and gentle and quiet, and never talked back to anyone, to Dave least of all, for she worshipped the very ground he walked on, and married him against all our wishes. She thought she could reform him!"

She said it sadly, but without bitterness.

"Was he good to her?" I asked. People draw near together in the stormy dark of a winter's morning, and the thought of Annie in her narrow box ahead robbed my question of any rudeness.

"He was good to her in his own way," Annie's mother said, trying to be quite just, "but it was a rough way. She had a fine, big, brick house to live in—it was a grand house, but it was a lonely house. He often went away and stayed for weeks, and her not knowin' where he was or how he would come home. He worried her always. The doctors said that was part of her trouble—worried her too much."

"Did he ever try to stop drinking?" I asked. I wanted to think better of him if I could.

"Yes, he did; he was sober once for nearly a year, and Annie's health was better than it had been for years, but the crowd around the hotel there in Rose Valley got after him every chance, and one Christmas Day they got him goin' again. Annie never could bear to mention about him drinkin' to anyone, not even me—it would ha' been easier on her if she could ha' talked about it, but she wasn't one of the talkin' kind."

We sat in silence, listening to the pounding of the rails.

"Everybody was kind to her in Rochester," she said, after a while. "When we were sittin' there waitin' our turn— you know how the sick people wait there in two long rows, waitin' to be taken in to the consultin' room, don't you? Well, when we were sittin' there Annie was sufferin' pretty bad, and we were still a long way from the top of the line. Dr. Judd was takin' them off as fast as he could, and the ambulances were drivin' off every few minutes, takin' them away to the hospital after the doctors had decided what was wrong with them. Some of them didn't need to go to the hospital at all—they're the best off, I think. We got talkin' to the people around us—they are there from all over the country, with all kinds of diseases, poor people. Well, there was a man from Kansas City who had been waitin' a week, but had got up now second to the end, and I noticed him lookin' at Annie. I was fannin' her and tryin' to keep her cheered up. Her face was a bad color from the pain she was in, and what did this man do but git up and come down to us and tell Annie she could have his place. He said he wasn't in very bad pain now, and he would take her place. He made very little of it, but it meant a lot to us, and to him, too, poor fellow. Annie didn't want to do it, but he insisted. Sick folks know how to be kind to sick folks, I tell you."

The dawn began to show blue behind the frost ferns on the window and the lamps overhead looked pale and sickly in the gray light.

"Annie had her operation on Monday," she went on after a long pause. "She was lookin' every day for a letter from Dave, and when the doctor told her they would operate on her on Monday morning early, she asked him if he would mind putting it off until noon. She thought there would be a letter from Dave, for sure, in that morning's mail. The doctor was very kind to her—they understand a lot, them Mayos—and he did put it off. In the ward with Annie there was a little woman from Saskatchewan that was a very bad case. She talked to us a lot about her man and her four children. She had a real good man by what she said. They were on a homestead near Quill Lake, and she was so sure she'd get well. The doctor was very hopeful of Annie, and said she had nine chances out of ten of getting better, but this little woman's was a worse case. Dr. Will Mayo told her she had just one chance in ten—but, dear me, she was a brave woman; she spoke right up quick, and says she, 'That's all I want; I'll get well if I've only half a chance. I've got to; Jim and the children can't do without me.' Jim was her man. When they came to take her out into the operatin' room they couldn't give her ether, some way. She grabbed the doctor's hand, and says she, kind of chokin' up, all at once,

'You'll do your best for Jim's sake, won't you?' and he says, says he, 'My dear woman, I'll do my best for your sake.' Busy and all as they are, they're the kindest men in the world, and just before they began to operate the nurse brought her a letter from Jim and read it to her, and she held it in her hand through it all, and when they wheeled her back into the ward after the operation, it was still in her hand, though she had fainted dead away."

"Did Annie get her letter?" I asked her.

My companion did not answer at once, but I knew very well that the letter had not come.

"She didn't ask for it at the last; she just looked at me before they put the gauze thing over her face. I knew what she meant. I had been down to see if it had come, and they told me all the mails were in for the day from the West. She just looked at me so pitiful, but it was like Annie not to ask. A letter from Dave would have comforted her so, but it didn't come, though I wired two days before telling him when the operation would be. Annie was wonderful cheerful and calm, but I was trembling like a leaf when they were givin' her the ether, and when they wheeled her out all so stiff and white I just seemed to feel I'd lost my girl."

I took the old lady's hand and tried to whisper words of comfort. She returned the pressure of my hand; her eyes were tearless, and her voice did not even waver, but the thought of poor Annie going into the valley unassured by any loving word gave free passage to my tears.

"Did Dave write or wire?" I asked when I could speak.

"No, not a word; he's likely off on a spree." The old lady spoke bitterly now. "Everybody was kind to my Annie but him, and it was a word from him that would have cheered her the most. Dr. Mayo came and sat beside her just an hour before she died, and says he, 'You still have a chance, Mrs. Johnston,' but Annie just thanked him again for his kindness and sort o' shook her head . . .

"The little woman from Saskatchewan didn't do well at all after the operation, and Dr. Mayo was afraid she wouldn't pull through. She asked him what chance she had,

and he told her straight—the Mayos always tell the truth—
that she had only one chance in a hundred. She was so weak
that he had to bend down to her whisperin', 'I'll take that
one chance!' "

"And did she?" I asked eagerly.

"She was still livin' when I left. She will get better, I
think. She has a very good man, by what she was tellin' us,
and a woman can stand a lot if she has a good man," the old
lady said, with the wisdom born of experience. "I've nursed
around a lot, and I've always noticed that!"

I have noticed it, too, though I've never "nursed
around."

"Dave came with us to the station the day we left
home. He was sober that day, and gave Annie plenty of
money. Annie told him to get a return ticket for her, too. I
said he'd better get just a single for her, for she might have
to stay longer than a month, all right. Dave seemed pleased
to hear her talk so cheerful. When she got her ticket she sat
lookin' at it a long time. I knew what she was thinkin'. She
never was a girl to talk mournful, and when the conductor
tore off the goin' down part she gave me the return piece,
and she says, 'You take this, mother.' I knew that she was
thinkin' what the return half might be used for."

We changed cars at Newton, and I stood with the old
lady and watched the trainmen unload the long box. They
threw off trunks, boxes, and valises almost viciously, but
when they lifted up the long box their manner changed and
they laid it down tenderly as if they had known something of
Annie and her troubled life.

We sent another telegram to Dave, and then sat down
in the waiting-room to wait for the west train. The wind
drove the snow in billows over the prairie, and the early twilight of the morning was bitterly cold.

Her train came first, and again the long box was gently
put aboard. On the wind-swept platform Annie's mother
and I shook hands without a word, and in another minute
the long train was sweeping swiftly across the white prairie.
I watched it idly, thinking of Annie and her sad home-going.

Just then the first pale beams of the morning sun glinted on the last coach, and touched with fine gold the long white smoke plume, which the wind carried far over the field. There is nothing so cheerful as the sunshine, and as I sat in the little gray waiting-room, watching the narrow gold beam that danced over the closed wicket, I could well believe that a rest remains for Annie, and that she is sure of a welcome at her journey's end. And as the sun's warmth began to thaw the tracery of frost on the window, I began to hope that God's grace may yet find out Dave, and that he too may "make good" in the years to come. As for the little woman from Quill Lake, who was still willing to take the one chance, I have never had the slightest doubt.

⚬

"The Return Ticket" was published in *The Canadian Ladies' Home Journal* (Summer 1910) and *The Black Creek Stopping-House, and Other Stories* (Toronto: William Briggs, 1912, 1919), 131–141.

The Runaway Grandmother

George Shaw came back to his desolate hearth, and, sitting by the untidy table, thought bitter things of women. The stove dripped ashes; the table overflowed with dirty dishes.

His last housekeeper had been gone a week—she had left by request. Incidentally there disappeared at the same time towels, pillow-covers, a few small tools, and many other articles which are of a size to go in a trunk.

His former housekeeper, second to the last, had been a teary-eyed English lady, who, as a child, had played with King George, and was well beloved by all the Royal family. She had a soul above work, and utterly despised Canadians. Once, when her employer remonstrated with her for wearing his best overcoat when she went to milk, she fell a-weeping and declared she wasn't going to be put on. Mr. Shaw said the same thing about his coat, and it led to unpleasantness. The next day he found her picking chips in his brown derby, and when he expressed his disapproval she told him it was no fit hat for a young man like him—he should have a topper. Mr. Shaw decided that he would try to do without her.

Before that he had had a red-cheeked Irishwoman, who cooked so well, scrubbed so industriously, that he had thought his troubles were all over. But one day she went to Millford, and came home in a state of wild exhilaration, with more of the same in a large black bottle. When Mr. Shaw came to put away the horse, she struck him over the head with her handbag, playfully blackening one of his eyes, and then begged him to come and make up—"kiss and forgit, like the swate pet that he was."

Exit Mrs. Murphy.

George Shaw decided to do his own cooking, but in three days every dish in the house was dirty, the teapot was full of leaves, the stove was full of ashes, and the floor was slippery.

George Shaw's farm lay parallel with the Souris river in that fertile region which lies between the Brandon and the Tiger Hills. His fields ran an unbroken mile, facing the Tiger Hills, blue with mist. He was a successful young farmer, and he should have been a happy man without a care in the world, but he did not look it as he sat wearily by his red stove, with the deep furrows of care on his young face.

The busy time was coming on; he needed another man, and he did hate trying to do the cooking himself.

As a last hope he decided to advertise. He hunted up his writing-pad and wrote hastily:

"Housekeeper wanted by a farmer; must be sober and steady. Good wages to the right person. Apply to George Shaw, Millford, Man."

He read it over reflectively. "There ought to be someone for me," he said. "I am not hard to please. Any good, steady old lady who will give me a bite to eat, not swear at me or wear my clothes or drink while on duty will answer my purpose."

Two days after his advertisement had appeared in the Brandon *Times*, "she" arrived.

Shaw saw a smart-looking woman gaily tripping along the road, and his heart failed.

As she drew near, however, he was relieved to find that her hair was snowy white.

"Good evening, Mr. Shaw!" she called to him as soon as she was within speaking distance.

"Good evening, madam," he replied, lifting his hat.

"I just asked along the road until I found you," she said, untying her bonnet strings; "I knew this lonesome little house must be the place. No trees, no flowers, no curtains, no washing on the line—I could tell there was no woman around." She was fixing her hair at his little glass as she spoke. "Now, son, run out and get a few chips for the fire, and we'll have a bite of supper in a few minutes."

Shaw brought the chips.

"Now, what do you say to pancakes for supper?"

Shaw declared that nothing would suit him so well as pancakes.

The fire crackled merrily under the kettle, and soon the two of them were sitting down to an appetizing meal of pancakes and syrup, boiled eggs, and tea.

"Land sakes, George, you must have had your own time with those housekeepers of yours! Some of them drank, eh? I could tell that by the piece you put in the paper. But never mind them now. I'll soon have you feeling fine as silk. How's your socks? Toes out, I'll bet. Well, I'll hunt you up a pair, if there's any to be found. If I can't find any you can go to bed when you get your chores done, and I'll wash out them you've on—I can't bear my men folks to have their toes out; a hole in the heel ain't so bad, it's behind you and you can forget it, but a hole in the toe is always in your way no matter which way you're going."

After supper, when Shaw was out doing his chores, he could see her bustling in and out of the house; now she was beating his bedclothes on the line; in another minute she was leaning far out of a bedroom window dusting a pillow.

When he came into the house she reported that her search for stockings, though vigorous, had been vain. He protested a little about having to go to bed when the sun was shining, but she insisted.

"I'm sorry, George," she said, "to have to make you go to bed, but it's the only thing we can do. You'll find your bed feels a lot better since I took the horse collar and the pair of rubber boots out from under the mattress. That's a poor place to keep things. Good-night now—don't read lying down."

When he went upstairs Shaw noticed with dismay that his lamp had gone from the box beside his bed. So he was not likely to disobey her last injunction—at least, not for any length of time.

Just at daylight the next morning there came a knock at his door.

"Come, George—time to get up!"

When he came in from feeding his horses a splendid breakfast was on the table.

"Here's your basin, George; go out and have a good wash. Here's your comb; it's been lost for quite awhile. I put a towel out there for you, too. Hurry up now and get your vittles while they are nice!"

When Shaw came to the table she regarded him with pleasure.

"You're a fine-looking boy, George, when you're slicked up," she said. "Now bow your head until we say grace! There, now pitch in and tell me how you like grandma's cooking."

Shaw ate heartily and praised everything.

A few days after she said, "Now, George, I guess I'll have to ask you to go to town and get some things we need for the house."

Shaw readily agreed, and took out his paper and pencil.

"Soap, starch, ten yards of cheesecloth—that's for curtains," she said. "I'll knit lace for them, and they'll look real dressy; toilet soap, sponge, and nailbrush—that's for your bath, George; you haven't been taking them as often as you should, or the hoops wouldn't have come off your tub. You can't cheat Nature, George; she always tells on you. Ten yards flannelette—that's for night-shirts; ten yards sheeting—that's for your bed—and your white shirts are pretty far gone."

"How do you know?" he asked in surprise. "They are all in my trunk."

"Yes, I know, and the key is in that old cup on the stand, and I know how to unlock a trunk, don't I?" she replied with dignity. "You need new shirts all right, but just get one. I never could bear them boughten shirts, they are so skimpy in the skirt; I'll make you some lovely ones, with blue and print flossin' down the front."

He looked up, alarmed.

"Then about collars," she went on serenely. "You have three, but they're not in very good shape, though, of course, you couldn't expect anything better of them, kept in that box with the nails—oh, I found them, George, you needn't look so surprised. You see, I know something about boys—I have three of my own." A shadow passed over her face and she sighed. "Well, I guess that is all for to-day. Be sure to get your mail and hurry home."

"Shall I tell the postmaster to put your mail in my box?" he asked.

"Oh, no, never mind—I ain't expectin' any," she said, and Shaw drove away wondering.

A few nights after she said, "Well, George, I suppose you are wonderin' now who this old lady is, though I am not to say real old either."

"Indeed you are not old," Shaw declared with considerable gallantry; "you are just in your prime."

She regarded him gratefully. "You're a real nice boy, George," she said, "and there ain't going to be no secrets between us. If you wet your feet, or tear your clothes, don't try to hide it. Don't keep nothing from me and I won't keep nothing from you. Now I'll tell you who I am and all about it. I am Mrs. Peter Harris, of Owen Sound, Ontario, and I have three sons here in the West. They've all done well, fur as money goes. I came up to visit them. I came from Bert's here. I couldn't stand the way Bert's folks live. Mind you, they burn their lights all night, and they told me it doesn't cost a cent more. Land o' liberty! They can't fool me. If lights burn, someone pays—and the amount of hired help they keep is something scandalous. Et, that is Bert's wife, is real smart, and they have two hired girls, besides their own two girls, and they get in a woman to wash besides. I wanted them to let the two girls go while I was there, but no, sir! Et says, 'Grandma, you didn't come here to work, you must just rest.' They wouldn't let me do a thing, and that brazen hired girl—the housemaid, they call her—one day even made my bed; and, mind you, George, she put the narrow hem on the sheet to the top, and she wasn't a bid ashamed when I told her. She said she hoped it didn't make me feel that I was standing on my head all night; and the way that woman hung out the clothes was a perfect scandal!" Her voice fell to an awed whisper. "She hangs the underwear in plain sight. I ain't never been used to the like of that! I could not stay. Bert is kind enough, so is Et, and they have one girl, Maud, that I really do like. She is twenty-one, but, of course, brought up the way she has been, she is awful ignorant for that age.

Mind you, that girl had never turned the heel of a stocking until I got her at it, but Maud can learn. I'd take that girl quick, and bring her up like my own, if Bert would let me. Well, anyway, I could not put up with the way they live, and I just ran away."

"You ran away!" echoed Shaw. "They'll be looking for you!"

"Let 'em look!" said the old lady, grimly. "They won't ever find me here."

"I'll hide you in the haymow, and if they come in here to search for you I'll declare I never knew you—I am prepared to do desperate things," Shaw declared.

"George, if they ever get in here—that is, Et anyway— she'll know who did the fixin' up. There ain't many that know how to do this Rocky Road to Dublin that is on your lounge. Et would know who'd been here."

"That settles it!" declared Shaw. "Et shall not enter. If Et gets in it shall be over my prostrate form, but maybe it would be better for you to take the Rocky Road with you to the hayloft!"

The old lady laughed heartily. "Ain't we happy, George, you and me? I've tried all my own, and they won't let me have one bit of my own way. Out at Edward's—he's a lawyer at Regina—I tried to get them all to go to bed at half-past ten—late enough, too, for decent people—and didn't Edward's wife get real miffed over it? And then I went to Tom's—he's a doctor down at Winnipeg, but he's all gone to politics; he was out night after night makin' speeches, and he had a young fellow lookin' after his practice who wouldn't know a corn from a gumboil only they grow in different places. Tom's pa and me spent good money on his education, and it's hard for us to see him makin' no use of it. He was nice enough to me, wanted me to stay and be company for Edith, but I told him he should try to be company for Edith himself. Well, he didn't get elected—that's one comfort. I believe it was an answer to prayer. Maybe he'll settle down to his doctorin' now. Then I went to Bert's and I soon saw I could not stay there. Just as soon as I saw your little bit in the paper, I says, 'The Lord has opened a door!' I gave Maud a hint that I would clear out some day and go where I would be let work, and the dear child says to me, 'Grandma, if I ever get a house of my own you can come and live with me, and you can do every bit of work, and everyone will have to do just what you say; they'll have to go to bed at sundown if you say so.' Maud's the best one I have belongin' to me. She'll give them a hint that I'm all right."

But Shaw was apprehensive. He knew who Bert was, and he had uncomfortable visions of Mr. Albert Harris driving up to his door some day and demanding that Mrs. Peter Harris, his mother, immediately come home with him; and the fear and dread of former housekeepers swept over George Shaw's soul. No, he would not give her up! Of course, there were times when he thought she was rather exacting, and then he felt some sympathy for Edward's wife for getting "miffed."

When she was with him about a week she announced that he must have a daily bath! "It is easier to wash you than the bed-clothes, that's one reason," she said, "and it's good for you besides. That's what's wrong with lots of young boys; they git careless and dirty, and then they take to smoking and drinking just natcherally. A clean hide, mind you, is next to a clean heart. Now go along upstairs; everything is ready for you."

Henceforth there was no danger of the hoops falling off the tub, for it was in daily use, and indeed, it was not many nights until George Shaw looked forward with pleasure to his nightly wash.

The old lady's face glowed with pleasure as she went about her work, or sat sewing in the shade of the house. At her instigation Shaw had put up a shed for his machinery, which formerly had littered the yard, and put his wood in even piles.

The ground fell away in a steep ravine, just in front of the house, and pink wild roses and columbine hung in profusion over the spring which gushed out of the bank. Away to the east were the sand-hills of the Assiniboine—the bad lands of the prairie, their surface peopled with stiff spruce trees that stand like sentries looking, always looking, out across the plain!

Mrs. Harris often sat with her work in the shade of the house, on pleasant afternoons, looking at this peaceful scene, and her heart was full of gladness and content.

The summer passed pleasantly for George Shaw and his cheery old housekeeper. Not a word did they hear from "Bert's" folks.

"I would like to see Maud," Mrs. Harris said one night to Shaw as she sat knitting a sock for him beside their cheerful fireside. He was reading.

"What is Maud like?" he asked.

"Maud favors my side of the house," she answered. "She's a pretty good-looking girl, very much the hi'th and complexion I used to be when I was her age. You'd like Maud fine if you saw her, George."

"I don't want to see her," Shaw replied, "for I am afraid that the coming of Maud might mean the departure of Grandma, and that would be a bad day for me."

"I ain't goin' to leave you, George, and I believe Maud would be reasonable if she did come! She'd see how happy we are!"

It was in the early autumn that Maud came. The grain had all been cut and stacked, and was waiting for the thresher to come on its rounds. Shaw was ploughing in the field in front of his house when Maud came walking briskly up the road just as her grandmother had done four months before! The trees in the poplar grove beside the road were turning red and yellow with autumn, and Maud, in her red-brown suit and hat, looked as if she belonged to the picture.

Some such thought as this struggled in Shaw's brain and shone in his eyes as he waited for her at the headland.

He raised his hat as she drew near. Maud went right into the subject.

"Have you my grandmother?" she asked.

Shaw hesitated—the dreaded moment had come. Visions of former housekeepers—dirty dishes, unmade beds, dust, flies, mice—rose before him and tempted him to say "no," but something stronger and better, perhaps it was the "clean hide" prompting the clean heart, spoke up in him.

"I have your grandmother," he said slowly, "and she is very well and happy."

"Will you give her up?" was Maud's next question.

"Never!" he answered stoutly, "and she won't give me up, either. Your grandmother and I are very fond of each other, I would like you to know—but come in and see her."

That night after supper, which proved to be a very merry meal in spite of the shadow which had fallen across the little home, Mrs. Harris said almost tearfully: "I can't leave this pore lamb, Maud—there's no knowin' what will happen to him."

"I will go straight back to the blanket and dog soup," Shaw declared with cheerful conviction. "You can't imagine the state things were in when your grandmother came—bed not made since Christmas, horsenails for buttons, comb and brush lost but not missed, wash basin rusty! Your grandmother, of course, has been severe with me—she makes me go to bed before sundown. Yet I refuse to part with her. Who takes your grandmother takes me; and now, Miss Maud, it is your move!"

That night when they sat in the small sitting-room with a bright fire burning in the shining stove, Maud felt her claim on her grandmother growing more and more shadowy. Mrs. Harris was in a radiant humor. She was knitting lace for the curtains, and chatted gaily as she worked.

"You see, Maud, I am never lonely here; it's a real heartsome place to live. There's the trains goin' by twice a day, and George here is a real good hand to read out to me. We're not near done with the book we're reading, and I am anxious to see if Adam got the girl. He was set on havin' her, but some of her folks were in for makin' trouble."

"Folks sometimes do!" said Shaw meaningly.

"Well, I can't go until we finish the book," the old lady declared, "and we see how the story comes out, and I don't believe Maud is the one to ask it."

Maud made a pretty picture as she sat with one shapely foot on the fender of the stove, the firelight dancing on her face and hair. Shaw, looking at her, forgot the errand on which she came—forgot everything, only that she was there.

"Light the lamp and read a bit of the book now," Mrs. Harris said. "Maud'll like it. I know. She's the greatest girl for books!"

Shaw began to read. It was "The Kentucky Cardinal" he read, that exquisite love-story that makes us lovers all, even if we never have been, or worse still, have forgotten. Shaw loved the book, and read it tenderly, and Maud, leaning back in her chair, found her heart warmed with a sudden great content.

A week later Shaw and Maud walked along the river bank and discussed the situation. Autumn leaves carpeted the ground beneath their feet, and the faint murmur of the river below as it slipped over its pebbly bed came faintly to their ears. In the sky above them, wild geese with flashing white wings honked away toward the south, and a meadowlark, that jolly fellow who comes early and stays late, on a red-leafed haw-tree poured out his little heart in melody.

"You see, Mr. Shaw," Maud was saying, "it doesn't look right for Grandma to be living with a stranger when she has so many of her own people. I know she is happy with you—happier that she has been with any of us—but what will people think? It looks as if we didn't care for her, and we do. She is the sweetest old lady in the world." Maud was very much in earnest.

Shaw's eyes followed the wild geese until they faded into tiny specks on the horizon. Then he turned and looked straight into her face.

"Maud," he said, with a strange vibration in his voice, "I know a way out of the difficulty; a real good, pleasant way, and by it your grandmother can continue to live with me, and still be with her own folks. Maud, can you guess it?"

The blush that spread over Maud's face indicated that she was a good guesser!

Then the meadowlark, all unnoticed, hopped a little nearer, and sang sweeter than ever. Not that anybody was listening, either!

～

"The Runaway Grandmother" was published in *The Globe* (Toronto: December, 1910), *The American Magazine* (n.d. [1910]), and *The Black Creek Stopping-House, and Other Stories* (Toronto: William Briggs, 1912, 1919), 113–138.

You Never Can Tell

It was at exactly half-past three in the afternoon of a hot June day that Mrs. Theodore Banks became smitten with the idea. Mrs. Banks often said afterwards she did not know how she came to be thinking about the Convention of the Arts and Crafts at all, although she is the Secretary. The idea was so compelling that Mrs. Banks rushed down town to tell Mr. Banks—she felt she could not depend on the telephone.

"Ted," she cried, when she opened the door of the office, "I have an idea!"

Theodore raised his eyelids.

Mrs. Banks was flushed and excited and looked well. Mrs. Banks was a handsome woman any time, and to-day her vivacity was quite genuine.

"You know the Convention of the Arts and Crafts—which begins on the twentieth."

"I've heard of it—somewhere."

"Well, it just came to me, Teddy, what a perfectly heavenly thing it would be to invite that little Mrs. Dawson, who writes reviews for one of the papers here—you remember, I told you about her—she is awfully clever and artistic and good-looking, and lives away off from every place, and her husband is not her equal at all—perfectly illiterate, I heard—uncultured, anyway. What a perfect joy it would be to her to have her come, and meet with people who are her equals. She's an Ottawa girl originally, I believe, and she does write the most perfectly sweet and darling things—you remember I've read them for you. Of course, she is probably very shabby and out of date in her clothes by this time. But it doesn't really matter what one wears, if one has heaps of brains. It is only dull women, really, who have to be terribly careful about what they wear, and spend so much money that way!"

"Dull women!" Theodore murmured. "Oh! is that why? I never really knew."

She laughed at his look of enlightened surprise. When Mrs. Banks laughed, there were three dimples plainly showing, which did not entirely discourage her merriment.

"And you know, Teddy, there is such a mystery about her marriage! She will really be quite an acquisition, and we'll have her on the programme."

"What mystery?" Mr. Banks asked.

"Oh, well, not mystery, maybe, but we all suppose she's not happy. How could she be with so few of the real pleasures of life, and still she stays with it, and actually goes places with her husband, and seems to be keeping it up, and you know, Ted, she has either three or four children!"

"Is it as bad as that?" he asked, solemnly.

"Oh, Ted! you know well enough what I mean—don't be such an owl! Just think of how tied down and horrible it must be for her out there in that desolate Alberta, with no neighbors at all for miles, and then only impossible people. I should think it would drive her mad. I must try to get her on the programme, too. She will at least be interesting, on account of her personality. Most of our speakers are horribly prosy, at least to me, but of course I never listen; I just look to see what they've on and then go straight back to my own thinking. I just thought I'd ask your advice, Teddy dear, before I asked the Committee, and so now I'll go to see Mrs. Trenton, the President. So glad you approve, dear! And really there will be a touch of romance in it, Ted, for Bruce Edwards knew her when she lived in Ottawa—it was he who told me so much about her. He simply raved about her to me—it seems he was quite mad about her once, and probably it was a lover's quarrel or something that drove her away to the West to forget—and now think of her meeting Bruce again. Isn't that a thriller?"

"If I thought Bruce Edwards had brains enough to care for any woman I'd say it was not right to bring her here," said Mr. Banks; "but he hasn't."

"Oh, of course," Mrs. Banks agreed, "he is quite over it now, no doubt. Things like that never last, but he'll be awfully nice to her, and give her a good time and take her around—you know what Bruce is like—he's so romantic and cynical, and such a perfect darling in his manners—always ready to open a door or pick up a handkerchief!"

"I am sure he would—if he needed the handkerchief," Theodore put in, quietly.

"Oh, Ted! you're a funny bunny! You've never liked Bruce—and I know why—and it's perfectly horrid of you, just because he has always been particularly nice to me—he really can't help being dreamy and devoted to any woman he is with, if she is not a positive fright."

Mrs. Trenton, the President of the Arts and Crafts, received Mrs. Banks' suggestion cautiously. Mrs. Trenton always asked, Is it right? Is it wise? Is it expedient? It was Mrs. Trenton's extreme cautiousness that had brought her the proud distinction of being the first President of the Arts and Crafts, where it was considered necessary to temper the impetuosity of the younger members; and, besides, Mrs. Trenton never carried her doubts and fears too far. She raised all possible objections, mentioned all possible contingencies, but in the end allowed the younger members to carry the day, which they did, with a clear and shriven conscience, feeling that they had been very discreet and careful and deliberate.

Mrs. Banks introduced her subject by telling Mrs. Trenton that she had come to ask her advice, whereupon Mrs. Trenton laid aside the work she was doing and signified her gracious willingness to be asked for counsel. When Mrs. Banks had carefully laid the matter before Mrs. Trenton, dwelling on the utter loneliness of the prairie woman's life, Mrs. Trenton called the Vice-President, Miss Hastings, who was an oil painter by profession, and a lady of large experience in matters of the heart. Mrs. Trenton asked Mrs. Banks to outline her plan again.

When she had finished, Mrs. Trenton asked:

"Is it wise—is it kind? She has chosen her life. Why bring her back? It will only fill her heart with vain repinings. This man, illiterate though he may be, is her lawful husband—she owes him a duty. Are we just to him?"

"Maybe she is perfectly happy," Miss Hastings said. "There is no accounting for love and its vagaries. Perhaps to her he is clothed in the rosy glow of romance, and all the inconveniences of her life are forgotten. I have read of it," she added in explanation, when she noticed Mrs. Trenton's look of incredulity.

Mrs. Trenton sighed, a long sigh that undulated the black lace on her capacious bosom.

"It has been written—it will continue to be written, but to-day marriage needs to be aided by modern—" she hesitated, and looked at Mrs. Banks for the word.

"Methods," Mrs. Banks supplied, promptly, "house-maids, cooks, autos, theatres, jewelry and chocolates."

"You put it so aptly, my dear," Mrs. Trenton smiled, as she patted her pearl bracelet, Mr. Trenton's last offering on the hymeneal altar. "It requires—" she paused again—Mrs. Trenton's pauses were a very important asset in her conversation—"it requires—"

"Collateral," said Mrs. Banks.

Miss Hastings shook her head.

"I believe in marriage—all the same," she said heroically.

"Now, how shall we do it?" Mrs. Banks was anxious to get the preliminaries over. "You have decided to invite her, of course."

Mrs. Trenton nodded.

"I feel we have no choice in the matter," she said slowly. "She is certainly a woman of artistic temperament—she must be, or she would succumb to the dreary prairie level. I have followed her career with interest and predict great things for her—have I not, Miss Hastings? We should not blame her if in a moment of girlish romance she turned her back on the life which now is. We, as officers of the Arts and Crafts, must extend our fellowship to all who are worthy. This joining of our ranks may show her what she lost by her girlish folly, but it is better for her to know life, and even feel regrets, than never to know."

"Better have a scarlet thread run through the dull gray pattern of life, even if it makes the gray all the duller," said Miss Hastings, who worked in oils.

And so it came about that an invitation was sent to Mrs. James Dawson, Auburn, Alberta, and in due time an acceptance was received.

From the time she alighted from the Pacific Express, a slight young woman in a very smart linen suit, she was a constant surprise to the Arts and Crafts. The principal cause of their surprise was that she seemed perfectly happy. There was not a shadow of regret in her clear gray eyes, nor any trace of drooping melancholy in her quick, business-like walk.

Naturally the Arts and Crafts had made quite a feature of the Alberta author and poet who would attend the Convention. Several of the enthusiastic members, anxious to advertise effectively, had interviewed the newspaper reporters on the subject, with the result that long articles were published in the Woman's Section of the city dailies, dealing principally with the loneliness of life on an Alberta ranch. Kate Dawson was credited with an heroic spirit that would have made her blush had she seen the flattering allusions. Robinson Crusoe on his lonely isle, before the advent of Friday, was not more isolated than she on her lonely Alberta ranch, according to the advance notices. Luckily she had not seen any of these, nor ever dreamed she was the centre of so much attention, and so it was a very self-possessed and unconscious young woman in a simple white gown who came before the Arts and Crafts.

It was the first open night of the Convention, and the auditorium was crowded. The air was heavy with the perfume of many flowers, and pulsed with dreamy music. Mrs. Trenton, in billows of black lace and glinting jet, presided with her usual graciousness. She introduced Mrs. Dawson briefly.

Whatever the attitude of the audience was at first, they soon followed her with eager interest as she told them, in her easy way, simple stories of the people she knew so well and so lovingly understood. There was no art in the telling, only a sweet naturalness and an apparent honesty—the honesty of purpose that comes to people in lonely places. Her stories were all of the class that magazine editors call "homely, heart-interest stuff," not deep or clever or problematical—the commonplace doings of common people—but it found an entrance into the hearts of men and women.

They found themselves looking with her at broad sun-lit spaces, where struggling hearts work out noble destinies, without any thought of heroism. They saw the moonlight and its drifting shadows on the wheat, and smelled again the ripening grain at dawn. They heard the whirr of prairie chickens' wings among the golden stubble on the hillside, and the glamor of some old forgotten afternoon stole over them. Men and women country-born who had forgotten the voices of their youth, heard them calling across the years, and heard them, too, with opened hearts and sudden tears. There was one pathetic story she told them, of the lonely prairie woman—the woman who wished she was back, the woman to whom the broad outlook and far horizon were terrible and full of fear. She told them how, at night, this lonely woman drew down the blinds and pinned them close to keep out the great white outside that stared at her through every chink with wide, pitiless eyes—the mocking voices that she heard behind her everywhere, day and night, whispering, mocking, plotting; and the awful shadows, black and terrible, that crouched behind her, just out of sight—never coming out in the open.

It was a weird and gloomy picture, that, but she did not leave it so. She told of the new neighbor who came to live near the lonely woman—the human companionship which drove the mocking voices away forever—the coming of the spring, when the world awoke from its white sleep and the thousand joyous living things that came into being at the touch of the good old sun!

At the reception after the programme, many crowded around her, expressing their sincere appreciation of her work. Bruce Edwards fully enjoyed the distinction which his former acquaintance with her gave him, and it was with quite an air of proprietorship that he introduced to her his friends.

Mrs. Trenton, Mrs. Banks, and other members of the Arts and Crafts, at a distance, discussed her with pride. She had made their open night a wonderful success—the papers would be full of it to-morrow.

"You can see how fitted she is for a life of culture," said Miss Hastings, the oil painter, "her shapely white hands were made for silver spoons, and not for handling butter ladles. What a perfect joy it must be for her to associate with people who are her equals!"

"I wonder," said Mrs. Banks, "what her rancher would say if he saw his handsome wife now. So much admiration from an old lover is not good for the peace of mind of even a serious-minded author—and such a fascinating man as Bruce! Look how well they look together! I wonder if she is mentally comparing her big, sunburned cattleman with Bruce, and thinking of what a different life she would have led if she had married him!"

"Do you suppose," said Mrs. Trenton, "that that was her own story that she told us? I think she must have felt it herself to be able to tell it so."

Just at that moment Bruce Edwards was asking her the same question.

"Oh, no," she answered, quickly, while an interested group drew near; "people never write their own sorrows— the broken heart does not sing—that's the sadness of it. If one can talk of their sorrows they soon cease to be. It's because I have not had any sorrows of my own that I have seen and been able to tell of the tragedies of life."

"Isn't she the jolly best bluffer you ever heard?" one of the men remarked to another. "Just think of that beautiful creature, born for admiration, living ten miles from any-where, on an Albertan ranch of all places, and saying she is happy. She could be a top-notcher in any society in Canada—why great Scott! any of us would have married that girl, and been glad to do it!" And under the glow of this generous declaration Mr. Stanley Carruthers lit his cigarette and watched her with unconcealed admiration.

As the Arts and Crafts had predicted, the newspapers gave considerable space to their open meeting, and the Alberta author came in for a large share of the reporters' finest spasms. It was the chance of a lifetime—here was local color—human interest—romance—thrills! Good old phrases, clover-scented and rosy-hued, that had lain in cold storage for years, were brought out and used with conscious pride.

There was one paper which hinted at what it called her "mésalliance," and drew a lurid picture of her domestic unhappiness, "so bravely borne." All the gossip of the convention was in it intensified and exaggerated—conjectures set down as known truths—the idle chatter of idle women crystallized in print!

And of this paper a copy was sent by some unknown person to James Dawson, Auburn, Alberta.

The rain was falling at Auburn, Alberta, with the dreary insistence of unwelcome harvest rain. Just a quiet drizzle—plenty more where this came from—no haste, no waste. It soaked the fields, keeping green the grain which should be ripening in a clear sun.

Kate Dawson had been gone a week, and it would still be a week before she came back. Just a week—seven days. Jim Dawson went over them in his mind as he drove the ten miles over the rain-soaked roads to Auburn to get his daily letter.

Every day she had written to him long letters, full of vital interest to him. He read them over and over again.

"Nobody really knows how well Kate can write, who had not seen her letters to me," he thought proudly. Absence had not made him fonder of his wife, for every day he lived was lived in devotion to her. The marvel of it all never left him, that such a woman as Kate Marks, who had spent her life in the city, surrounded by cultured friends, should be contented to live the lonely life of a rancher's wife.

He got his first disappointment when there was no letter for him. He told himself it was some unavoidable delay in the mails—Kate had written all right—there would be two letters for him to-morrow. Then he noticed the paper addressed to him in a strange hand.

He opened it eagerly. A wavy ink-line caught his eye. "Western author delights large audience." Jim Dawson's face glowed with pride. "My girl!" he murmured, happily. "I knew it." He wanted to be alone when he read it, and, folding it hastily, put it in his pocket and did not look at it again until he was on the way home. The rain still fell drearily and spattered the page as he read.

His heart beat fast with pride as he read the flattering words—his girl had made good, you bet!

Suddenly he started, almost crushing the paper in his hands, and every bit of color went from his face. "What's this? 'Unhappily married'—'borne with heroic cheerfulness'." He read it through to the end.

He stopped his horses and looked around—he did not know, himself, what thought was in his mind. Jim Dawson had always been able to settle his disputes without difficulty or delay. There was something to be done now. The muscles swelled in his arms. Surely something could be done! . . .

Then the wanton cruelty, the utter brutality of the printed page, came home to him—there was no way, no answer.

Strange to say, he felt no resentment for himself; even the paragraph about the old lover, with its hidden and sinister meaning, angered him only in its relation to her. Why shouldn't the man admire her if he was an old lover?—Kate must have had dozens of men in love with her—why shouldn't any man admire her?

So he talked and reasoned with himself, trying to keep the cruel hurt of the words out of his heart.

Everyone in his household was asleep when he reached home. He stabled his team with the help of his lantern, and then, going into the comfortable kitchen, he found the lunch the housekeeper had left for him. He thought of the many merry meals he and Kate had had on this same kitchen table, but now it seemed a poor, cold thing to sit down and eat alone and in silence.

With his customary thoughtfulness he cleared away the lunch before going to his room. Then, lamp in hand, he went, as he and Kate had always done, to the children's room, and looked long and lovingly at his boy and girl asleep in their cots—the boy so like himself, with his broad forehead and brown curls. He bent over him and kissed him tenderly—Kate's boy.

Then he turned to the little girl, so like her mother, with her tangle of red curls on the pillow. Picking her up in his arms, he carried her to his room and put her in his own bed.

"Mother isn't putting up a bluff on us, is she, dearie?" he whispered as he kissed the soft little cheek beside his own. "Mother loves us, surely—it is pretty rough on us if she doesn't—and it's rougher still on mother!"

The child stirred in her sleep, and her arms tightened around his neck.

"I love my mother—and my dear daddy," she murmured drowsily.

All night long Jim Dawson lay wide-eyed, staring into the darkness with his little sleeping girl in his arms, not doubting his wife for a moment, but wondering—all night long—wondering!

The next evening Jim did not go for his mail, but one of the neighbors driving by volunteered to get it for him.

It was nearly midnight when the sound of wheels roused him from his reverie. He opened the door, and in the square of light the horses stopped.

"Hello, Jim—is that you?" called the neighbor. "I've got something for you."

Jim came out bareheaded. He tried to thank the neighbor for his kindness, but his throat was dry with suppressed excitement—Kate had written!

The buggy was still in the shadow, and he could not see its occupant.

"I have a letter for you, Jim," said his friend, with a suspicious twinkle in his voice, "a big one, registered and special delivery—a right nice letter, I should say."

Then her voice rang out in the darkness.

"Come, Jim, and help me out."

Commonplace words, too, but to Jim Dawson they were sweeter than the chiming of silver bells . . .

An hour later they still sat over their late supper on the kitchen table. She had told him many things.

"I just got lonely, Jim—plain, straight homesick for you and the children. I couldn't stay out the week. The people were kind to me, and said nice things about my work. I was glad to hear and see things, of course. Bruce Edwards was there, you know—I've told you about Bruce. He took me around quite a bit, and was nice enough, only I couldn't lose him—you know that kind, Jim, always saying tiresome, plastery sort of things. He thinks that women like to be fussed over all the time. The women I met dress beautifully and all talk the same—and at once. Everything is 'perfectly sweet' and 'darling' to them. They are clever women all right, and were kind to me, and all that, but oh, Jim, they are not for mine—and the men I met while I was away all looked small and poor and trifling to me because I have been looking for the last ten years at one who is big and brown and useful. I compared them all with you, and they measured up badly. Jim, do you know what it would feel like to live on popcorn and chocolates for two weeks and try to make a meal of them—what do you think you would be hungry for?"

Jim Dawson watched his wife, his eyes aglow with love and pride. Not until she repeated her question did he answer her.

"I think, perhaps, a slice of brown bread would be what was wanted," he answered smiling. The glamor of her presence was upon him.

Then she came over to him and drew his face close to hers.

"Please pass the brown bread!" she said.

◞

"You Never Can Tell" was published in *Saturday Night* (Toronto: n.d.) and *The Black Creek Stopping-House, and Other Stories* (Toronto: William Briggs, 1912, 1919), 159–176.

THE ELUSIVE VOTE: AN UNVARNISHED TALE OF SEPTEMBER 21ST, 1911

John Thomas Green did not look like a man on whom great issues might turn. His was a gentle soul encased in ill-fitting armor. Heavy blue eyes, teary and sad, gave a wintry droop to his countenance; his nose showed evidence of much wiping, and the need of more. When he spoke, which was infrequent, he stammered; when he walked he toed in.

He was a great and glorious argument in favor of woman suffrage; he was the last word, the *pièce de résistance*; he was a living, walking, yellow banner, which shouted, "Votes for Women," for in spite of his many limitations there was one day when he towered high above the mightiest woman in the land; one day that the plain John Thomas was clothed with majesty and power; one day when he emerged from obscurity and placed an impress on the annals of our country. Once every four years John Thomas Green came forth (at the earnest solicitation of friends) and stood before kings.

The Reciprocity fight was on, and nowhere did it rage more hotly than in Morton, where Tom Brown, the well-beloved and much-hated Conservative member, fought for his seat with all the intensity of his Irish blood. Politics were an incident to Tom—the real thing was the fight! and so fearlessly did he go after his assailants—and they were many—that every day greater enthusiasm prevailed among his followers, who felt it a privilege to fight for a man who fought so well for himself.

The night before the election the Committee sat in the Committee Rooms and went carefully over the lists. They were hopeful but not hilarious—there had been disappointments, desertions, lapses!

Billy Weaver, loyal to the cause, but of pessimistic nature, testified that Sam Cowery had been "talkin' pretty shrewd about Reciprocity," by which Billy did not mean "shrewd" at all, but rather crooked and adverse. However, there was no mistaking Billy's meaning of the word when one heard him say it with his inimitable "down-the-Ottaway" accent. It is only the feeble written word which requires explanation.

George Burns was reported to have said he did not care whether he voted or not; if it were a wet day he might, but if it were weather for stacking he'd stack, you bet! This was a gross insult to the President of the Conservative Association, whose farm he had rented and lived on for the last five years, during which time there had been two elections, at both of which he had voted "right." The President had not thought it necessary to interview him at all this time, feeling sure that he was within the pale. But now it seemed that some trifler had told him that he would get more for his barley and not have to pay so much for his tobacco if Reciprocity carried, and it was reported that he had been heard to say, with picturesque eloquence, that you could hardly expect a man to cut his throat both ways by voting against it!

These and other kindred reports filled the Committee with apprehension.

The most unmoved member of the company was the redoubtable Tom himself, who, stretched upon the slippery black leather lounge, hoarse as a frog from much addressing of obdurate electors, was endeavoring to sing "Just Before the Battle, Mother," hitting the tune only in the most inconspicuous places!

The Secretary, with the list in his hand, went over the names:

"Jim Stewart—Jim's solid; he doesn't want Reciprocity, because he sent to the States once for a washing machine for his wife, and smuggled it through from St. Vincent, and when he got it here his wife wouldn't use it!

"Abe Collins—Abe's not right and never will be—he saw Sir Wilfrid once—

"John Thomas Green—say, how about Jack? Surely we can corral Jack. He's working for you, Milt, isn't he?" addressing one of the scrutineers.

"Leave him to me," said Milt, with an air of mystery, "there's not one has more influence with Jack than me. No, he isn't with me just now, he's over with my brother Angus; but when he comes in to vote I'll be there, and all I'll have to do is to lift my eyes like this" (he showed them the way it would be done) "and he'll vote—right."

"How do you know he will come, though?" asked the Secretary, who had learned by much experience that many and devious are the bypaths which lead away from the polls!

"Yer brother Angus will be sure to bring him in, won't he, Milt?" asked John Gray, the trusting one, who believed all men to be brothers.

There was a tense silence.

Milt took his pipe from his mouth. "My brother Angus," he began dramatically, girding himself for the effort—for Milt was an orator of Twelfth of July fame— "Angus Kennedy, my brother, bred and reared, and reared and bred, in the principles of Conservatism, as my poor old father often says, has gone over—has deserted our banners, has steeped himself in the false teachings of the Grits. Angus, my brother," he concluded, impressively, "is—not right!"

"What's wrong with him?" asked Jim Grover, who was of an analytical turn of mind.

"Too late to discuss that now!" broke in the Secretary. "We cannot trace Angus's downfall, but we can send out and get in John Thomas. We need his vote—it's just as good as anybody's."

Jimmy Rice volunteered to go out and get him. Jimmy did not believe in leaving anything to chance. He had been running an auto all week and would just as soon work at night as any other time. Big Jack Moore, another enthusiastic Conservative, agreed to go with him.

When they made the ten-mile run to the home of the apostate Angus, they met him coming down the path with a lantern in his hand on the way to feed his horses.

They, being plain, blunt men, unaccustomed to the amenities of election time, and not knowing how to skilfully approach a subject of this kind, simply announced that they had come for John Thomas.

"He's not here," said Angus, looking around the circle of light that the lantern threw.

"Are you sure?" asked James Rice, after a painful pause.

"Yes," said Angus, with exaggerated ease, affecting not to notice the significance of the question. "Jack went to Nelson to-day, and he ain't back yet. He went about three o'clock," went on Angus, endeavoring to patch up a shaky story with a little interesting detail. "He took over a bunch of pigs for me that I am shippin' into Winnipeg, and he was goin' to bring back some lumber."

"I was in Nelson to-day, Angus," said John Moore, sternly; "Just came from there, and I did not see John Thomas."

Angus, though fallen and misguided, was not entirely unregenerate; a lie sat awkwardly on his honest lips, and now that his feeble effort at deception had miscarried, he felt himself adrift on a boundless sea. He wildly felt around for a reply, and was greatly relieved by the arrival of his father on the scene, who, seeing the lights of the auto in the yard, had come out hurriedly to see what was the matter. Grandpa Kennedy, although nearing his ninetieth birthday, was still a man of affairs, and, what was still more important on this occasion, a lifelong Conservative. Grandpa knew it was the night before the election; he also had seen what he had seen. Grandpa might be getting on, but he could see as far through a cellar door as the next one. Angus, glad of a chance to escape, went on to the stable, leaving the visiting gentlemen to be entertained by Grandpa.

Grandpa was a diplomat; he wanted to have no hard feelings with anyone.

"Good-night, boys," he cried, in his shrill voice; he recognized the occupants of the auto and his quick brain took in the situation. "Don't it beat all how the frost keeps off? This reminds me of the fall, 'leven years ago—we had no frost till the end of the month. I ripened three bushels of Golden Queen tomatoes!" All this was delivered in a very high voice for Angus's benefit—to show him, if he were listening, how perfectly innocent the conversation was.

Then as Angus's lantern disappeared behind the stable, the old man's voice was lowered, and he gave forth this cryptic utterance:

"John Thomas is in the cellar."

Then he gaily resumed his chatter, although Angus was safe in the stable; but Grandpa knew what he knew, and Angus's woman might be listening at the back door. "Much election talk in town, boys?" he asked, breezily.

They answered him at random. Then his voice fell again. "Angie's dead against Brown—won't let you have John Thomas—put him down cellar soon as he saw yer lights; Angie's woman is sittin' on the door knittin'—she's wors'n him—don't let on I give it away—I don't want no words with her!—Yes, it's grand weather for threshin'; won't you come on away in? I guess yer horse will stand." The old man roared with laughter at his own joke.

John Moore and James Rice went back to headquarters for further advice. Angus's woman sitting on the cellar door knitting was a contingency that required to be met with guile.

Consternation sat on the face of the Committee when they told their story. They had not counted on this. The wildest plans were discussed. Tom Stubbins began a lengthy story of an elopement that happened down at the "Carp," where the bride made a rope of the sheets and came down from an upstairs window. Tom was not allowed to finish his narrative, though, for it was felt that the cases were not similar.

No one seemed to be particularly anxious to go back and interrupt Mrs. Angus's knitting.

Then there came into the assembly one of the latest additions to the Conservative ranks, William Batters, a converted and reformed Liberal. He had been an active member of the Liberal Party for many years, but at the last election he had been entirely convinced of their unworthiness by the close-fisted and niggardly way in which they dispensed the election money.

He heard the situation discussed in all its aspects. Milton Kennedy, with inflamed oratory, bitterly bewailed his brother's defection—"not only wrong himself, but leadin' others, and them innocent lambs!"—but he did not offer to go out and see his brother. The lady who sat knitting on the cellar door seemed to be the difficulty with all of them.

The reformed Liberal had a plan.

"I will go for him," said he. "Angus will trust me—he doesn't know I have turned. I'll go for John Thomas, and Angus will give him to me without a word, thinkin' I'm a friend," he concluded, brazenly.

"Look at that now!" exclaimed the member elect. "Say, boys, you'd know he had been a Grit—no honest, open-faced Conservative would ever think of a trick like that!"

"There is nothing like experience to make a man able to see every side," said the reformed one, with becoming modesty.

An hour later Angus was roused from his bed by a loud knock on the door. Angus had gone to bed with his clothes on, knowing that these were troublesome times.

"What's the row?" he asked, when he had cautiously opened the door.

"Row!" exclaimed the friend who was no longer a friend. "You're the man that's makin' the row. The Conservatives have 'phoned in to the Attorney-General's Department to-night to see what's to be done with you for standin' between a man and his heaven-born birthright, keepin' and confinin' of a man in a cellar, owned by and closed by you!"

This had something the air of a summons, and Angus was duly impressed.

"I don't want to see you get into trouble, Angus," Mr. Batters went on; "and the only way to keep out of it is to give him to me, and then when they come out here with a search-warrant they won't find nothin'."

Angus thanked him warmly, and, going upstairs, roused the innocent John from his virtuous slumbers. He had some trouble persuading John, who was a profound sleeper, that he must arise and go hence; but many things were strange to him, and he rose and dressed without very much protest.

Angus was distinctly relieved when he got John Thomas off his hands—he felt he had had a merciful deliverance.

On the way to town, roused by the night air, John Thomas became communicative.

"Them lads in the automobile, they wanted me pretty bad, you bet," he chuckled, with the conscious pride of the much-sought-after; "but gosh, Angus fixed them. He just slammed down the cellar door on me, and says he, 'Not a word out of you, Jack; you've as good a right to vote the way you want to as anybody, and you'll get it, too, you bet'."

The reformed Liberal knitted his brows. What was this simple child of nature driving at?

John Thomas rambled on: "Tom Brown can't fool people with brains, you bet you—Angus's woman explained it all to me. She says to me, 'Don't let nobody run you, Jack—and vote for Hastings. You're all right, Jack—and remember Hastings is the man. Never mind why—don't bother your head—you don't have to—but vote for Hastings.' Says she, 'Don't let on to Milt, or any of his folks, or Grandpa, but vote the way you want to, and that's for Hastings!' "

When they arrived in town the reformed Liberal took John Thomas at once to the Conservative Hotel, and put him in a room, and told him to go to bed, which John cheerfully did. Then he went for the Secretary, who was also in bed. "I've got John Thomas," he announced, "but he says he's a Grit and is going to vote for Hastings. I can't put a dint in him—he thinks I'm a Grit, too. He's only got one idea, but it's a solid one, and that is 'Vote for Hastings'."

The Secretary yawned sleepily. "I'll not go near him. It's me for sleep. You can go and see if any of the other fellows want a job. They're all down at a ball at the station. Get one of those wakeful spirits to reason with John."

The conspirator made his way stealthily to the station, from whence there issued the sound of music and dancing. Not wishing to alarm the Grits, many of whom were joining in the festivities, and who would have been quick to suspect that something was on foot, if they saw him prowling around, he crept up to the window and waited until one of the faithful came near. Gently tapping on the glass, he got the attention of the editor, the very man he wanted, and, in pantomime, gave him to understand that his presence was requested. The editor, pleading a terrific headache, said good-night, or rather good-morning, to his hostess, and withdrew. From his fellow-worker who waited in the shadow of the trees outside, he learned that John Thomas had been secured in body but not in spirit.

The newspaper man readily agreed to labor with the erring brother and hoped to be able to deliver his soul alive.

Once again was John Thomas roused from his slumbers, and not by a familiar voice this time, but by an unknown vision in evening dress.

The editor was a convincing man in his way, whether upon the subject of Reciprocity or apostolic succession, but John was plainly bored from the beginning, and though he offered no resistance, his repeated "I know that!" "That's what I said!" were more disconcerting than the most vigorous opposition. At daylight the editor left John, and he really had the headache that he had feigned a few hours before.

Then John Thomas tried to get a few winks of unmolested repose, but it was election day, and the house was early astir. Loud voices sounded through the hall. Innumerable people, it seemed, mistook his room for their own. Jack rose at last, thoroughly indignant and disposed to quarrel. He had a blame good notion to vote for Brown after all, after the way he had been treated.

When he had hastily dressed himself, discussing his grievances in a loud voice, he endeavored to leave the room, but found the door securely locked. Then his anger knew no bounds. He lustily kicked on the lower panel of the door and fairly shrieked his indignation and rage.

The chambermaid, passing, remonstrated with him by beating on the other side of the door. She was a pert young woman with a squeaky voice, and she thought she knew what was wrong with the occupant of number seventeen. She had heard kicks on doors before.

"Quiet down, you, mister, or you'll get yourself put in the cooler—that's the best place for noisy drunks."

This, of course, annoyed the innocent man beyond measure, but she was gone far down the hall before he could think of the retort suitable.

When she finished her upstairs work and came downstairs to peel the potatoes, she mentioned casually to the bartender that whoever he had in number seventeen was "smashin' things up pretty lively!"

The bartender went up and liberated the indignant voter, who by this time had his mind made up to vote against both Brown and Hastings, and furthermore to renounce politics in all its aspects for evermore.

However, a good breakfast and the sincere apologies of the hotel people did much to restore his good humor. But a certain haziness grew in his mind as to who was who, and at times the disquieting thought skidded through his murky brain that he might be in the enemy's camp for all he knew. Angus and Mrs. Angus had said, "Do what you think is right and vote for Hastings," and that was plain and simple and easily understood. But now things seemed to be all mixed up.

The Committee were ill at ease about him. The way he wagged his head and declared he knew what was what, you bet, was very disquieting, and the horrible fear haunted them that they were perchance cherishing a serpent in their bosom.

The Secretary had a proposal: "Take him out to Milt Kennedy's. Milt said he could work him. Take him out there! Milt said all he had to do was to raise his eyes and John Thomas would vote right."

The erstwhile Liberal again went on the road with John Thomas, to deliver him over to the authority of Milt Kennedy. If Milt could get results by simply elevating his eyebrows, Milt was the man who was needed.

Arriving at Milt's, he left the voter sitting in the buggy, while he went in search of the one who could control John's erring judgement.

While sitting there alone, another wandering thought zig-zagged through John's brain. They were making a fool of him, some way! Well, he'd let them see, b'gosh!

He jumped out of the buggy, and hastily climbed into the hay-mow. It was a safe and quiet spot, and was possessed of several convenient eye-holes through which he could watch with interest the search which immediately began.

He saw the two men coming up to the barn, and as they passed almost below him, he heard Milt say, "Oh, sure, John Thomas will vote right—I can run him all right!—he'll do as I say. Hello, John! Where is he?"

They went into the house—they searched the barn— they called, coaxed, entreated. They ran down to the road to see if he had started back to town; he was as much gone as if he had never been!

"Are you dead sure you brought him?" Milt asked at last in desperation, as he turned over a pile of sacks in the granary.

"Gosh! ain't they lookin' some!" chuckled the elusive voter, as he watched with delight their unsuccessful endeavors to locate him. "But there's lots of places yet that they hain't thought of; they hain't half looked for me yet. I may be in the well for all they know." Then he began to sing to himself, "I know something I won't tell!"

It was not every day that John Thomas Green found himself the centre of attraction, and he enjoyed the sensation.

Having lost so much sleep the night before, a great drowsiness fell on John Thomas, and curling himself up in the hay, he sank into a sweet, sound sleep.

While he lay there, safe from alarms, the neighborhood was shaken with a profound sensation. John Thomas was lost. Lost, and his vote lost with him!

Milton Kennedy, who had to act as scrutineer at the poll in town, was forced to leave home with the mystery unsolved. Before going, he 'phoned to Billy Adams, one of the faithful, and in guarded speech, knowing that he was surrounded by a cloud of witnesses, broke the news! Billy Adams immediately left his stacking, and set off to find his lost compatriot.

Mrs. Alex Porter lived on the next farm to Billy Adams, and being a lady of some leisure, she usually managed to get in on most of the 'phone conversations. Billy Adams' calls were very seldom overlooked by her, for she was on the other side of politics, and it was always well to know what was going on. Although she did not know all that was said by the two men, she heard enough to assure her that crooked work was going on. Mrs. Alex Porter declared she was not surprised. She threw her apron over her head and went to the field and told Alex. Alex was not surprised. In fact, it seems Alex had expected it!

They 'phoned in cipher to Angus, Mrs. Angus being a sister of Mrs. Alex Porter. Mrs. Angus told them to speak out plain, and say what they wanted to, even if all the Conservatives on the line were listening. Then Mrs. Porter said that John Thomas was lost over at Milt Kennedy's. They had probably drugged him or something.

Then Angus's wife said he was safe enough. Billy Batters had come and got him the night before. At the mention of Billy Batters there was a sound of suppressed mirth all along the line. Mrs. Angus's sister fairly shrieked. "Billy Batters! Don't you know he has turned Conservative!—he's working tooth and nail for Brown." Mrs. Angus called Angus excitedly. Everybody talked at once; somebody laughed; one or two swore. Mrs. Porter told Milt Kennedy's wife she'd caught her eavesdropping this time sure. She'd know her cackle any place, and Milt's wife told Mrs. Porter to shut up—she needn't talk about eavesdroppers—good land! and Mrs. Porter told Mrs. Milt she should try something for that voice of hers, and recommended machine oil, and central rang in and told them they'd all have their 'phones taken out if they didn't stop quarreling; and John Thomas, in the hay-mow, slept on, as peacefully as an innocent babe!

In the Committee rooms, Jack's disappearance was excitedly discussed. The Conservatives were not sure that Billy Batters was not giving them the double cross—once a Grit, always a Grit! Angus was threatening to have him arrested for abduction—he had beguiled John Thomas from the home of his friends, and then carelessly lost him.

William Batters realized that he had lost favor in both places, and anxiously longed for a sight of John Thomas's red face, vote or no vote.

At four o'clock John Thomas awoke much refreshed, but very hungry. He went into the house in search of something to eat. Milton and his wife had gone into town many hours before, but he found what he wanted, and was going back to the hay-mow to finish his sleep, just as Billy Adams was going home after having cast his vote.

Billy Adams seized him eagerly, and rapidly drove back to town. Jack's vote would yet be saved to the party!

It was with pardonable pride that Billy Adams reined in his foaming team, and rushed John Thomas into the polling booth, where he was greeted with loud cheers. Nobody dare ask him where he had been—time was too precious. Milton Kennedy, scrutineer, lifted his eyebrows as per agreement. Jack replied with a petulant shrug of his good shoulder and passed in to the inner chamber.

The Conservatives were sure they had him. The Liberals were sure, too. Mrs. Angus was sure Jack would vote right after the way she had reasoned with him and showed him!

When the ballots were counted, there were several spoiled ones, of course. But there was one that was rather unique. After the name of Thomas Brown, there was written in lead pencil, "None of yer business!" which might have indicated a preference for the other name of John Hastings, only for the fact that opposite his name was the curt remark, "None of yer business, either!"

Some thought the ballot was John Thomas Green's.

✍

"The Elusive Vote: An Unvarnished Tale of September 21st, 1911" was published in *Saturday Night* (Toronto: n.d.) and *The Black Creek Stopping-House, and Other Stories* (Toronto: William Briggs, 1912, 1919), 187–205.

RED AND WHITE

I

Mrs. Rosie Starblanket, taking the pipe from her mouth and narrowing her black eyes into two smudgy lines, listened to the footsteps of her son as he approached the parental dwelling. Mrs. Starblanket did not understand the language of flowers or of precious stones, and had not heard of the handkerchief flirtation, but she did know something of the language of footsteps; and on this occasion, as her son came quickly down the boardwalk, Mrs. Starblanket reached a quick conclusion—she thought she knew what the joyousness of his approach meant.

Now it happened that Mrs. Starblanket was for once astray in her diagnosis, but, as her historian, I hasten to exonerate her from blame.

Johnny Starblanket's footsteps on this particular blue-black midnight in July were of amazing lightness. There was evidently some great source of exaltation which had shod his feet with wings.

Mrs. Rosie Starblanket, his mother, knew but one form of exaltation, now that the great days of buffalo hunts were over. Exaltation, as she knew it, came in one form, and one only—conical in shape, dark green in color, with the maker's name in gold letters, and a gold seal below. So Mrs. Starblanket, intently listening, assumed—falsely, as it proved—that her son had been drinking.

Johnny had been to "the Beach" for the evening, and as this was prior to prohibition days, and four adequately equipped bars were diligently striving to alleviate the thirst of the population from eight o'clock in the morning until twelve o'clock at night, Mrs. Starblanket had another extenuating circumstance to condone her mistake.

The air was heavy, and electrical with thunder-storms. Lightning stabbed the big clouds which lay over Blueberry Island, across the Lake. Above her head, in the velvety blackness of the night, a hive of mosquitoes circled and spread, monotonously chanting their complaints; but none came near Mrs. Rosie Starblanket, whom mosquitoes had long since passed up as a tough proposition.

When Johnny stepped off the walk and turned into the gate, which was always left open, his mother greeted him. There was no word spoken—just a sound, but the sound had in it all the essentials of a kindly greeting. Interpreted, it ran: "There you are—I see you! Where have you been? and how are you?"

Johnny replied by another sound, which meant, "I'm jake! How's yourself?"

Ordinarily this was all that would have passed between them, for Mrs. Starblanket had learned, in a long-term school, that it is no time for talking when the exalted mood was upon any of the male members of her house.

But to-night it was Johnny who did the talking. He had been hoping his mother would be in her accustomed place at the west end of the white-washed log-house, for he wanted to talk to her. Great events had transpired, and his mother must know of them.

"Maw," he said, "I got a girl."

Mrs. Starblanket deliberately lit her pipe before replying. If that was all that was wrong it would keep until she got her pipe going. Then she made another sound, which meant, "I suppose it had to come sometime, so go on and let me know the worst."

John had been educated at the Industrial School, and had learned the use of language. He was now Assistant Station Agent at the Beach.

"She is one Jim-dandy girl, Maw," he began; "you know her. It is Minnie Hardcastle. You knew her mother, didn't you?"

Mrs. Starblanket nodded, but it was so dark Johnny could not see the signal of acquiescence, and he repeated the question.

His mother offered no denial.

"She went to the school, you know, when I did, at Brandon, but she was small then. She is just eighteen years old now, and smart—say, Maw, you should see her wait on table there! She's at 'The Homestead,' and all the fellows are after her. But to-night at the dance I asked her out straight, and she likes me better than any of them!"

His mother smoked on, but Johnny did not resent her apparent indifference.

There was a long silence between them, then Mrs. Starblanket carefully knocked the ashes from her pipe, put it in her blue print dress pocket, and began to talk. "Her father was white man," she said.

Johnny caught the implied disparagement. "But her mother was Indian, all Indian—Cree, too," he said eagerly. "You know the Lily people; they were good Indians, Maw— good Indians, like our folks." There was an appeal in the boy's voice that he knew would bring his mother around. "Fathers don't count like mothers," he continued; "you know that."

Mrs. Starblanket, of course, did not deny this. She was willing to admit, like all other students of sociology, that the virtues of the mother are sometimes visited on the children.

"She's pure Indian in everything but looks," urged Johnny, "and doesn't like white men a bit. You see, she takes me when she could have lots of white men; told me she would never marry a white man—wants pure Indian. She remembers her father, and just hates him—says she hopes he's dead, and all that."

"Humph!" Mrs. Starblanket swung around on her stool and addressed the place in the dark where her son was sitting. "What about Maggie?" she asked.

Johnny made an impatient gesture, which his mother felt as plainly as if she had seen it. "Maggie ain't got no style to her—and she toes in too bad," he said.

His mother shifted uneasily in her seat and drew her own moccasined feet under her skirt.

"Anyway, she's got another fellow," said Johnny, "a big freight handler on the train. She wouldn't look at me last night at the dance, just made a face at me when I passed. Maggie isn't caring a cent about me."

"Maybe not," said his mother, "maybe so. You better go slow on this other girl—she's too white for us, Johnny. It don't do any good, these mixtures. White is all right; Indian all right; I don't like breeds."

Mrs. Starblanket spoke with deep scorn. Why not? In her veins ran the blood of princes, and it was her great comfort that all her children had intermarried with undefiled Indian families. Johnny, her youngest and dearest, must not be allowed to stumble. Everything else had been taken from her but her pride of blood, and the slumbering resentment against the conquering race which had robbed the red man of everything but his honor awoke with increasing passion.

"Maggie's the best girl for you," she said; "you can't depend on white ones—some day they'll see another fellow and let you slide—I know! You can't count on white ones, they change."

"What about Maggie, then?" cried the boy, indignantly. "She's the one that has changed; she's the one that makes faces at her old fellow."

"You left her first," said his mother, severely. "I not blame Maggie—I'm glad she has another fellow. Maggie's a good girl—she make moccasin, basket, everything. White girls all for spend and dance."

A sudden crash of thunder, following upon a blinding flash of lightning, drove them indoors, and the rain, which had been threatening all evening, poured down in torrents. It ran in floods down the square-paned windows, and poured in and out of the barrels which Mrs. Starblanket had placed at the corner of the house for her supply of soft water.

Johnny Starblanket lighted a small coal-oil lamp and began to make his preparations for slumber. This well-dressed young man, resplendent in new tan boots and red tie, seemed like a casual caller in the whitewashed cabin, on whose walls hung many a trophy of the brave old days. He hung his collar and tie on the horns of an antelope, threw his boots on a tanned buffalo hide, and flung himself on a canvas stretcher in the corner of the room.

The raging of the storm made further conversation impossible, and for this Johnny was not sorry, for he knew his mother's moods too well to try to change them. In a vague, boyish way Johnny had compassion for his mother. He knew that life had grown gray and uneventful for her since the cottages had been built all around the Lake and the whole place had become filled with white people, to whom his mother was simply an Indian woman who occasionally did a washing for them.

He could remember the time, long ago it seemed now, when their house was the only one on the Lake as far as he could see, and when the hunters gathered with his father and big brothers around the fire in the winter evenings, and all the talk was of big game and shooting.

He could still recall the joy of being carried on his mother's back through the woods, when the acrid smell of the camp-fire got in his eyes as she stooped over to stir something in a pot. Around them he could hear the howling of the wolves, but he was not afraid.

The change had come suddenly, with the building of the railroad to the Beach, and the hunters had gone North. Soon after his father had died, and he had gone to school in Brandon to begin his education from books and teachers.

At the end of four years he had come back to his mother's white-washed house beside the Lake and begun his work in the Station.

At first the excitement of trains leaving and arriving, the surging crowd, the dances in the evenings, the bands which came out from the City and played in the Pavilion, all seemed like a wild dream of delight after the rigid discipline of the School; and yet, when he went back to his mother's cabin at midnight and listened to her stories of buffalo hunts and the felling of big game, his soul longed for the silent ways of the forest. By day he was Jack Starblanket, in all respects a white man, doing a white man's work in the throbbing avenues of trade; at night, with the sound of the

Lake licking the gray boulders on the shore, mingling with his mother's soft voice as she told him the stories of his people, he was an Indian, descendant of Chief Starblanket, and to whom the far country called.

Mrs. Starblanket lived again the thrilling scenes of life as she told them to her son. Civilization, which had closed in about her so terribly in the last four years, seemed now to choke and stifle her; and it was only in these dark nights, when the kind mantle of darkness blotted out the offending evidences, that her tongue was loosened and something of the old joy of living came back to her.

In daylight she could not look out without seeing the desecrated woods, the patches of clearing, the circle of red and white cottages which had broken out like a rash on the fair surface of the sandy shore. There were fences and flag-poles and sidewalks and running wells on all sides. There was an automobile road from the City, over which the honking, chucking, ill-smelling dragons of autos raced and jostled each other. No wonder that so many of the birds and squirrels had fled in terror.

"Too many people," Mrs. Starblanket often mourned to herself as she walked in the early morning along the sandy shore. Behind the cottages there was a boardwalk, and a good road, but she scorned them in her heart; and besides, she liked the crunch of the white gravel under moccasined feet.

The late night and the early morning were the times she liked best, for then the cottage dwellers were within doors, and the calm face of the Lake was not disfigured with their presence, and the horrible clatter of the screaming, laughing bathers was stilled.

In the morning, too, her own birds, the meadowlarks, flickers and thrushes, feeling much the way she did, claimed the woods for their own, and drove their songs of defiance into the open windows of the late-sleeping cottagers.

Some of these had even brought their own birds with them, as if the wild ones were not good enough for them, and these wretched little creatures, some of whom sang bravely in their gilded cages, hanging on the painted verandas, drew forth Mrs. Starblanket's pity and scorn.

"They take everything," she muttered to herself; "they can't let anything be. Ain't a bird singing in the trees better than a poor thing sitting on a roost? But the bird in the woods is free, and its own boss, and they want to be boss of everything. Nobody is safe now—they grab everything."

That night, after Johnny had gone to bed, Mrs. Starblanket long lay winking at the darkness. There was an unwonted bitterness in her heart as she thought of what her son had told her. He wanted to marry this white girl, for white she was to Mrs. Starblanket in spite of Johnny's spirited defence of her Indian parentage.

"White!" Mrs. Starblanket muttered, "and she'll lie in bed till noon, and wear rags on her head when she gets up, and paint her cheeks, and go out all afternoon to sit on some other woman's veranda and gab and cackle. She'll not make moccasin or tan hide, and when she has a kid she'll be sick a year before and a year after, and then never have another."

Mrs. Starblanket scorned the lady-like weaknesses of the Beach dwellers, which she had so often heard discussed by them with great frankness. She often wanted to tell them of the twelve children she had raised—and "never lay in bed a day" in her life. They surely were the good-for-nothing set, these white women, with their pains and their nerves and their operations.

And now Johnny was going to marry one of them, and his good wages would be spent on doctor's bills and operations and crazy frilled things. The sore touch to Mrs. Starblanket in all this was that her brightest and best dream was shattered by this new turn in her son's affairs. There was no chance now of Johnny going back to the life to which all Indians belonged—to the life of his father and his grandfather and the older brothers, who had fled before civilization's choking breath. Johnny, the powerful, the fleet of foot and strong of arm, who, when he was five years old, could put his arrows into a tree like a man and ride the worst pony at the Fair—she could see Johnny pushing a baby carriage up and down the sidewalk while his wife played cards with other white women and told them "how many stitches she had put in the last time." She supposed a place would be found for her in the kitchen, where she could wash and iron, and polish the slippery floors. It looked like a life sentence for both Johnny and her.

Mrs. Starblanket made no sign of all this the next morning, but was especially attentive to Johnny when she got ready his breakfast of eggs and bacon. Poor Johnny, he would soon be cooking his own—her's too; while his mother had him she would "use him good."

The mother's solicitude was unnoticed, for John Starblanket's heart was busy with other matters. Like most men, Indian and white alike, the attention of his women-folk was only noticeable in its absence. But Mrs. Starblanket was not worrying or even thinking about this. Indian women do not live on words of praise and honeyed phrases.

The storm of the previous night had left the Lake fretful and complaining, although the sun had come up in a cloudless sky and the wind had gone down. But the waves rolled in upon the shore petulantly, whimpering of the night and what its fury had done.

Johnny went gaily whistling out of the gate, but suddenly remembered something which he wished to say to his mother. Coming back to the door, he called to her: "I'll bring Minnie down to see you, Maw. She's real Indian—you'll see! She's been asking about you."

His mother made a sound in her throat which Johnny knew meant assent, and he resumed his whistling. "I won't come home tonight," he said, "but we'll both come down tomorrow night for supper. We'll come in canoe mos' likely. Oh, yes, there's something else I want to say. The papers say there's going to be war over in Europe. There's lots of talk goin' round, and the fellows say we'll all have to go mos' likely."

Mrs. Starblanket nodded. War! That was more of a man's job than handing out train tickets like Johnny was doing now. War! She remembered when her grandfather had painted his face and gone out early . . . War! What was she thinking of? "They won't fight!" she said in contempt. "White men won't fight; they're too soft, too lazy, too fond of easy things!"

II

The instinct to house-clean is inherent in women. It is a sure wall of defence against the arrows of fortune, for with a clean house a woman can face the world even though it turns to her a frowning countenance.

Mrs. Starblanket's first impulse now was to set to work to clean the house so that Minnie Hardcastle would see that Johnny was the son of a woman who knew how to make a man comfortable. The floor would be none the worse of a scrubbing; the windows, cleaned though they had been a few days before, were now spotted with flies; the stove could easily be made a brighter black; there were weeds in the garden, too, which Mrs. Starblanket could remove.

She rose hurriedly and began to set away the remains of the breakfast, with many plans for improving the appearance of her house, and glad of the two whole free days in which she had to do it. She'd let this white man's daughter see that John Starblanket had been "fetched up good," and if he picked up with lazy women now it wasn't because he had been used to them.

Mrs. Starblanket knew well the ways of cleaning a house. Though she would not have admitted it, the cottage dwellers had taught her many things; and if her heart had been heavier since their coming, her house at any rate had been cleaner. Curtains had appeared at the small windows, and vegetable dishes had mysteriously supplemented the functions of the black pot in which her potatoes and cabbages were boiled. Better methods of washing, too, had superseded the fire on the shore and the rubbing of clothes by hand on a stone.

For two days Mrs. Starblanket practised all her skill in household arts. Every treasure of her house was brought to light. Johnny would not feel badly about his mother and her Indian ways. The beaded suit with the gauntlets to match was hung carelessly on the head of Johnny's bed, just as if beaded suits were but incidents in his life. The bearskins were beaten on the line until no more dust could be dislodged, and the one and only houseplant, given to Mrs. Starblanket by one of her last year's patronesses, and carefully brought through the winter by heavy newspaper coverings on the coldest nights, was turned around to show the best side of its luxuriant leaves, and of the jardiniere she had made for it from some silver paper she had picked up on the shore.

"Mos' likely they'll be hungry," she said to herself as she went over to one of the cottages to negotiate for a chicken. Chicken, she knew, was the proper offering when company was coming. White though she was, Johnny's girl would be "treated good."

If Mrs. Starblanket had not watched herself closely she would have grown quite happy over her preparations, but she kept up a scornful attitude to the whole proceedings. She put tiger-lilies in a pickle bottle on the table for a cen-tre-piece; she brought out all her plates and washed them in soapy water, and polished them till they shone. She knew the more dishes people use at a meal the "sweller" it is. She folded white paper napkins into teepees before each plate, and had her steel knives scoured to look like silver. Mrs. Starblanket was feminine enough to prepare more thor-oughly for an enemy than a friend.

If it had been Maggie, the basket-maker, who was coming for a meal—Maggie, her choice for a daughter-in-law—there would have been none of this; but for this white girl there would be nothing amiss, and no need for apolo-gies. She would let Johnny's girl see that she knew how a meal should be cooked!

That evening, while Minnie served dinner in the long dining-room of the Winnipeg Beach Hotel, overlooking the blue waters of the Lake, she was watched by at least two pairs of masculine eyes. Johnny's deep-set, languorous gaze fol-lowed her graceful movements with admiring prideful looks.

She was his girl, the swellest girl at the Beach, and his. He gloried in her somewhat haughty beauty, her well-poised head, her neatly coiled hair, the springiness of her step, and the neatness of her attire. But Johnny did not analyze her appearance—all his adoration of her was covered when he told himself "she sure is a swell girl!"

The other pair of eyes was gray and oyster-lidded—not so young or so bright as Johnny's, not so honest in their admiration. They belonged to a man, thick-set and prosperous-looking, who had come on the evening train.

He spoke to a younger man who sat beside him. "Great place they have here!" he said, looking about the long dining-room approvingly, with its many tables. "This place was virgin wilderness the last time I saw it. Just nineteen years ago a bunch of us were out hunting for a week—lived with the Indians and shot big game—feared neither God nor man. We sure were wild young colts. That was the time a fellow could have a good time; there were no laws, no ten commandments, and no consequences. The present was everything." He laughed reminiscently. "I wish I could see it as it was then. The Indians were in great form. They took us up the Lake in canoes, and showed us how to tan hides and make moccasins. There were some pretty girls among them, with shy brown eyes and red cheeks. That girl," pointing to the next table, where Minnie was serving, "reminds me of one of them—same carriage and same dignified manner. By Jove! she is a pretty girl."

"Hush!" said the other man, with some embarrassment, "she'll hear you."

"That won't hurt her—they all like to hear it, young or old. Don't worry about me. I make no mistakes with women. There's just one system with them, young man. Go after them—they like to be chased—and lay on the blarney. You can't put it on too thick. Now, watch me if you want to see how it's done."

When Minnie passed the table at which he was sitting he lifted his hand to attract her attention. "How are you, my dear?" he said blandly, regarding her with a beaming smile.

A full ten seconds passed before she replied, and then her answer came deliberately: "I am quite well." The voice was serenely calm and level, and would have been disconcerting to a less self-assured man.

"My dear," he beamed, "I did not need to ask. All I needed to do was to look and see the roses on your cheeks and the sparkle in your eye. My dear girl, to look at you makes me young again."

Minnie's eyes were narrowing as he spoke, and the two dull red angry spots which rose in her cheeks emphasized the high cheek-bones. There was something about him that gave her a feeling of nausea. Not that Minnie Hardcastle had not been made love to in public before—she too long had been a waitress in a summer hotel to experience any surprise at the foolishness of men, young or old, and had thought herself prepared for anything—but there was something in the tone of the stranger's voice, a sort of vaseline softness, that stirred bitter memories.

"What do you want to eat?" she asked hurriedly, forgetting her accustomed courteous manner in her intense desire to return to a strictly business basis with this well-favored guest whose eyes were turned upon her in such bold admiration.

"Eat?" he laughed noisily, "I have not got to that yet, my dear. I am too busy admiring the roses. I am walking in the garden in the cool of the evening—don't hurry me. My dear, will you tell me, were you born up here in this wild country, or have you stepped out of a picture, or where did you come from?"

Minnie's eyes were half-closed as she asked, "Are you fresh, or just foolish?"

The younger man laughed, and looked at his companion to see if his composure had wilted at all. But the bland face revealed nothing.

"I'm just foolish," he said, still smiling.

"In that case," said Minnie testily, "I do not mind telling you I was born near here. My mother is dead and my father is, too, I hope."

"Bless its heart!" he cried, bursting into a laugh as if some witty word had been spoken—a great throaty laugh which had no mirth in it—the sort of laugh in which no one joins. "It has a temper for all it looks so mild. Well, well, we won't press the point any further."

"Ham and eggs, roast beef, pork chops, sausage," repeated Minnie mechanically, and with no hint in her voice of any emotion other than the desire to serve the two men and get it over as quickly as possible.

The guests decided in favor of roast beef, and when Minnie had gone the older man had just a hint of anger in his heavy eyes. The younger man adroitly ignored the incident, and began to talk of other things.

The portly gentleman, however, had been wounded in a tender spot, and could not easily forget it. "It's all a part of this damned uplift business!" he snarled, attacking the roll beside his plate with unnecessary violence. "There is no place where a man has any liberty any more. Here, even here in this neck of the woods, the half-breed girls after a year or two in these infernal industrial schools get the airs of a duchess, and imbibe notions entirely beyond their place. There are no shy, modest little girls any more, who blush when they are spoken to and know how to take a compliment. Now they stare back and talk back, and I'll bet that black-eyed jade wants to vote, and all the rest of it. A real man might as well be dead as live in this world when the bars go and every last woman is of this independent kind. Good Lord! where's the fun of living? What will we do after ten o'clock—tell me that. We might as well go to war and kill Germans as stay at home here and drink ice-water . . . the darned women get my goat, anyway; there's a few of them in this country that ought to be deported."

He was growing more and more inflamed as he went on.

"Now, this part of it—this half-breed waitress talking back, handing it to me like a queen. There was a time when a girl would lose her job for this, but now the laboring people have the whip hand on us, and we have to keep civil, even to these mongrel half-breeds!"

Without knowing it he had raised his voice.

When he was through speaking a shadow fell across his table, and, looking up, he found himself looking into the face of Johnny Starblanket, who, without apparent motion, had made the distance across the dining-room.

Indian-like, Johnny had made no sound, but stood facing the other man waiting for him to speak.

"Well," said the big man, harshly, "what do you want?"

"I heard you speak of half-breed waitress," said Johnny, slowly. "I just wanted to say—I just want you to hear—that there's no such word as 'half-breed' in this country. If you think there is you had better forget it quick. If you are afraid you can't forget you had better get out. It ain't healthy here for people who can't forget the word. That girl you spoke to is Indian girl—straight Indian. Her mother was daughter of a chief; her father don't matter—he was nothing."

"What about her father?" the white man asked, insolently.

"Her father don't count," said Johnny, slowly, "he was just yellow dog of white man, the kind we see some time at the hotel—fresh guy that talks too much."

Johnny waited motionless for a reply to his words, staring into the muddy depths of the fat man's eyes. There was tense silence in the room. The air was electrical. Anything might happen. Everyone had heard Johnny's words.

The big man tried to bluster a reply, but there was a slumbrous fire in the inky blackness of the Indian boy's eyes which caused him to change his mind.

"All right, all right, my boy," he stammered, "no harm done, I hope."

"No harm done!" Johnny, repeated, with emphasis, "no harm done—just thought of, but not done," and with the same gliding motion he returned to his seat.

The meal proceeded in silence, the older man giving his orders in sulky monosyllables. But his eyes devoured the girl's face, following her graceful movements as she cleared the table next to them.

From his corner Johnny Starblanket sat and watched, and drew his own conclusions. He had heard of men like this, whose desires were evil, and who regarded all young, innocent things as their legitimate prey. Johnny had even known bad Indians, though not many. On all such he poured the contempt of his young heart. He would kill them gladly, joyously, as his father had once with his bare hands killed the wildcat which attacked little Rose, his sister. But his love for Minnie drove out all baser thoughts, and the paramount emotion of his passionate young heart was the joy of possession. Minnie, the admired one, was his girl; she liked him best of all the boys.

In the construction he put upon the white man's admiration for Minnie, Johnny was not exactly correct in his assumption that it was entirely evil. Evil it certainly was at first, as most of the man's impulses were, but as he watched her now deftly clearing away the dishes from the table near at hand he was conscious of another emotion. It was not exactly remorse or memory—it was a sudden growing wonder.

When the meal was over Johnny strolled out to the veranda, quite conscious of his striking figure and elegant new clothes; conscious also of the sensation that had been produced by his words to the flashy stranger. The Indian love of admiration was strong in Johnny. Young, fine-looking, earning money, Johnny Starblanket felt a thrill of pride and joy such as his ancestors had felt in the supreme moment of the chase.

He stretched himself in one of the folding canvas chairs which stood on the screened-in veranda overlooking the Lake, and cast his black eyes out over the water. Blueberry Island, where he had often gone in pursuit of the berries which gave it its name, stretched blue and misty on the eastern sky-line. White-winged boats, with an occasional colored parasol above them, dotted the placid surface of the Lake. It was the quiet hour at the Beach, the hush that came before the clamorous arrival of the city trains. Leisurely he took the evening paper from his pocket and casually glanced at the headlines.

"England sends ultimatum to Germany," he read, and whistled, not in surprise, but just because he liked whistling and felt the need of doing something. The trouble in Europe made no ripple on the complacent soul of John Starblanket, yet he read the front-page article through with a growing feeling of wonder. War was plainly hinted at, and yet war seemed to belong to a glorious day long past.

He read the article again, then folded the paper, replaced it in his pocket, and made his way to the back door to see if he could get a word with Minnie. A restlessness had seized him, a strange thrilling excitement. He wanted some one to applaud him—praise him—admire him!

Minnie was filling her tray from the oilcloth-covered table, and skilfully keeping the flies at bay at the same time, when Johnny filled the doorway of the kitchen. Minnie's quick smile seemed to fill the room with radiance.

"Come on, Minnie," he said, "it's dandy out. Can't you get a spell off? You've often let the other girls out before it was all over. As long as you slave away they'll let you, girl—take that from me."

"We're short to-night," Minnie said, lifting her tray. "I hear them calling, Jack. Just wait till I place these and I'll come back. Won't you sit down?"

"No, thanks, I don't fancy hanging around a kitchen. I'll go over and wait at the bandstand. But hurry up—I want to get out in the canoe—I want to tell you something."

"I must go and get in this pie," said Minnie, "they're waiting. But I'll come to the bandstand as soon as I can get out. Wait for me there."

"You bet!" was the hearty response, and Johnny strolled leisurely across the green grass plot to the main street, where the first of the evening trains was arriving.

The same old holiday crowd surged through the doors and eddied out to the platform, milling and weaving the same gorgeous coloring of sweaters and blazers and sailor hats, amid the same holiday chatter, the idle things so joyously spoken by people whose day's work is done and who are off for a "time."

John Starblanket moved among them with something of the grace of the old Chief, his great-grandfather, when the tribe had assembled to do him honor—absolutely aloof and unconcerned in appearance, and yet alive to every nod or word or glance of approval.

"Gee! ain't it good to get away from those darned pavements and get a sniff of real air instead of that fanned stuff!" The speaker, making her way past Johnny, was one of the smartest dressers in the "Notions," with the widest hat, the shortest skirt, and the thinnest blouse. "Now, why can't I get a job out here? Gee! I'd do anything, catch frogs, hold clothes for the bathers, or even sling hash, to get here. Say, girls, honest, I know a girl out here that waits on tables and is all done at eight o'clock, and she sure has as fine a time as I ever saw a girl with."

They were making their way to the Pavilion, being among the passengers from the first section of the "Moonlight."

"Say, Speers, your language is lovely," said the tallest girl of the group, a salesgirl from the hardware section. "Now, I've seen girls with lots of things—I've seen them with beaus, and with jags even, but I never saw one with a 'time'!"

"Oh, shut up, Brown, you highbrow!" snapped the little one. "You know what I mean. That's what's keepin' you back—you know too darned much, and every one's afraid to talk before you only me."

She was ruffling a curl which had lost some of its beauty in the heat, holding one hair lightly and sending all the others up the pole by a skilful movement of her thumb and finger.

"Don't be sore, kid," said the tall girl; "you're not much on language, but you get there all the same. I'm jealous of you—that's all that's wrong with me. Don't be sore on a wallflower."

"Many a true word is spoken in jest," said the little cashier, gravely, as she applied a pink chamois to her nose; "but if you wanted to be human I believe you could do it, and you'd sure be a world-beater with those long lashes of yours. Only you're so stiff and prim, and have a way of making people feel small. That won't go with men—you have to make them feel sporty and smart and beamy. You have to look at them with mute admiration in your eyes—and, gee-whizz, when I can do it with these peepers of mine, what couldn't you do with those Mazda lights of yours? Why don't you try it once, Brown, just for fun?"

Brown shook her head gravely. "What's fun for the bad little boys is death to the frogs," she replied.

"There you go again, quoting poetry and makin' me feel ignorant because I don't know what it's all about, though of course I get the run of it. But no one likes to be put in the wrong. Now, look, Brownie, do you see that good-looking Indian boy over there?"

John Starblanket had walked by slowly, moving with all the grace and suppleness of his race.

Miss Brown looked after him with interest.

"Some kid, eh?" said the cashier. "Do you want to see how it is done, Brown? If so, follow me, but not so close as to get in the machinery. Safety first! This is a time for skilful treatment."

"Oh, say, Speers!" Miss Brown spoke with animation now. "Leave the Indian boy alone—I'll bet he's got a girl some place. Have a heart, woman, and don't cut in on the native race. There ought to be a law against it, the same as selling liquor to them."

"Well, there is no law, my lady, no law but the law of get what you can and how you can. The world is your parish, so to speak. I'm a dead shot, a real go-getter, and I get what I go after."

"Leave the Indian boy alone," urged Miss Brown, gravely, "he looks like a nice kid."

"Well, I won't bite him; I won't even scratch him; I only want to have him around for a spare. I've got my permanents and regulars, haven't I? An ice-cream soda won't break him. I'll let him go back to his Minnehaha all right. I just want to make things pleasant for him. Can you find any fault with that?"

The second section of the "Moonlight" came in, and another surging crowd of the city's youth in their nightly quest for pleasure gravitated to the Pavilion, where the "Officers of the Day" march called to them to come and dance.

John Starblanket, leisurely smoking a long cigar, leaned against the bandstand, still conscious of the admiring glances of the girls who passed him, but unmoved by them, for in his heart there was only one flame burning.

"They ain't one, two, three alongside Minnie," he was thinking, as they danced past him, "they haven't got the style she has, nor the set-up."

But he did wish she would hurry, for he, too, wanted to dance. The music fairly hurt him, it was so sweet and piercing. Why couldn't she get out like other girls instead of sticking in that furnace of a kitchen washing dishes? She'll stay till the last dish is dried, too—that's her kind.

The second dance was called, and still Minnie had not appeared, and Johnny's annoyance was growing every minute. He moved down towards the entrance so that he would see her when she came in.

The dance was a weird sort of shuffling two-step, which has since become very popular, with runs and glides quite bewildering. Johnny had not seen it before, and now took his cigar from his mouth to watch. There was something fascinating about it.

The cashier, who glided by dancing with one of the delivery men, was drawing more attention than any other girl on the floor. Her blouse was the thinnest in texture and the lowest in cut, her skirt the shortest and tightest, and her hold of her partner the closest and most gripping. She had often said that what she did she did well, and her style of fox-trotting bore out the statement.

"Some fine stepper," Johnny said to himself.

It so happened that when the music stopped she was right beside him, and as she turned to find a seat brushed closely against his coat-sleeve, exuding the sweet odor of violets. Quite unconsciously she raised her eyes, and suddenly let the lids fall in apparent confusion.

"You sure can dance," Johnny said, wondering at his own boldness, as he motioned her to take his seat.

"Oh, do you think so?" she murmured. "I love it, you know. Don't you?"

Her voice was as sweet as the tinkle of the Mission bells. She was fixing a wandering hairpin as she spoke.

"We never danced much at the Mission," Johnny said, blushing pleasurably.

"It's no trick to learn," volunteered the cashier. "I'm sure I could show you how—not here in this mob of course; but if we had a little more room I could show you. I've showed lots of boys, but I have to have room. If you come out on the veranda, where there ain't so many dancers, I'll show you in no time. I just know it would be easy for you."

Johnny didn't know just how it happened. There is a word for it—several words with Latin derivation, but all meaning the same. It is a sort of temporary displacement of affection—not serious if rearranged in time. The evening air from the Lake was soft as velvet and resonant with laughter and gaiety; the band played the sort of music which sends rhythmic thrills through the heart; something like a cut-out was sounding in Johnny's impressionable heart. The flattery in the cashier's eyes was irresistible.

When the dancing lesson, accompanied by much laughter and ragging from an interested group of spectators, was over, and Johnny, who had a quick ear and sense of rhythm, was complete master of the fox-trot, Miss Speers archly hinted at an ice-cream soda, declaring that after a hot dance it was the thing she was fondest of.

To her surprise her companion, with a hurried word of thanks, abruptly declared he had forgotten all about a friend of his who was waiting for him, and that he must go.

"It's my girl," he said, with a quick blush of boyish confusion. "Gee, I don't know what she'll say!" and he was gone.

Miss Speers' look of surprise was so apparent that the crowd around laughed good-humoredly.

"Stung, kiddo!" they cried.

"Well, what do you know about that for ingratitude?" said one.

"He hasn't a girl at all, I'll bet—he just wanted to save the two-bits," ventured another.

"He's nothing but a cheapskate," added a third.

"Come and teach me," one big fellow said, laughing, "and I'll pay in advance. I won't leave you high and dry without even a cone at the end of the lesson, either. I'll treat teacher both times."

Miss Speers made a brave attempt to join in the fun, but her pride had received a severe shock in the Indian boy's abrupt departure.

"Gee-whizz!" she said to Miss Brown, who was one of the company. "Did I dream it, or is it true? Tell me, Brown, did that boy turn me down? Did he actually say he had a girl some place, another girl? What right has he to be thinking of another girl when I'm giving full time to him? I feel like a defeated candidate, Brown."

"Oh, leave the Indian boy alone, Speers," said her friend; "I like him all the better because he did remember his girl. You've already got more fellows than you've got time for."

"Sure Mike!" said Miss Speers, modestly, "but it's the principle of the thing. I can't afford to lose my punch, Brown. You don't understand—it's professional pride with me. And now, listen, draw near and hear. This will cost him more than the price of a soda before he's done with me. He started something when he put me in the place where people had the laugh on me!"

III

Johnny, meanwhile, quite unconscious of the storm he had left behind him, went to the place where Minnie had said she would meet him, and, not finding her, proceeded to the hotel to find the reason for delay.

The summer evening was going; already purple shadows of night were wrapping the shores, and the lights on the motor-boats glittered in the darkening twilight. Cautious mothers were making their way to the shore with coats and sweaters for their ungrateful children, for the first breath of autumn had come. The faint sadness which it brings touched Johnny's young heart, and he shivered with a vague sense of dread. "Darn it all!" he muttered to himself. "Why can't things last? We've had no summer yet."

A sense of disappointment filled his heart. The evening had gone wrong, and it was all Minnie's fault—she would stick around there until the last pan was washed. She was too honest, Minnie was; she went hunting work, and did more than any two of the other girls.

On his way to the hotel Johnny met the stranger whose remarks regarding half-breeds had called forth his indignation. The stout gentleman was in an amiable and apologetic mood, and had his own reasons for a conference with the Indian boy. Since the scene in the dining-room the placid though muddy waters of his soul had been ruffled, and conscience, long since atrophied from disuse, was vaguely stirring in its long sleep. The Indian boy probably knew certain things—or didn't know—and he was glad of this chance meeting, which would give the appearance of casualness to the whole incident which was so necessary. He would find out, if he could, how much was known of the pretty waitress's history.

"I say," he began affably, "I want to thank you for putting me right in there. I meant no harm, you know. It's just my nature to jolly the girls along—nothing to it but a bit of fun. You came on me so quick I couldn't gather my wits together fast enough to apologize, but I do it now. You were quite right, and I was wrong."

The stranger put out a flabby hand, and Johnny took it readily. The older man's apology fell agreeably on his ears. He was evidently a person of importance. The well-ironed crease in his trousers; the russet shoes, well-polished and pointed; the Panama hat with its well-blocked crown, and the white hands, so far removed from toil, gave evidence of his standing in the world of men, and a new feeling of power came over John Starblanket. This man, wealthy and important as he undoubtedly was, had apologized to him.

The Indian is always magnanimous and gracious. "The incident is forgotten," said Johnny, in the stately manner of his great-grandfather.

"Perhaps you would tell me something about this very beautiful girl. Beauty interests everyone, and I cannot pass a flower, a tree, or a beautiful scene, without stopping to admire it. It is my habit of mind. This girl with her ease and grace of movement would attract attention in New York City. Am I asking too much if I ask you to tell me about her?"

"There is nothing much to tell," said Johnny. "She attended the Mission school when I did, and she has good people on her mother's side. They are the Fox Hills Indians. Her mother was one of the chief's daughters, and she was born here nineteen years ago, I think."

"But what about her father?" the white man asked, and if Johnny had been looking closely he would have noticed that the flabby hands twitched nervously.

"No one knows much about him," said Johnny, slowly. "She doesn't talk, neither does her mother; it is forgotten. Indian women do not tell their troubles," he concluded proudly.

A wave of relief swept over the other man's face. "Indian women do not tell their troubles"—behind that kindly wall his craven soul cowered and felt itself hidden. Just for a moment, then the thought came tormentingly from somewhere that it was just possible the Indian boy knew more that he was telling. It might be well to find out for sure. There was one way of loosening any man's tongue, Indian or white, one sure way to make a man tell what was in his heart. It was just an off-chance, this suspicion of his—most improbable, and yet not impossible—and for his own satisfaction he wanted to know how much was known.

"Miss Hardcastle is engaged to be married to me," said Johnny, after a pause. "We expect to be married at Christmas if I get the promotion I am looking for."

"My boy," said the older man, warmly, and in his desire to accomplish his object his words sounded almost sincere; "my boy, I congratulate you, and wish you the very best of life's good things. You deserve them all, too, you and your beautiful young lady. And now let us have a drink to your best happiness."

He turned towards the door of the bar, but Johnny stopped him. "You forget," he said, "that Indians cannot be supplied with liquor in public bars."

The other man laughed. "Oh, no, my boy, I wasn't forgetting, and I wasn't going near the bar. I carry a little all the time for emergencies, my boy—cramps, snake-bites, weddings, christenings, engagements—I'm prepared! This seems to be one of the times. Rotten tough luck, too, not to be able to get a drink like other people—rank injustice, I say. But if these infernal temperance cranks get their way we'll all be in the same boat in a year from now, so let us get a drink while we can."

"I'm sorry," said Johnny, hastily, "but I am looking for Miss Hardcastle now. I have missed her some way, and I don't want to keep her waiting."

"Say, boy," said the older man, lowering his voice, "don't run after 'em too much. They're all the same. Keep 'em guessing—that's the system—don't let 'em be too sure of you. Now, I've had my own way with women all my life, and I've let them do the chasing if there was any to be done."

"She's different," said the Indian boy, simply; "she's independent and high-tempered—she not stand anything. There's too many fellows after her—white men, too, lots of them. She never looks at any of them, though."

The older man laughed in a way that made Johnny feel very young and green and countrified.

"Lad, you've got a lot to learn about women. Now, come with me; my room is on the first floor. It will only take a minute, and remember, a year from now there may not be any in the country, so take a snort while you can, I say. It will make you enjoy your evening all the more. I'm as dry as a covered bridge, so come on."

In half an hour Johnny and his companion came back to the Pavilion, the latter, accustomed as he was to the effect of liquor, comfortably warmed and stimulated, feeling himself rather a fine fellow, with only the weaknesses of other fine fellows; all very attractive failings, too, and excusable on the ground of frail humanity.

John Starblanket's outlook on life had suffered more. The fine passionate tenderness of his heart was driven out by something coarse, sensual, and selfish—something which made him, his wishes and desires, the centre of his little world, instead of the girl whom he had loved so well. Toward her now he had a feeling of annoyance, disappointment, even anger, and he asked himself over and over again, "Why wasn't she here when she promised?" No one had seen her.

His annoyance soon passed in the glamor of the lights and the music, and in the exaltation which was growing in his heart, for John Starblanket's training and education had broken down temporarily, and all the primitive savage instincts were surging within him. He wanted action, noise, motion, excitement, admiration. If it had been forty years earlier he could have painted his face, sharpened his tomahawk, and found an outlet for this turbulent soul in stalking some of the young braves of another tribe. But this was in the year of grace nineteen fourteen, and there were laws and conventions to be considered.

To all intents John Starblanket was a white man, an employee of a great Railway, a young man of promise, who held a position of trust. The law had placed a ban on the evil thing that had the power to set aside his training and turn him back to savagery again. But even the law cannot control that elusive, uncertain, and variable factor which enters into every human equation. Individuals can find a way to evade and elude the law, and so make its good purposes of no effect. The law had tried to save John Starblanket from his enemy, but the law had failed.

As Johnny swung gaily in among the dancers, who now surged around the Pavilion in a promenade, it so happened that the cashier from the "Notions" was the first person he saw, and she, for her own purposes, smiled up at him in a way that made his eyes shine with a mistier light.

When Minnie had finished her work she had hastily changed her white uniform for a muslin dress and come out to find Johnny. She had a guilty feeling of having delayed too long, and already had words of explanation prepared with which to soothe his impatient spirit.

At the bandstand, where she expected to find him, she found an empty chair, which she carried down to the shore below the Pavilion. Sinking gratefully into its green and white striped seat, she suddenly realized how utterly tired and footsore she was. The music fell about her in a refreshing shower, under which the feeling of weariness and lonesomeness gradually gave way. She was not alone any more in this great rushing, excited throng of people that surged and milled and chattered and danced and ate. Minnie could not regard them quite the same as one who did not have to feed them, but, happily enough, she reflected, she would not always have to carry trays and sweep off crumbs. Johnny would get a raise at Christmas, and already she had saved enough to buy herself a dress and a fur coat.

Minnie's life had been a singularly lonely one on account of her unhappy parentage and the Indian's dislike of half-breeds. Her mother's people had tolerated her, and that was all. All the anguish of the child who is not liked had been her portion—the nameless, unspoken, crushing weight of being different from other children, though it was not until she went to school at the Mission that she knew the reason. Then it was Maggie Hoskin, arrogantly proud of her pure red blood, who had scornfully classified her, using the evil word that had gone crashing through her young heart with its benumbing cruelty.

Then Minnie understood for the first time, in a flash of blinding horror, why it was that she was never given first place in any of the games; why her grandmother had never taken her with her as she did her other cousins when she went visiting "up the Lake," never even seeming to look at her; and why her mother had often crushed her in her arms with fierce tenderness, and then hastily pushed her away as if she could not bear the sight of her.

When the teacher at the Mission, noticing her troubled face, had gently sought the cause, Minnie, Indian-like, had hid her grief and bravely lied about it. The place in her heart was too sore for even Miss Bowden's tender hands, so she missed the consolation that might have been hers.

Tonight as she sat by the shore and listened to the band and the rhythmic movement of the feet of the dancers, with the velvety coolness of the evening on her face and in her mouth, which somehow seemed to satisfy her like a drink of water, and with the blue Lake spread at their feet, reflecting the sun-flecked clouds, Minnie's heart was filled with a great peace.

All her life, even in the saddest times of her lonely childhood, the open spaces, the water, trees, and birds had comforted her, whispering to her a message of hope. Nothing mattered, these said, nothing. The sun would shine; the gentle, cooling breezes, bearing perfume, would come; the birds' wings would go flashing by. Nature was always all right—it was only people who were bad and cruel.

But since Johnny Starblanket had come into her life Minnie's times of sadness had almost disappeared. Johnny knew everything about her, and he didn't mind. Johnny's approval was enough to banish every bitter thought, and in his towering strength, so abundant, so assured, Minnie's trembling heart had found rest.

Only one thought now troubled her, but this she tried to put from her as being disloyal. Sometimes Johnny had frightened her with his fierce love-making, when his eyes burned deep and his breath smelled like that of a white man. Among the Indians, she knew, liquor was forbidden, and at the Mission she had been taught that liquor drinking was very wicked, and would do dreadful things to the lining of the stomach, for Miss Bowden had shown them a picture of it; but she wished that Johnny would not drink it, for when he had the burning eyes he was not gentle and kind to her, but had a way that made her afraid. But Johnny had said that when they were married he would never think of it, because he would not have time to think of anything but her, and at the memory of his words Minnie's heart was flooded with a tender sweetness.

She knew that if she could only get him to come away from the Railway, away up into the big woods, where the rivers sweep down to the sea, and the woods are crimson in autumn, and the nights are filled with silence, he would be all her own, and she would never be afraid. Here there were too many people, too much talk and noise, too many things moving, and no peace and quiet.

Johnny would get tired of it all, too, just as she was, and then they would take the two canoes and go down North—north to the big country—and live their lives as her people and his had lived theirs before all these troublesome, noisy things had come upon them.

With these quieting and comforting thoughts filling her mind Minnie's lithe young body relaxed in the comfortable canvas chair, and her tired hands lay at rest on her lap. The music seemed to grow softer and softer and to drift farther away. Now it was only the roar of the big river that she heard—the big falls where the rainbow throws its lovely arch across the foam—and soothed by the sound she fell asleep.

Minnie was awakened by the passing of many feet. The crowd was swarming out of the Pavilion toward the train, which stood on a siding with its engine gently throbbing its impatience to be on the way. The dance was over. Rousing herself, she stood up, chilled by the night air, stiff and miserable. Slowly her thoughts came back. Where was Johnny? And why hadn't he met her? Something must have happened to Johnny!

Fear drove out every other thought as she turned toward the Pavilion, from which the crowd still poured. Who could she ask? Not a familiar face did she see.

Suddenly she became rigid as a piece of iron, and with ancestral instinct flattened herself against the white wall of the Pavilion, watching with eyes that glinted like dagger-points. Johnny was passing, with the cashier beside him. Johnny was talking too loudly, gesticulating and rolling in his walk, and his eyes were burning, deep and glowing, like a campfire in the black night. His hand held the white girl's bare elbow, and he bent over her caressingly.

Then it was well for little Miss Speers that Minnie had no instrument of death in her hand, for Minnie's mind held but one thought. She was pure Indian now, with no restraint or compunction, and would have killed the girl joyously as her grandfather had killed the bear at the falls where the rainbow throws its radiance.

Like a ghost Minnie darted after them through the throng, and saw them enter the train. Then she watched from the shelter of a tree for Johnny's return. She was partly white now, and reasoned with herself that, failing to find her, Johnny had danced with the girl and was now putting her on the train—that was all. It was right that he should do this; Johnny was the sort that would always be kind and polite to any girl. The surging flood of anger had left her pale and trembling, and in her thin summer dress she shivered in the night air. She argued, reasoned, tried to persuade herself it was all right. She must be fair, and always fair.

It was a night brilliant with stars, but with no moon, and the big arc lamp at the Station threw a brassy light on the trees around, whose leaves rippled and whispered in the shore wind. It seemed to Minnie that she had slept for days, maybe weeks, her joints were so stiff and cold, and the events of the day were so far removed.

Johnny would be sorry and concerned over her, and afraid that she might have a cold. It was nice to have someone who cared. Her mind alternated with lightning rapidity from one attitude to the other. Rage and jealousy, that made her veins run fire, were succeeded by a calm mood in which she told herself she must be true to Johnny whatever happened, and must continue to believe in him.

While Minnie fought with her emotions the "Moonlight" rapidly took on its passengers, a throng of shouting, laughing young people, whose excitement still prevented them from thinking of the tired time ahead of them. Thoughts of the morning after, with its languor and fatigue, had no power to blight tonight's pleasure; there was only one time for them, and that was tonight, with its flirtations, music, and fun.

Minnie darted forward as the engine shrieked its last warning and the train bell began to ring. With noiseless steps she ran over the deserted platform in the faint hope that Johnny might have gone in another car; but as the cars passed by her one by one, gathering speed as the great engine plowed its way into the night, no one came off, and no one noticed the slim wraith of a girl who stood wringing her hands in mute agony.

Faster and faster the train swept by, every window revealing happy young faces, hateful to her as she glimpsed them passing, and appearing to mock and scorn her in her misery.

She stood there until the last car had disappeared around the turn and the roar of the train had been swallowed up in the night sounds. Motionless she stood, like one who had forgotten her surroundings, forgotten everything. On her face was a puzzled look of childish fear, pain, and wonder. Then she turned and ran through the deserted street to the back entrance of the hotel, and up the three flights of stairs to her little room under the rafters.

The night, with its wells of blackness and its cruel silence and weird noises, is a hard time to be brave. The whole scheme of things seems so big and black and all-embracing, so utterly heartless, so inexorable and hard to entreat. Most of us are cowards until the sun comes back.

When the inky blackness of the night filled the room under the rafters Minnie could find no way out of her troubles. The bitter truth, no matter how she tried to explain it, could not be set aside—Johnny had gone away with another girl. He had been drinking, too, and he was gone! He would lose his place in the Station for this, for the boss had told him he would not have a man who drank. All their plans for getting a home back in the woods, where she could raise vegetables to sell to the campers, and earn money for nice curtains, and maybe a parlor rug, were broken down . . . It was hard to give up all the things she had planned as they passed before her now in melancholy review.

Minnie was nineteen years old, and every day, every hour of that time, there had been a longing in her heart for something. First it was a vague wish for a place in her family; then for a father and mother, like other children; and, after she knew that this could never be, for a home of her own, and someone for her very own.

John Starblanket, the handsome young Indian, with his strength and his devotion to her, had seemed to make possible all the dreams and hopes of the nineteen years. And now the picture was broken—the game was hopeless—the cards were not coming right.

All this was while it was dark. But as morning approached over the Lake came the blue light of dawn, reddening as the sun drew nearer, until two bands of color lay along the eastern shore-line, the deep blue of the night and the blood-red of coming day. Below them the Lake lay calm and placid, and every minute the red band widened and grew more luminous.

Minnie washed her face in the little blue enamel basin, and as she carefully arranged her hair, with her gaze on the coming day, new thoughts were taking shape in her mind. The sunrise began to have its effect on her, and to tell her about new days, new beginnings. It was impossible to look at the glory that was growing across the Lake and not respond to it.

"When the cards do not come right what do you do?" she asked the sunrise. "There's no use holding them and trying and trying, is there?" She knew what her mother had done—she had held the cards in her hands, just held them, confessing herself beaten.

"What do you do?" she asked of her image in the mirror, fixing upon it a sternly compelling eye which refused to be evaded.

"You shuffle the cards all over again," replied the image in the glass; "you just shuffle them, and then try again!"

Minnie nodded her approval of the answer, and, turning, greeted with new hope the rising sun.

She dressed herself in her best suit, not knowing where the day might lead her, and went hastily downstairs. She had but the one thought in her mind—she would shuffle the cards again; she would not hold them as they were.

Mrs. Pelatski, the proprietor, meeting her in the hall, asked kindly, "How are you and Johnny coming on?"

From the solicitude in her voice Minnie suspected that she knew something, and a momentary impulse came to cry out all her trouble to the older woman; but close upon this again came the Indian impulse to say nothing, but bravely hide all, lying, if necessary, that the sore spot in her heart might remain hidden. Forcing herself to speak, she stammered, "I don't know what happened to him last night."

Mrs. Pelatski came to the rescue. "Look here, Minnie, I want to tell you about that. That old rake who tried to get fresh with you in the dining-room last night took Johnny to his room and gave him liquor. That's a criminal offence, and we now have it on him for future use. He is a Member of Parliament from the East, and naturally doesn't want to go to jail. We have the evidence on him all right, for two of the girls saw him, and I'm just telling you in case you need it. And here's another thing. His brother is Magistrate Brown, in the City. That's a good thing to know, too."

Mrs. Pelatski passed on into the kitchen to give her orders for the day. Men might come or men might go, but meals go on forever.

Minnie had made a sudden resolve. Following Mrs. Pelatski into the kitchen, she asked abruptly, "Can you spare me to-day? I would like to go to the City—I need to go. I will come back in good time."

Mrs. Pelatski looked at her closely, a kindly glance, full of sympathy and having in it a promise of help. "Sure, Minnie, run along," she said. "Have you enough money, and everything you need?"

Minnie nodded and ran back to her room. The first train would be leaving in a few minutes. Her preparations were simple. From a locked drawer she took a revolver, loaded it, and slipped it into her handbag; then hastily pinning a hat on her shining black hair, she ran downstairs and over to the Station.

IV

When John Starblanket wakened from his fitful slumber that morning he was at first under the delusion that an earthquake had occurred and some large building had fallen on him. His head ached, his hands appeared to be powerless, every joint was stiff and sore, and one eye refused to open. Thinking, too, proved to be such a painful process that he abandoned it and lay perfectly still, looking at a small barred window through which a sickly indoor light was filtering.

The only thing he knew about his surroundings was that he had never been in this place before, with its cellar-like air, foul and reeking with evil odors. It nauseated him, and with a painful effort he sat up to look about him. This revealed to him the astonishing fact that he was handcuffed!

Slowly the mental process began, and John Starblanket recalled step by step the devious path which had led him thither. He recalled the dance at the Pavilion, the girl who dared him to come with her on the train, the big delivery man who had brought her to the Beach and who got fresh with him and had to be dealt with. Johnny recalled a breaking window on the train, and a shower of glass which cut his hands. Feeling a bump on his cheek-bone, which was very tender and sore, he wondered what the delivery man was feeling like this morning, and if he had got his features back into place. John Starblanket recalled with a fleeting thrill of satisfaction that the delivery man had crumbled up like a disabled jack-knife at the first blow, and that the friends who came to his assistance had seemed equally brittle.

From the floor of the cell John Starblanket, hand-cuffed, swollen of cheek, and black of eye, recalled these scenes with a measure of pride which was in no way dimmed by his surroundings. It had taken four policemen to bring him there, he remembered, and he had given them plenty to do. So, all things considered, and remembering, too, how the night had ended, he still felt it had been a great night.

He had not yet reached the repentant mood, for an Indian does not repent easily, especially of what he does while under the influence of liquor. Liquor-drinking to an Indian is a great joyous adventure, so hard to achieve, so hilarious and glorious while it lasts, that repentance is a small part of the experience; and John Starblanket as he lay handcuffed and bruised and sore in No. 7 cell in the Police Station had all the blissfully exultant heart glow of one who comes to the end of a perfect day.

Suddenly he thought of Minnie, and at the thought the high light of exhilaration began to pale. Minnie would be sore about this. He could not explain it to her, either; she wouldn't understand how it felt or how it all happened. Minnie was too white to know about certain things. She would likely cry and fuss around and make a row, like white women do, though Johnny admitted that he had never known Minnie to cry. Still, he felt sure she could, and he became very uncomfortable in thinking of what was ahead of him.

Then there was his mother, too—she didn't like this at all. She would not cry, of course, but she would have a sore heart and look down and say nothing.

Johnny's sensation of glamor began to fade when he thought of his women folks; his spirits drooped, and the deep dejection of "the morning after" claimed him for its own.

When Minnie reached the City and made her way to the Police Station she found that a charge of being drunk and disorderly, also of assault and battery against the person of John Salter, driver of the T. Eaton Co., Ltd., and further, of assault against the person of Thomas Smith, train conductor, had been preferred against John Starblanket, baggage man, and would be heard that afternoon at three o'clock before Magistrate Brown.

The clerk in charge kindly asked her if she wished to see the prisoner, but she said she did not. She only wanted to know when the case would be heard, and would he please give her Magistrate Brown's street and number. The clerk was a leather-faced little chap, with beady eyes, and he showed himself quite willing to talk to the well-dressed half-breed girl, but Minnie passed quickly out into the street.

The noise and confusion of the street traffic beat upon her mercilessly; the hurrying people, clanging streetcars, darting automobiles that roared at each other their shrill threats and warnings; newsboys calling "Extra," delivery men wedged in the traffic—a familiar street scene on a busy morning, but to Minnie a scene of terror.

A white husky dog, with wolf's ears and a collie nose, ran nervously through the throng, yelping his fear and terror—a poor lost thing, belonging, like herself, to the kindly open spaces. She watched him, terrified, as he darted across the street only to meet a fire-engine as it came swiftly through an alley, and with an almost human shriek run blindly under its wheels! She turned away, sickened at the sight.

Reaching the home of Magistrate Brown, Minnie rang the bell, wondering at her own boldness. There was no fear in her heart now. She could dare anything, do anything, like the settlers in fire-swept regions, who rush from the burning forest knowing the Lake is just beyond—the Lake with its cool green waters, where they will find rest and safety.

Magistrate Brown was at home, and received her in his dimly lighted library. Minnie had no words prepared, but the quiet dignity of her race was in her manner, and this impressed him favorably.

"There is an Indian boy in the cells waiting for you to hear his case this afternoon," she said. "He got drunk at the Beach, and came in on the 'Moonlight,' acting very bad, and fighting. He is my man, and I want you not to send him to jail, but let him come back with me. I will look after him."

Magistrate Brown was a kindly man, but he was also a magistrate, sworn to uphold the law. It was not the first time that a woman had pleaded for her man. He cleared his throat in his magisterial manner, and said, shaking his head: "But, my dear girl, I can't do this. If the man has been guilty of an offence the offence must be punished. I'm sorry for you, as I am always sorry for the relatives of offenders, but it is my duty to uphold law and order."

While he was speaking Minnie could see again the white husky caught and mangled under the wheels, and her words came fast. "But you don't understand," she said, lapsing into the Indian manner of speech, "he is good boy— never drinks—saving his money—nice—but white man takes him up to his room and gives him drink out of bottle—then white girl gets him at dance—coaxes him away into City here. He's good boy if damn whites only leave him alone."

"Oh, I see," the magistrate said, soothingly; "that is too bad. If we could prove that against the white man it is a criminal offence, for which the penalty is two years. I do not see how that can mitigate this Indian's offence, but if you would like to prefer a charge against the white man it will be heard. Do you know who he is?"

Minnie nodded, her eyes narrowing wickedly. "His name is Brown," she said, her words falling in a marked staccato; "he's a Member of Parliament from East long piece away."

The magistrate sprang from his chair. "Nonsense!" he cried, "you don't know what you are saying."

Indian-like, Minnie made no reply, but gently smoothed her hand-bag.

The magistrate quickly recovered his composure. "Now, look here, my girl," he said, and his voice had a rougher tone, "I'll be as easy as I can on this Indian boy, but law is law, and he has to be punished. He must learn to take the consequences. I am under oath to enforce laws. Your charge against this man Brown would be hard to prove. Brown is a very common name, and he would be hard to find. Your Indian will be dealt with leniently, and the lesson will do him good."

The magistrate rose and motioned her to the door with a gesture that he had found efficacious in ending interviews. However, this time it missed fire.

"Let out my man to-day—let him go free," she said. "I take him away, far away; this is no place for Indians. It was great country once—all grass and trees and buffaloes—all our country. You came, you white men, with guns and killed us—drove us out—stole our land. All right—keep it! You've made it great country, I guess—lots of money, lots of cars, lots of noise, lots of lies. It suits you—it don't suit us—let us go. We'll go away down North—far away—we won't come back. Let us go!"

Just at that moment the magistrate's brother, who had arrived on the late train from the Beach and had slept late, came into the library, yawning and rubbing his hands. In the dim light he did not notice the girl, and began to talk to his brother.

"You'll have a full docket this afternoon, Dan, I think. We had a lively time coming in on the train from the Beach with a drunken Indian boy who ran amuck and pushed the conductor through a window. I was in another car, but I heard about it at the station. Fortunately no person was much hurt; but there were three or four arrested. Sorry I missed all the fun."

He laughed good-naturedly. The West was surely the place to get excitement.

Minnie took a step forward, and as the pallid light from a heavily curtained window fell on her the magistrate's brother gave an exclamation of surprise.

"You'll not miss all the fun," she said, in an even voice. "You will be at the trial to-day, and you will be asked where the Indian boy got his liquor. It would be a pity for you to miss all the fun."

Minnie had regained her composure, and spoke now as she had been taught at the Mission.

The magistrate looked from one to the other—then made a quick resolve. "When the case against your friend is called to-day it will be dismissed," he said to Minnie without turning around, and when he turned to see if she understood what he had said she was gone.

The sun had gone down in a haze of golden glory behind the trees along the Lake-shore, and from the upper sky, where every cloud had a lining of flame, there fell a radiance on the placid water. But Mrs. Starblanket's eyes, peering sharply over the Lake, were only vaguely conscious of its beauty, for she looked for a canoe bringing the visitors for whom she had been preparing the last two days.

The chicken was fried to a golden brown, and the boiled potatoes were steaming on the back of the well-polished stove. The water pitcher, with real ice in it, stood on the table. Every plate in the house was in readiness.

The first train from the Beach roared past, not even stopping at the Station, but rushing through the trees behind her house with a shrieking whistle that filled the evening air with tatters of sound.

Mrs. Starblanket shivered as she listened. Never had a train seemed so overbearing and hostile. "It sure don't give a damn!" she said to herself as she watched the funnel of smoke that caught the evening glory and carried it away to the City.

Vaguely disappointed because Johnny and his girl were late, she built up her fire, mashed the potatoes with a gem-jar, and went outside to her favorite seat behind the house. They could come or they could stay away; she was ready anyway. But a grave loneliness was on her soul, and her pipe went out unnoticed.

On the eight o'clock train from the City, which crossed the Beach train, they came, and in her excitement Mrs. Starblanket did not notice that Johnny's face was swollen on one side, or that his good blue suit was baggy and crumpled. Her eyes were all for Johnny's girl, so neat and stylish in her well-made suit.

Mrs. Starblanket was afraid of her at first, but when they sat down to eat, and Minnie seemed so pleased with everything, praising the cooking, and making Johnny compliment his mother's art, too, the older woman's heart melted toward the handsome girl whose only fault was that she was partly white.

"Johnny will sleep soundly tonight, Mrs. Starblanket," said Minnie, as they washed the dishes together. "He has had a hard day. It is too hard work at the Railway—too many heavy things to handle—and sometimes glass breaks and cuts one's hands so bad. Even Johnny gets tired sometimes, strong as he is. Anyway, he is thinking of quitting the Railway. He is going to give notice tomorrow."

Mrs. Starblanket gave an exclamation of surprise. So did Johnny, his surprise mixed with protest.

Minnie's eyes commanded silence. "Yes," she went on, "Johnny told me about the place down North where your other sons are, and how you would like to go, too. I know I would like it. There are too many people here, too much noise and crowds all the time, and never any quiet time any more. It's a right place for white people, but no good for Indians."

When the dishes were washed the three sat in silence on the shore and watched the night come down in purple splendor, hushing the world, even the noisy Beach world, to sleep. Long after midnight they sat there, rarely speaking, but each one happy in thinking of the big country "down North" beckoning to them with its promise of peace and plenty and good hunting—three happy Indians about to enter into their native heritage of open air and open sky.

∽

"Red and White" was published in *Western Home Monthly* (November, December, 1921; January, February, 1922) and *All We Like Sheep, and Other Stories* (Toronto: Thomas Allen, 1926), 128–175.

BANKING IN LONDON

I determined to deposit my money. I knew that was an easy thing to do, even pleasant, the simplest form of banking operation; and so with my money in my black bag I entered a bank.

To the young lady behind the wicket I addressed myself. "I wish to open an account," I said. I spoke casually. I wanted her to understand that banking money was a daily experience with me.

"Yes, madam," she said, but not in that eager, welcoming way I had expected, "but you must see the manager."

"Where is he?" I asked, looking around at the many men I saw through the brass lattice, perched upon their high stools.

"You must wait for him in the waiting-room," she said. Her manner was dignified and grave. I gathered from it that a bank manager was not to be achieved at a single bound, but must be won by patient waiting.

Through the blue velvet hangings she directed me to the waiting-room. It was dark, small, and empty. I waited. The steady rumble of London's afternoon traffic went by. When my eyes grew accustomed to the gloom I found the heavily shrouded window, and, drawing the funeral hangings, I gazed into the street. I counted the buses; I figured out my expenses for the day—and I waited.

A door led from the waiting-room. It was marked "Private." I believed it led to the retreat of the manager whom I would see. I watched it hopefully; it might open at any moment. Time passed.

Suddenly I looked at my watch: it was after half-past two. The place seemed to be deserted. A fear broke over me—they had locked up and gone home—they had forgotten me! The night watchman would find me, here, with this money! He might shoot me!

I was leaving the waiting-room hurriedly, but to my relief I found no one had gone. The young lady was still in the cage, the occupants of the high stools were still repeating sums of money to each other. Fear making me bold, I again addressed the young lady.

"Tell me," I said, "what the delay is? I see I have begun wrong some way. I am a stranger, you see, and I do not know your ways. Perhaps you do not take money on Mondays; maybe you have all the money you want. Or should I give a three-days notice of motion, or wire ahead for a reservation? I see I am wrong, but please tell me how to go on from here."

She looked at me wonderingly.

"Has it anything to do with Lent," I said, "or full moon, or the Lord Mayor's show?"

"Oh, no," she replied, puzzled, "not at all. The manager will see you presently. I will tell him again."

"Yes, do," I said; "and please tell him I do not want to borrow money, but to deposit it. I think you could not have made that plain. I know people who want to borrow money have to wait, but not depositors."

"Certainly, madam," she said, politely.

Again I went back to the dim little room, and again time passed. A man came out of the private door, hat in hand, and passed into the street, but still the door turned its inhospitable back on me. The shadows lengthened in the street as the afternoon wore away.

I looked out through the blue hangings to reassure myself that the staff were still at work, and saw one fellow untwisting his legs from around the shank of his stool. It looked to me as if he were getting ready to go.

A sudden impulse seized me. I would see what was behind the closed door. She had said the manager would see me presently. All right. He would if his eyesight happened to be good—he would see me! I knocked.

The door opened, and a tall man in gray stood in the murky doorway.

"Well?" he asked. His tone betokened a certain amount of resignation, not untinged with annoyance.

"Did the girl at the wicket tell you I was here?" I asked, trying to speak haughtily, but finding my courage seeping away. I began to see that it was presumptuous of me to bother the staff with my little personal affairs.

He disdained my question. "Now what is it, exactly, that you want?" he asked.

"I want to open an account," I said, "and I made the mistake of thinking this was a bank. It is marked so, but it must be a mistake."

"Do come in," he said.

I came in.

"Now, do sit down." His tone gave me to understand that my habit of not coming in and not sitting down was very annoying.

I sat down.

He spread his hands on the table as if it were a *séance*.

"Now, tell me what it is," he said patiently.

"I want to open an account," I said doggedly. "I still want to, and it's the same account I wanted to open an hour ago."

"Very good," he said, "very good. We are not refusing money, but you must give me a reference."

I began all over again.

"I must be using the wrong words," I said, "you have misunderstood me. But see, I have the money, and I want you to take it and keep it for me. I don't want you to loan me money; I have it here in Bank of England notes."

"Even so," he said, "we must have a reference."

I could think of nothing that would be both suitable and becoming.

"What do you want a reference for?" I asked at last. "Are you collecting references?"

"It is our rule," he said with finality.

I put the money in my bag and stood up.

"Good afternoon," I said. "I'm sorry I have to go. I've had a pleasant time, but it is getting late, and I really must find a bank."

"This is a bank," he said, "and you will have to give a reference wherever you go in England. Don't you know someone in London?"

"Give me time," I said, "I have only been here since Saturday."

"You must know someone," he persisted.

"I do," I replied, "I know Lady Astor."

"Who is she?" he asked wearily. I knew now I was undergoing an intelligence test.

I shook my head. "If you have never heard of the British House of Commons," I said severely, "it's too long a story for me to begin."

"Who else do you know?" he asked. "Some business man perhaps?"

"Yes," I said, "I know Sir Charles Starmer."

There was no gleam of intelligence in the cold eyes that regarded me. I must explain further.

"Sir Charles Starmer," I said reproachfully, "is the editor of the *Northern Echo* and twenty-six other newspapers." (I was not really sure about my figures, but I felt it was no time to be mean with Sir Charles over a few newspapers.)

"I have not heard of him," he said.

"Well," I said, "it's your turn now, anyway. Who do you know?"

We looked at each other through the dusky light of the room, and it seemed like a deadlock in the proceedings.

"Look here," he began, with a sudden flash of intelligence, "have you a passport?"

I had.

When he had it spread before him he read it aloud: "McClung, Nellie Letitia; married; eyes brown, mouth large."

He looked at me closely.

"By Jove! that's right," he cried. "Hair brown—slightly gray. That's right, too," apparently surprised at the coincidence.

Then he studied the photograph, comparing it with me.

"Don't you think it's a good picture?" I said.

He refused to commit himself. "It appears," he said at last, guardedly, "that you are the person described in this passport."

"Don't be rash," I said, "I would not like you to lose your job over this."

My sarcasm was lost.

"There is very little chance for fraud," he said, still regarding me critically.

"Fraud!" I cried hotly. "Fraud! You make me tired. Do you know, I can borrow money in any bank in Canada with less bother than this!"

"Quite!" he agreed with me. "Quite! I have always heard that the banking in Canada is done in very loose fashion. Very well, then," he said, "we will take your money."

Then it was my turn.

"Oh, indeed!" I said, "but remember I have my family traditions, too. You must convince me that you are to be trusted. Who are you? and what did your grandmother die of? I cannot leave my money with unauthorized people."

"Quite!" he said again, and solemnly placed before me the financial statement of the bank.

"And now," he said, "I will have to have a specimen signature for reference."

"Would you like a lock of my hair?" I asked.

"It will not be necessary," he replied gravely.

"And now, how shall we open this account?" I asked gaily. "Having gone so far I certainly want to see it done right. Just do whatever your custom is. Do we open with the National Anthem? Or, under the circumstances, would it not be better to use 'O Canada'?"

His air of perplexity deepened.

All went well until the day when I returned to draw out my balance. Again I had to wait to see the manager.

"Look here," he began, "do I understand you are going away?"

"I am going on Friday," I said, "and I came in to draw my balance."

"This is Monday," he said, shutting one eye and transfixing me sternly with the other.

"Am I wrong again?" I asked. "Is Monday the wrong day to draw money?"

He pursed his mouth reflectively and beat his chin with his forefinger. "You should have given us more notice," he said at last.

I gasped. "Notice to draw fifty pounds?" I said. "Will you miss my account as much as that?"

"Certainly not," he corrected me, "but how are we to tell how many cheques you have issued?"

"You do not need to tell," I said. "I can talk, and I will tell you. The stubs in the cheque book will tell you."

"You may have written more than these," he persisted.

"But I didn't," I said.

"And it would be very embarrassing to have them presented after you had taken your money," he continued without heeding my interruption.

"It would be embarrassing for the holder of the cheque," I said, "but not for you."

"It would certainly embarrass us," he said virtuously, and here he looked at me with grave reproof, "and I should think it would embarrass you."

"Well, it won't," I said, "because I haven't written any but these."

He still hesitated.

"Well," I said, "do you think I had better cancel my sailing and stay another month to see if any other cheques come in?"

"Oh, no, I do not advise that," he said.

"Well, then," I said, "get along in there and tell me my balance, and I'll write a cheque to cover it. I know what it is, but I just want to know if you do. Now chase yourself, my lad, for, pleasant as it is, I cannot stay all day talking to you."

He seemed to loom taller and grayer than ever, and the look he gave me was one of the deepest wonder.

But I got the money.

When our business relations were at an end he grew almost genial. "You will come again, I hope," he said; "and if you do I hope you will again open up an account with us."

"Oh, yes," I agreed, "surely I will. I wouldn't think of going anywhere else. I would not care to break in another bank manager at my time of life. I will surely come to you—but do be careful," I said.

I know he will not be there when I go back. All depositors are not as long suffering as I am. Someone will shoot him.

⤶

"Banking in London," originally titled "Banking in England," was published in *Macleans* (15 December 1923) and *All We Like Sheep, and Other Stories* (Toronto: Thomas Allen, 1926), 176–183.

THE NEUTRAL FUSE

In the East Golding neighborhood where she lived she was called the "Bride" until her first baby came, and then it hardly seemed a fitting title; but she was so dainty and be-frilled and sweet, with her London clothes and her foolish little hats that were never made for the windy prairie, that the neighbors felt the need of some word that would be adequate.

She won her way into the hearts of the people because there was nothing that she could not do. What she could not do when she came she immediately set about to learn. After taking one lesson from Mrs. Hiram Smith in making bread, she astonished the neighborhood by taking the prize at the Fair, even though her teacher was among the competitors. No one was more delighted than Mrs. Smith. To have anyone else win from her would have been a downfall, but to have her own pupil do this—that was distinction.

The young women of the neighborhood were just a little inclined to resentment at first. No English bride had any right to be as good-looking as she was! A slight figure; a head of syrupy yellow hair that just "went right" all the time, and always looked as if it had just been done; blue eyes with black lashes, and dimples, and a voice that was so sweet and soft that no one minded the accent, and the tiniest feet. No English girl had any right to feet like hers. But in spite of these handicaps the Bride won her way.

She got the children on her side first, for of course they did not understand that she was a stranger and from another country, and therefore to be held in suspicion until she proved herself worthy of a place in the East Golding society. They only knew that she showed them the most wonderful games and puzzles; she knew songs and tricks with handkerchiefs, and had come to the school on a dull, cloudy afternoon soon after she had arrived and wanted to play with the children "if the teacher did not mind." After that she came every Friday afternoon, and soon there was a general attendance of the older people, who just happened to drop in.

Having been a school-mistress in England (though she hardly looked old enough to be out of school herself), she gave the children physical culture exercises which were of the contagious kind, and soon the whole neighborhood were touching their toes and swaying from side to side as they counted "one–two–three–four."

All but Mrs. Ewing! Mrs. Ewing was not going to touch her toes and act silly even if everyone else was doing it. What would she touch her toes for anyway? It was some time since Mrs. Ewing had even seen her toes, and that may have had something to do with her reluctance, but Mrs. Ewing did not admit it. She took the ground strongly that good, decent toes did not need to be touched; she also darkly muttered that a new broom sweeps clean, and that there was such a thing as being too sweet to be wholesome and too good to be true.

Mrs. Ewing had come from London herself many years ago, and confided out of her deep knowledge of that great city to her friend Mrs. Winters that there were plenty of these "dashing kind of play-actin' girls over there just waitin' a chance to marry a decent man and get to Canadar; and though they could fool the Canadians that had never seen their like, they were very far from foolin' Marthar Ewing!" Mrs. Winters, her friend, gave to this statement hearty and immediate assent, and added that she would like to see the person who *could* fool Marthar Ewing, for if there was such a person on land or sea one thing was certain sure, that such person had never been seen or as much as heard of by Sarah Winters! Then the two ladies had a cup of tea, and just a little mite of fruitcake to go with it—"the white kind that never lays heavy on your stomach"—and spent a very happy and neighborly time.

All unconscious that she had been weighed by Mrs. Ewing, her countrywoman, and found wanting, the Bride went joyously on her way. She liked everyone, and expected that they would like her. There was no one so popular at the parties, but she made a different use of her popularity from anyone else. When Ted Smith, who considered himself quite the best dancer in East Golding, came to claim a dance with her she reminded him that he had not yet danced with his hostess or her guest, and the gay Mr. Smith thereby received a lesson in courtesy which he sorely needed. Many a girl who got only dances with brothers-in-law, uncles, and other girls, was pleasantly surprised to find her card full, not knowing that the Bride gave her dances conditionally. People who had stayed away from the dances because they had had such dull times at them before her coming now began to attend, and it was on these that the Bride bestowed her attention.

She had an intuitive instinct for detecting loneliness or embarrassment or awkwardness, and a magical way of dispelling it. Even good old John Baker, who had the firemark on his face, so badly disfiguring it that he shrank from meeting anyone, was beguiled by her to come to a party at her house, and he had such a good time that he did not miss a dance all that winter, and in the spring got up his courage to write a proposal to the elder Miss Spink. Some said the Bride put him up to it, but that was never known for sure. Be that as it may, the proposal was accepted, and two people who had thought they were past hope were made very happy.

Not only at the dances did she shine. She played the organ for the church services, and taught a class of admiring girls in Sunday-school; and her eager face, so full of interest and sympathy, was many a young minister's inspiration and help when he tried to preach to the East Golding congregation and found some of them sound asleep and others looking dreamily out of the windows, their thoughts busy with the growing crops or the price of hogs—anything except the wanderings of the children of Israel. Her attention never appeared to wander, and her kindly greeting was sure. There was also a good dinner for the minister, and the use of her tiny little parlor, where a gaily flowered couch could be made into a bed at a moment's notice.

The capitulation of Mrs. Martha Ewing happened in threshing time. The mill was coming to her farm, and at the last minute the girl that was going to come from town to help to cook for the men fell sick—"the way they always do," said Mrs. Ewing.

Mrs. Ewing was in deep distress. She said she could have done it all herself only her feet got so sore now since she "had fallen into flesh." The party telephone just hummed with her complaints. There was scarlet fever in the neighborhood just then and several were in quarantine.

The Bride rose to the occasion. In pink and white house dress, with pink stockings and white canvas shoes, she arrived two hours before dinner time and gathered the disordered household together in her capable little hands, and had the dinner on the table when the avalanche of men swept in from the field. The owner of the outfit was John Baker, whose heart was tender toward the woman who had shown him kindness. John immediately released his best English boy to help her in the house, and the three days that the threshing lasted passed very pleasantly. Mrs. Ewing was able to sit at the kitchen table in billowy importance and have all the things brought to her that she needed to bake with, resting her feet on the stool made of tomato cans. In this way was her supremacy maintained.

Speaking to her friend Mrs. Winters of the incident, she said, "I could tell she was a good girl when I saw her save all the small potatoes and peel them to fry at night for the men— lots of 'ussies would have pitched them out, but not she. Oh, I say, when you get a good English girl there is nothing like her on earth—that is what poor Ewing so often said to me."

For fifteen years she has lived in East Golding. No one calls her the Bride now. The London clothes and the flirty little hats have all disappeared, and their successors, too. The last seven years have been lean and sad ones, and hard times have come to the good people of East Golding, which is in the drought area of the West. The women who knew her as the Bride have never called her Mrs. Benton. She is "Sadie" to them, and it is to her that they are always able to tell all their troubles. She never fails to see some way of comforting them. She always has time for other people's troubles, for she does not seem to have any of her own.

"I sure wish I had your nerve, Sadie," the Regent of the Daughters of the Empire said to her one day, "the way you can stay alone with just the children and work all the time without getting cranky beats me—and you not brought up to it the way we were. How do you do it? I guess you have better stuff in you than the rest of us."

"Oh! I do get cranky, too," was the reply, "but I try not to show it. It would break Joe's heart if I were cross with him, and it would be a shame to do that, for he is the best fellow in the world. And I am sure I never could be cranky with my good neighbors; and it would be a crime to work it off on the two boys. So there you are—what can a poor woman do?"

That night, after the work was done, she sat at the west window looking at the flaming sky, wondering about life with all its cares and disappointments. It was at this time of day that she allowed herself the luxury of thinking her own thoughts. In the little red book which she kept in the drawer of her sewing-machine she wrote:

> "Why am I chained to pots and pans,
> Dishes to wash and meals to get?
> Heavy white dishes and drab farm hands,
> Reeking of stables and heavy with sweat?
> Dust in clouds that go past my door
> And winds that fret and fret and fret?—
> Winds that scream past the house at night,
> Whispering things that they have no right
> Even to think of, much less say.
> I hate the wind with its evil spite,
> And it hates me with a hate as deep,
> And hisses and jeers when I try to sleep."

"There, now," she said, "I feel better; it is a good way to work off a fit of the blues, and it does not hurt anyone."

After a fiercely windy night she added the following lines:

> "When the wind seizes the window frames,
> Raving and cursing and calling them names,
> Cruel as only the wind can be,

It isn't the windows it's shaking—
   It's me!"

The last seven years have left their mark on the Bride, and not much of her girlish beauty remains other than her wonderful blue eyes. The golden hair is broken now and dulled with gray; the joints of the little hands are coarsened with hard work, and the backs of them have many brown spots. Outside work has darkened her face, but the fair, white skin appears again in her two fine boys, now aged fourteen and twelve.

In spite of all their hard times and disappointments, the Bride of the early years has never admitted defeat. "No one is beaten until he acknowledges it," she often tells her husband, "and we are a long way from admitting it yet."

Often she repeats the words of her creed: "I believe that the bad years are behind me. I believe the rain will come, and prosperity, as much of it as we need, will come to us. If we had never had a set-back we might have grown purse-proud and haughty. Let us be thankful we are well and strong."

The biggest disappointment was missing the trip to England which they had planned. They were going to go to England for a year, put the boys in school, and motor through Kent, where she was born; but the year set for the trip was the first of the dry years, and, as each year was worse than the last, the trip faded farther and farther away.

There was one year of the seven when the prospects were of the best until the middle of July, and then in twenty minutes all the year's work and hopes lay in ruins, for hail-stones, jagged and cruel and big as hen's eggs, had battered every growing thing into the ground, and had even broken down the young trees which they had planted. The Bentons were the hardest hit in the whole neighborhood, for all their crop was gone, their farm lying straight in the path of the storm.

But it was Sadie Benton who thought of a use for the hailstones. With the help of the two boys she gathered a pail-ful of them for freezing a can of ice-cream, and called in the neighbors. And after they had gone away some of them said it was well to see her so cheerful. Wasn't it well for people who could take things so lightly? But they did not see, of course, what she wrote in her little red book that night after they were all gone.

"I don't think I would mind it so much," she wrote, "if we had lost our crop by a prairie fire, or a spark from an engine, or any way that was caused by the carelessness of human beings; but when God sends destruction it is terrifying. I thought we were good friends with God. I thought He liked to see us working and getting ahead. I wish I could ask someone about this. I am trying to keep on believing, for it is a wicked thing to sow the seeds of unbelief, and I will not say a word to anyone."

The hail had done its work so completely that there was no feed for the cattle that year, and as they had quite a large herd of pure-bred Holsteins it became necessary to buy from their more fortunate neighbors to provide for these. This expense made a serious drain on their savings, and as the next year was one of the driest, the prospects grew darker and darker. However, there was enough short straw to feed the cattle, and that was something. Many a night, after the children had gone to bed, Joe and his wife had done much figuring as they sat at the kitchen table.

"I wish now I had not told the boys so much about the old country," she said one night; "it would not then have been such a disappointment."

"Never mind that, Girl," her husband said soothingly. "We would all have been dead if it had not been for your stories. I hope we will get enough to let you go anyway, for you can bring back the story of what you saw, and the whole neighborhood will have it secondhand; and I don't know but to hear you tell it is just about as good as to go—and far cheaper!"

She came over and put her arms around his neck. "Joe, do you think I would go without you? Do you think I could leave you here alone to cook and do everything. Why, Joe, your poor, lonely face would haunt me some night when I was dining at the Piccadilly, and in the midst of all the festivity I would be found with my eyes set and staring into one of the crystal chandeliers, and all the people would rush to me, crying, 'Oh! what is it? What is she looking at?' They would see nothing, of course, but I would be staring at you—gaunt, unshaven, starved, and wild—and then I would go mad and have to be sent home in a strait-jacket!"

Joe laughed and patted her head. "Well, Sadie, so long as your imagination holds out I believe we will pull through, but if you ever get dull and gray like the other women I will just curl up and die. Now, remember you have to hold out, no matter what happens, for everyone in this neighborhood depends on you."

"I will try, Joe, I will try; but, oh, dear, why doesn't God send rain? If I had as much rain as God—for He has the oceans, the rivers, and the seas and the lakes, and all the machinery to haul it up into the clouds and sprinkle it down on us—I could not keep from sending it, even if no one was asking; for I would see the flowers fading and hear the cattle bawling, and I would push all the buttons at once and call off even the Recording Angel from his books. It would be 'All hands to the pumps' if I were God!"

She stopped suddenly and shuddered.

"Maybe I shouldn't talk like this, Joe—does it sound wicked to you? You know, sometimes at night when I lie awake listening to the wind I get frightened and think the wind has it in for me some way. It—it threatens me, Joe!"

"Now, old dear," said Joe, "that is all imagination. You are just beginning to get nervous, and you have simply got to get away for a little while to get back your nerve. I get goofy sometimes, too, but I have you to cheer me up, and you, poor girl, have no one. I am no more good to cheer you than the man in the moon."

"Oh, yes, you are," she said. "I never feel frightened when you are at home; it comes when I am alone in the house and the wind is blowing. I know there is no truth in it, but I do hear things, Joe, that are horrible."

"Poor little Sade!" he answered tenderly, "I wish I could take you away from the wind and the dust and this land of heart-break."

At once she became the comforter again.

"It will all come right, Joe. I know it will. Every country has its bad years, and ours will pass and all our dreams will come true yet. I believe in God. Remember how Job was tried and he sinned not, and it was all made up to him. So it will be to us, and all this long dreary time we have not been utterly cast down. We have each other and our two fine boys, and we can go to our beds at night, as Robert Louis Stevenson said, 'weary and undishonored'—that is something."

A few days after this conversation—hot and terrible days, when the grain seemed to stand motionless and parched—Joe got an offer to go to the town ten miles away to help in a bankrupt sale which was being held. He was glad of the chance to earn a little money, which would at least get some groceries. He got a Galician who had worked for him before to go on with the summer-fallowing.

"You will be all right, Sade," he said when he told her he had the offer. "Get the Daughters to come over when your flowers are in bloom. I don't know what you will give them to eat, but I never saw you stuck yet, and you can give them such a good time they won't know whether you have fed them or not."

She laughed a little wearily.

"I will do it, Joe," she said, "if the wind will just leave my flowers until they bloom. I think maybe the wind will be man enough to see that I have not asked for favors, carrying all the water myself. Don't you think I deserve to have a few flowers?"

"You deserve the finest and loveliest flowers in the world, Sade, and I believe the wind is ready to admit it."

Joe left on Monday morning, not without some misgivings, for he could see that she was not feeling just like herself; but she assured him that it would be foolish to lose a chance of earning some money when they were in such need of it.

The day he left there was some promise of rain, for thick, murky clouds came up in the West, darkening the afternoon sun and giving some comfort in the grateful shade which fell on the burning country.

Sheltered from the west wind, at the front of the house were the flowers, on which she had bestowed the care usually attributed to an efficient guardian angel; and they had answered to her affection, for they were now glossy and healthy, and their buds were beginning to show the color. Dark-red climbing nasturtiums were next to the wall, with everything in readiness for their upward journey. In front of them were the dwarf nasturtiums in mixed colours, bordered with mignonette and sweet alyssum, whose dainty white flowerets would set off the brilliant coloring of their bolder brothers.

She had imagined the effect, and thrilled over it every time she thought of it, and, now that the blossoms were actually showing, her pleasure was so poignant it hurt. Her heart beat too quickly and chokingly. There was always the chance of a horrible wind that would swagger into her little garden, tramp over it with hob-nailed boots, tear it to pieces, and go thundering on, like Marie Corelli's motorists who kill children in English villages.

"I'll enjoy them while I can," she murmured apprehensively as she brought out her potatoes in a pan for peeling, and her little canvas stool. There she sat and worshipped at her little altar of beauty, praying with frenzied earnestness that the God of the falling sparrow might be their God and hers, and stay the ruthless hand of the wind. Another day would see them out, and then she would call her friends and have the party; but it seemed to her beauty-loving and fearful heart that she must have the flowers first. She was so near them now she could think of nothing else.

All afternoon the world seemed to stand still. The air was heavy and close, like the smother of furs in summer. The clouds, cavernous and full of navy-blue shadows, stood over the baking earth, charged with rain, yet withholding it, taunting the parching grain with the nearness of relief, as torturing as the trickle of water to a man dying of thirst in the desert.

"Oh, God, I do not understand! Let not my heart break trying to," prayed Sadie Benton in an agony as she wandered from window to window.

Sadie sat up till midnight watching the sky, which had begun to seethe and roll. Strange patches of light from the departed sun glowed on the mountainous clouds, revealing their weird and restless movements.

Falling asleep as soon as she went to bed, she dreamed of rain—rain that ran down the window panes, making a pleasant throaty gurgle as it ran in foaming streams into the cracks of the dry ground; rain falling on parching fields and lifting up the drooping heads of stunted crops that were ready to die; rain so gentle and tender that the cattle held up their faces to receive its soft caress; rain that washed her precious flowers with fingers gentler even than her own.

Then something harsh and terrible wakened her. It was the wind, shaking the windows in its great knotted, battling fists—the wind, fierce, and without mercy. She put her hands over her ears.

In the morning she wrote again in her little book below her last entry:

> "I might have known—I might have known
> That the wind would wait till my flowers had grown;
> And then come roaring down the trail
> To beat my flowers with its threshing flail.
> And there they lie—and my heart is stone.
> I know it isn't the flowers alone
> That the wind has murdered in roaring glee;
> It isn't the flowers that are lying dead
> With blackened body and bleeding head—
> It's me!"

The Daughters of the Empire had a hurried meeting—an emergency had arisen. They must send Sadie Benton to the

Convention in the City. The Regent had called them together and reported that when she went over to see Mrs. Benton the morning after the storm, she found her serene and calm, but queer. Mrs. Pollard, not being much of a psychiatrist, could not explain very well, but was certain that Mrs. Benton was "queer."

"It was the flowers that just finished her off," said Mrs. Pollard. "The roof blowing off the machine-house didn't seem to bother her; but she had buried the flowers, mind you, not a trace of them is to be seen. She said it seemed to be the decent thing to do, and she was writing when I went in, in her little book. Now, we didn't intend to send a delegate, on account of the expense, but we just will. Sadie has to go. It will cheer her up, and she sure needs it. Mind you, she brought me in for breakfast, and was as cheerful as ever to the boys and got them off for school, but she's queer. She said: 'I don't suppose the flowers mind being dead. It's really rather nice to be dead.' Now, that's queer talk from Sadie . . . so we've just got to persuade her to go; and we have enough money to send her and give her ten dollars to spend."

The women agreed, and set off in a body to persuade Sadie to be their delegate. Rules of procedure did not harass the Daughters; they got things done by "unanimous consent."

Two weeks later the train brought Sadie Benton to the station in the big City eighty miles from East Golding. Some of the old sparkle was in her eyes and she came through the iron gate where the blue-coated policeman with a white helmet directed the traffic which passed between the two banked walls of humanity. All the fatigue of her long day and of the long years seemed to have fallen from her, and she was only conscious of a great elation.

The four great double doors on each side of the station were opened outward, and through them swept the summer breeze refreshingly. Unaccustomed smells were in her nostrils as she sat on one of the cool oak seats to watch the stream of people who passed. Oranges, cherry-cheer, gum, mingled with stale tobacco-smoke and the old bread and mouldy cheese of forgotten lunches. Disinfectants, mothballs, and last weeks' clothes blended with the heavy perfume of the powder of a painted lady who stood close by furtively watching the door, painfully standing on her spike heels, which someway made the swollen ankles look more swollen. Sadie watched her, fascinated by the crimson redness of her lips, vivid as a wound that will not heal, and even then was conscious of the thrill of delight which color always brought to her.

A group of women had come to bid a friend goodbye—women in bright sports suits, so boldly colored and gay that Sadie wanted to stroke them in gratitude for the gleam they made on the grim gray floor. When a child in a rose romper tried to slide across the tiled floor Sadie's hands went out to catch him. He seemed like a gorgeous butterfly. Magazines with colored covers hung by their corners around the news booth, and bottles of brightly colored drinks in glass cases seemed to beckon to her. Over in a corner, above the open box where a woman with the arms of a purple sweater tied around her neck listened to the wires, there stood a thin white china glass globe which every few seconds was filled with golden light, which held a moment and then faded. When it gleamed she noticed the word "Telegraph" in bold black letters. She watched the bright light come and go, come and go, bright, then dark, until it seemed that she would have to go and beg them not to put the light out at all.

Suddenly she realized that she had been sitting there a long time, for the lights were burning in the inverted alabaster bowls overhead, and although the room was as bright as ever and the stream of people still surged between the wide doors, she could tell that night had fallen. She wondered vaguely if she had been asleep but she was not alarmed or greatly concerned, for a new and delightful sense of detachment was upon her. It seemed so strange to have nothing to do. The women had told her they wanted her to "just loaf" for the three days before the Convention began, and get well rested, so she would be able to enjoy every minute of it and bring home a good story of everything that happened. They had said that, now that there was so much to discourage them, they felt they must get something to cheer them up from the outside, and that was why they were sending her, for she would bring back the best story. They did not once hint that she needed the trip; but Sadie knew what was in their hearts, and she loved them for not saying it, and determined to do her best for them. She knew they would like to hear what the women were wearing, and what she had to eat, and just what the other women looked like, in addition to the regular work of the Convention.

An impulse to go to the lunch-counter and get a cup of coffee came to her, but her great weariness inclined her to find a bed; and besides, she wanted to get so many things that even the ten cents which the coffee would cost was a consideration. She would be quite all right until morning, and then she would get a good breakfast.

She arose with some difficulty, her limbs stiff from the unaccustomed inactivity, and made her way to the big doors of the station, and there when she looked into the street her heart bounded with joy, for the rain, blessed rain, was falling in tiny parallel lines between her and the street lights, and the pavement was shining-wet. An automobile which rolled away from the station trailed behind it a crimson ribbon until it turned west on Eighth Avenue.

Just across the street a friendly window, bright with red geraniums and white star of Bethlehem, beckoned her, and she felt that there she would find rest and a welcome for the night. It was soon arranged, and the obliging clerk carried the straw valise upstairs to a room in the front of the house.

"This is the only room we have," he said, "and I am afraid you may find it pretty noisy—there are a lot of trains and cars go by in the night."

"Oh, I will like that," she said eagerly, "then I will not be able to hear the wind."

He looked at her closely. "I guess they won't bother you," he said kindly, "you sure do look tired."

A gleaming brass bed by the open window offered rest for her weariness, and without undressing she lay down with a great sigh of relief. She was so tired that it seemed to her that she had spread herself all over the bed.

After hours of deep sleep—or so it seemed—she noticed that the bed did not stand still as a bed should, but moved with a motion of a train, and vibrated with the grinding of the wheels on iron rails; but it was quite pleasant and she was not alarmed, for she knew such a big and handsome bed would know its business and know where it should go. City ways were surely wonderful, and she was determined to see all she could!

The bed certainly knew where to take her, for it brought her into the most wonderful garden she had seen since she left England. It was a very friendly garden, for the flowers she looked at came right into her hands. Crimson roses were everywhere, and they were coaxing her to take them. It did not seem polite to refuse them. And then she noticed the beads hanging on little trees in glittering strings. She remembered that it was beads she wanted for the two little Bates girls, whose mother had died. Lily must have a blue string to match her eyes—and she was sure that Nellie would like the red ones. While she was making her selection she noticed that a girl with short, bushy hair was standing beside her, and it seemed that she was asking her something, but it was hard to understand. It was something about paying, and just for a minute it frightened her. Then she remembered that she had plenty of money. A delicious sense of great wealth came to her. It was a new and delightful feeling.

"I have the gold of the sunset, the silver of eve, up my sleeve," she said. She smiled when she noticed the rhyme she had made, and, seeing the girl's look of surprise, patted her hand reassuringly.

She now noticed for the first time that she had not her valise, and for a moment she wondered where it was. Then she remembered, but the delightful feeling of abundance shut out every other feeling. She knew she would never lack anything again. Her heart was so full of joy that she could not keep from singing:

> "My Father is rich in houses and lands;
> He holdeth the wealth of the world in His hands:
> Of rubies and diamonds, of silver and gold,
> His coffers are full—He has riches untold."

Her voice had a mellowness it never had before and rolled away from her in billows of sound, not one voice only, but a full choir of heavenly singers. Even after the words were sung she could hear the melody weaving around her, folding her in crimson waves of sweetness. She shut her eyes with the rapture of it. When she opened them she found people staring at her curiously, and she tried to smile at them. She had an impulse to sing again and start the wonderful melody, but her lips were cracked and stiff.

Then came a voice—like the wind which wakened her when she was dreaming of rain—a voice harsh and terrible like the wind: "Madam, I arrest you! You are shoplifting!"

The words went crashing through her brain, each one exploding like a dum-dum bullet. And yet she saw everything around her with the vividness of a flash of lightning.

On the counter before her there were strings of beads displayed on high holding rods, in great variety of colors. A girl in a brown dress and with bobbed hair stood behind them, her mouth wide open. Three women stood in the aisle, clutching each other as if in fear. Beside her stood the young man whose hand was still laid on her arm.

"Where am I?" she asked.

The young man looked at her closely. He knew that question. They all ask it.

"You are in the Fifteen-cent Store," he told her, "and you must come with me."

"What have I done?" she asked him.

"Look in your bag," he said quietly.

Then she saw that her bag was full of the crimson roses which she had seen, but they were not real roses, only paper ones. In her hands were the two strings of beads.

"You must come with me to the Police Station," he said.

Again the words crashed through her like a jagged streak of lightning, leaving behind them the very darkness of the pit, into which her soul sank without even a cry.

The next day in the Police Court there were three cases of shoplifting. Hers was heard first.

Not having slept or eaten, her eyes were bloodshot and wild, her hat was crooked, and her clothes were badly wrinkled.

"How do you plead?" asked the Judge.

The question had to be explained.

"Guilty," she faltered.

"Now, there are far too many cases of this kind coming before me," said the Judge, "and I am going to give each of them the limit. We will see if we cannot put a stop to this petty thieving. You admit that you are guilty. Three months. Next case!"

(Now, by all the rules of short-story writing, this is the place to end the story, and this is the logical ending. In many cities this would have been the ending, but it so happened in the city of which I am writing that the ending was on this wise—)

"How do you plead?" asked the Judge.

The question had to be explained.

"Guilty," she faltered.

The Judge wrinkled her forehead. She was an attractive woman, with a neat gray silk hat and a rose-colored silk dress. Her brown eyes had grown a little weary and sad from looking on human misery in the manifold forms in which it came before her, but she had never grown accustomed to it, and now her tender heart was stabbed by the hopelessness in Sadie Benton's face.

"Detective Smithers," she said, "will you tell me what you know of this case?"

Detective Smithers was only too glad to tell.

"I was called on the 'phone," he said, "to the Fifteen-cent Store, your Honor, yesterday morning. They told me this woman had come in as soon as the store opened and wandered about aimlessly. When she came to the artificial flowers she took some in her hands. One of the girls asked her if she wished to buy, but she did not seem to understand. The girl asked her if she had any money, and she gave some outlandish answer about gold and silver and houses and lands. Then she began to put them in her bag—not like a thief, your Honor, the girls said, but just as if she were picking flowers. Then she took two strings of beads. I was sent for and can say the same, for I watched her. She was like a woman picking flowers in her own garden, leisurely and because she loved them. She's no common shoplifter, your Honor."

"Thank you, Detective Smithers," said the Judge, "I think you are right."

"I am going to suspend sentence, Mrs. Benton," said the Judge kindly, "but I want you to stay three days with a friend of mine, Dr. Crossley."

"But I only want to die," said the prisoner. "I have been arrested for shoplifting. I can't go on living."

"You'll not feel that way about it when you have had three days with Mrs. Crossley. She is a doctor who understands mental processes. She'll show you what happened."

Sadie sat huddled in her chair. The Crown Prosecutor touched her shoulder.

"Don't feel too badly over this, ma'am," he said. "You musn't take it too hard. We feel sure you are honest. Just something slipped in your brain. Brains are queer things—they can go out of order just like stomachs, or livers, or gasoline engines."

Sadie's eyes grew wider with astonishment. "I never knew people in police courts were kind like this—kind to—" she could not frame the word.

Mrs. Crossley came in then, a big woman with a deep voice.

"Where's my patient?" she asked.

She and the Judge had a hurried consultation in the next room, then she led Sadie to her car and drove her to her home in the suburbs of the City.

Somehow it was easy to talk to Mrs. Crossley, and in her big, white bed, so downy and soft, with a stone crock full of lilacs on the floor beside it, it was easy to sleep.

While Sadie slept Mrs. Crossley studied her case. The straw valise revealed many secrets. There were the lists from different neighbors, samples to match and things to buy, and then her little red book with its entries.

When Sadie awoke after ten hours' sleep Mrs. Crossley had considerable knowledge of her case. Indeed she knew more of Sadie Benton than did any of the East Golding people, with whom Sadie had lived for fifteen years.

When she awakened a maid came in and dressed her hair, and put a blue silk gown on her, with brightly colored birds embroidered on it, and brought her a dainty breakfast on a tray. Sadie had not tasted food for forty-eight hours, and in spite of her troubles she ate it all. Then her hostess came in to talk to her.

"When does your husband expect you home?"

"On Saturday," Sadie replied. "He will come to meet me, but how can I go home? Everyone will know."

"No one knows, dear," said her hostess. "The Judge gives out no information from her Court. Her Court is a sort of mental hospital, not a place of punishment. We try to find out what is wrong with our people and how it happened—and how to prevent its happening again. Now, I want you to tell me all about yourself. You know those albums which ask the guests to write in their favorite flower and quotation, and how they take their coffee, and all that. Just talk about yourself."

"There's nothing to tell," said Sadie, "I have a good man and two fine boys, and a lot of nice neighbors. I have brought disgrace on them. Who will believe me when I say I have no recollection of being in that store?"

"I will," said Mrs. Crossley; "I know it is true."

"Did anyone else ever do it?" Sadie asked eagerly.

"Yes, and people have done other things that were much worse. You haven't hurt anyone—no one has lost even five cents."

"But to be arrested!" said Sadie in horror.

"Now, listen," said Mrs. Crossley. "It was a good thing you were arrested. It gives us a chance to tell you what is wrong. You came into the city for a week. You did a week's work the day before you left, didn't you? Tell me all you did."

"I made a shirt for Frank, baked bread, boiled a ham, made pies, and churned. I had to leave things for the men, you know."

"Yes. What time were you up the morning you left?"

"Well, I couldn't sleep, anyway. I was excited about coming, and so I got up at four and scrubbed the floor and washed a few tea-towels and things."

"Yes, and then drove ten miles and rode eighty on the train. Did you eat anything on the train?"

"I wasn't hungry," said Sadie, "and besides, I needed the money I had for other things."

"You haven't eaten anything, then, since you left home until just now?"

"No, but—"

"Yes, I see. Now, tell me, how do you put in your time when you are at home? When do you get up in the morning?"

"At five in the summer. You see, there's the cows— and I like it. It's lovely in the morning. Sometimes the dawn is all rose and amber, and the dew on the grass sparkles like diamonds . . . Work is beautiful," she finished lamely.

"Up late, too, sometimes?"

"Oh, yes, when someone comes in. We like to see our neighbors."

"You board the teacher, do you?"

"Sometimes."

"And you have men working for you in harvest and seeding. Then you do some things for the neighbors. When that woman was sick—I forget her name—"

"Do you mean Mrs. Porter, or Mrs. Snider?"

"Yes," said Mrs. Crossley, "both. Just what did you do for them?"

"Only what any neighbor would."

"But for how long?"

"Mrs. Porter was in bed a month, and Mrs. Snider is sick yet. I sent her some things the day I left."

"And you had a good bit of trouble about a girl once?"

Sadie's face was full of fear.

"I cannot talk about that," she said, "it's a secret."

"It troubled you quite a bit," said Mrs. Crossley kindly, "and you worried over it. Was it you who had to tell her mother at last?"

"No one else would, and I knew how I would feel, but—"

"It was hard on you," interrupted Mrs. Crossley.

"Oh, but think of the poor mother!" said Sadie.

"Then that couple who couldn't agree—you were in that, too. You tried to get them to make up?"

"They did make it up," said Sadie proudly. "They only needed someone to talk to them. But how did you know? I never told anyone."

"I didn't know," said Mrs. Crossley, "but I read faces, and I have lived in country neighborhoods. You are worn out bearing other people's burdens, setting aside your own comfort, stifling your own desires, belittling your own disappointments, though you seem to have borne every kind. If your man drank you would have borne that, too. I knew you were a burden-bearer when I saw in your bag all the commissions you have taken for other people.

"You have been giving out all your life, laying up treasures in Heaven sure enough, but running close to mental bankruptcy here. You have issued big cheques on your mental bank when you had a very small reserve, and had many an overdraft that was always honored before, and you managed to meet it someway; but this time, when you put still heavier burdens on yourself, just for a few minutes the bank stopped payment and left you in the lurch. It had to come— it was bound to come!"

"Now, I'll illustrate it in another way," continued Mrs. Crossley, going to the switch and turning on the three lights in the room. "You see," she said, "they are all burning evenly—one light is as strong as another. But watch. Just outside in the hall is the switchboard. I am going to do something there. The lights will not go out, but they will be changed."

Mrs. Crossley went into the hall for a second. Then one light grew very bright, and the other two quite dim.

"What did you do?" Sadie asked interestedly.

"I took off a little thing called the neutral fuse. Now one is very bright and two are dull."

"Can you bring them right?" asked Sadie.

"Just as easily, by putting back the equalizer. Just for a little while the equalizer in your brain went off. Imagination, love of pretty things, your desire to give pleasure, all of which are strong in you at any time, burned very bright, like this light; caution and discretion, and the desire to pay your way, burned dim. During that time you saw lovely colors in flowers and beads, and you wanted them to make people happy. You forgot that you must pay for them—that faculty was burning dimly, and the bright light had its way with you. If the dim light made any protest you didn't hear it. This little lapse is a danger signal. It will not come back again unless you let yourself get as tired and exhausted as you were. It's no disgrace to have a brain go out of order; you would not feel disgraced if your liver went on strike or your stomach refused to function. It is quite aristocratic to have a heart that misses a beat, so why should anyone feel so disgraced to have a brain that falters in its work? Indeed, it is a wonder that women on the farm do not all develop mental trouble, they work so hard, and have had, in the last few years particularly, so many disappointments."

"Then I am not a thief!" cried Sadie Benton, sitting very straight in her chair.

"No, you are not. You worked at such high tension, bearing everyone's troubles, trying to do the work of two or three people, you blew out your neutral fuse and had to run into the service station to get fixed up.

"Now you know the danger and will be more careful. You are not going to the Convention; you are going to stay here with me until the end of the week, and then you will go home feeling better. I will give you a certificate to show that you were not able to attend the Convention."

The two women's eyes met in a long understanding gaze. From Sadie Benton's face the clouds of trouble rolled back and were gone. "You are something like God," she said softly, "in the way you understand."

And so it happened that Sadie Benton, who had helped many in their day of trouble, was not left desolate when her own black hour came upon her.

❧

"The Neutral Fuse" was published in *Macleans* (December 1924) and *All We Like Sheep, and Other Stories* (Toronto: Thomas Allen, 1926), 100–127.

CARRIED FORWARD

I

The silence of a funeral is like no other silence in all the world. Even the work-horses knew there was something wrong, and, coming to the bars of the pasture, had put their heads through, and stood in a solemn, unblinking row, as motionless and subdued as undertakers, watching the yard filling with the horses and buggies which were bringing the neighbors.

On a knoll in the back pasture which commanded a view of the premises the cows had assembled in a startled group, drawn together in the fellowship of mystery. The sheep grazing on the summer fallow seemed to be trying to curb the uncouth caperings of their offspring, with a lack of success that was almost human.

Leaving the door-yard, whose silence they found oppressive, the hens led their broods down the bank of the creek and passed unmolested into the freshly plowed garden, rich in fishworms, where in opulent undertones they tried to direct the activities of the clamorous crowds that followed them.

In the yard the neighbors' horses dozed comfortably in the soft May sunshine, undisturbed by any questionings of life or death. They only knew it was quiet and warm and that it was good to be at rest, with the clutch of the harness gone from their tired shoulders. As the neighbors arrived in their wagons and buggies the women went at once into the house, using the back door; but the men went to the big barn, where Luke Berry, the bereaved husband, received their sympathy, which, though awkwardly expressed, was none the less sincere.

Luke had dressed himself in his "other suit" and put on a stiff collar. The latter irritated him somewhat, causing him to chafe at its narrow confines. He was a good-looking, thick-set man, with dark-blue eyes, in which to-day there was a look of deep bewilderment.

"It isn't as if she had been sick and I was prepared for this," he said brokenly, "but here she was two days ago as well as one could expect, helping me to cut potatoes, complaining a little of a pain in her side; but that was nothing more than I would expect . . . She was not exactly a delicate woman either . . . never lay in bed more than three days with any of the children. By gosh, I don't see how having a baby should kill a woman. It's natural and right that they should have them, and, of course, we all know they suffer, but they shouldn't die! . . . Women don't seem to have the sand in them they used to have; my mother raised fifteen and lost five, and I have often heard my father say they never had a doctor in the house, and never needed one . . . I got the doctor as soon as Mrs. Peters said there was something wrong, and he said as soon as he came that it was too late to do anything—that he should have been called as soon as she took sick. He said something, too, about a month or two ago being the right time to call him in. But how in thunder did I know there was going to be any trouble! . . . Well, anyway, here I am, left with all these children, all girls, too; and even the baby is alive and well—and her gone!"

After relieving his feeling thus Mr. Berry rested on his elbows on the half-door and, leaning back, searched the faces of his neighbors for an explanation. "This is a pretty how-do-you-do, boys, now, isn't it?" he asked after a pause.

The men shook their heads gravely. It was quite evident that Luke Berry had been badly treated.

"We are all sorry, Luke," said Bob Walters, who, being an auctioneer, was readier of speech than the others, and naturally became the spokesman of the party. "It sure is an awful blow for a man to be left with a family, and all young. I don't suppose you know what you will do yet!"

With unerring instinct Bob knew that it was best to get this sad event on an earthly plane. The problem of a housekeeper was earthly enough.

"God knows," said Luke bitterly; "I don't. I never thought I would come to the place when I was looking for a housekeeper—and it don't seem fair. Here I am, a man who has always worked hard; never took a holiday the way lots of men do, just slaved and worked and paid my debts; and here, just when I was getting on my feet, with most of my machinery paid for, and that new quarter of school land, look what has happened to me! It's not a square deal. I didn't deserve this, boys."

The huge windmill on the barn was throwing its gaunt arms against the slight breeze that had sprung up, and filling the tank above with much creaking and groaning of machinery, throwing a shower of water on the ground around them.

"Stop it, Dave," Luke said impatiently to the hired man; "it don't seem right to have so much noise even here in the barnyard, and, anyway, don't you know the tank is full enough? There is no use wasting water."

He went back to the subject that was so heavy on his heart, and searched the faces of his neighbors for corroboration of his case.

"Talk about a set-back, boys, well, here's where I get mine! It would have been easier to have lost every horse in the place and had the barn burned . . . And what beats me is I don't see why it had to happen. I have been a square shooter, and I think I have been a decent neighbor. I never was any hand for going to church, because with machinery to look after and chores to do I never seem to get the time. There was always something to get ready, and Sunday seemed like the time to get it done. God knows I never spared myself, and seems to me God should be willing to give a man a chance when he sees he is willing to work . . . I can't square this in my mind with common fair play!" He was pounding his closed fist as he spoke on the half-door of the box stall, and continued to do it as again he looked for light or some explanation in the faces before him. Even the auctioneer could only shake his head and venture the opinion that "it sure was tough."

Lifting the discussion out of the trembling fog of metaphysics into which it had now fallen, and where none of the company felt at ease, Mr. Walters, with a deft stroke, placed it safely on the solid ground of economics once more.

"The worst thing about a man losing his wife," he began, stopping long enough here to light his pipe and carefully drop the match in one of the water pails, "is the housekeepers that he has to put up with. There may be good women who go out working, but, by George, no one can tell that to my brother Dan. Dan lost his wife just a year again now, and he has had five women already. First he tried a man and his wife. They were just married and looked strong and likely. Everything went well for about a week, and then one morning the woman did not get up—it was the man that got the breakfast. Dan might'uv stood that, but when he saw the man getting ready to carry her breakfast to bed it looked a little much of a good thing. He did not say anything until it had happened three times, and then he told her what he thought. He told her his wife had never had a meal in bed in her life only when the children were born; and, by George, do you know what that saucy lump snapped back at him? 'I quite believe you, Mr. Walters,' she said, 'your wife was different in lots of ways from me, but remember this when you are making comparisons, that she died at thirty-three. Get that? She died, and I am not figuring on an early grave and leaving a flock of orphans!' Gee, that cut Dan, and he paid them off right there. Now he has a red-haired dame that never gives him a civil word, though she is good to the kids. But she makes him get the men's shirts done up in town, and buy all the bread, and he has to do the milking all himself. But she knows he is in a corner, and you bet she hands it to him rough, and her pulling down forty dollars a month."

Conversation became general then, for each of the men had contributions to offer on this subject.

In the house the big room, from which the sunshine was shut out by the dark-green Holland blinds, was filled with women, all somberly dressed in black; big, deep-bosomed women, most of them, with sunburnt faces and thick red hands that worried their owners to-day in their uncertainty just where to put them. Good hands they were, kind, skilful, and ready when there was work to be done; but to-day every woman was unpleasantly conscious of their size and their redness, and of the difficulty of concealment in the absence of aprons. The pervading odor of the house was that of freshly scrubbed floors mingled with camphor, and, after the arrival of Grandma Brown, mothballs, for Grandma Brown had on her widow's veil, which was taken from its bed of mothballs only for funerals, with the one exception of the Sunday that the Masonic Lodge attended Divine Worship. Grandpa Brown had been laid away with Masonic honors thirty years before, and since then his widow had felt that she belonged to the Order, and faithfully attended the one open meeting of the year, wearing the veil as a token of membership.

To-day she did not stay in the front room, where the silence was rather terrifying, but went to the rooms above, where the work of dressing the children and making them ready for the funeral was going on.

The neighbors had made a thorough cleaning of the house according to the unwritten laws of neighborhoods, and there was hardly a trace of the smell of small babies and unwashed milk-cans which had prevailed prior to this upheaval.

Conversational efforts were made at intervals by the women in the darkened room, but, although held up bravely for a few moments, these soon flickered, languished, wavered and went out, and silence fell deeper than ever. Even the children, who sat uncomfortably on the edges of their chairs, were motionless and dumb, as if they did not wish by their activity to cast aspersions on the inactivity of the dead. The clock, which stood on a shelf of its own, with an elaborately scalloped newspaper drape, seemed to feel the solemnity of the hour, and, after clearing its throat to strike, changed its mind, gurgled once, and went on with its ticking.

The company in the front room increased with the coming of each buggy. Many had come from a distance to pay their respects to the dead and look their last on her white face, telling each other in sighing whispers that she looked "natural."

Upstairs a frightened group of children, all washed and brushed, were herded together in one of the bedrooms, and warned to stay clean by Mrs. Peters, who had taken charge of the proceedings. They sat dully on the bed, awed by the silence of the house. Suddenly little Julia began to cry.

Mrs. Walters undertook to scold her. "Bad little girl to be crying," she said, "and the whole house full of people! Bad little girl, crying, and her poor mother lying dead downstairs!"

At this Julia's grief flowed afresh.

Grandma Brown, who had laid aside the crepe veil to be better able to lend a hand, took the sobbing child on her knee and stoutly defended her. "Well, Missus Walters," she said, "I don't know just how you look at these things, but I should say there is no one has any more right to cry than young Julia here. I would say this is her funeral, if you get my meaning, and if she feels like crying I am not going to try to stop her. I lost my mother when I was about her age, and the neighbors told me afterwards that I whooped it up for fair, and none of them could stop me; and looking back now, I know I had good reason, and I am glad I knew enough to cry. I had two stepmothers, and I guess they did the best they could, poor things—I am not holding anything against them—but I never tell a kid to stop crying. I don't blame them for howling any time."

"Why, Grandma Brown, whatever makes you talk like that? Life isn't as bad as all that, even if there are hard places in it, like the one we are at to-day," said Mrs. Peters, soothingly. Mrs. Peters was a placid woman, with straw-colored hair, not a strand of which was ever out of place.

"Life is hard on the people who cannot take their own part," the old lady persisted; "that's what happened to the poor girl downstairs. She never grumbled—never got mad—took it all. Did without things all her life. Stayed at home and fed pigs while Luke went out to buy more land and more pigs. Had a baby every year, and broke her heart when they died. To be sure Luke was a good man; he never beat her or starved her. There are others ways of killing a woman. Annie was dumb and Luke was blind—and this is what happened."

"But Annie was fond of him, too. He was good to her in his own way," said Mrs. Walters.

"Yes, she was fond of him," Mrs. Brown admitted. "That is what beats me. It is so easy for women to be fond of someone. Their affections go out with a little hook on the end, like a wild cucumber vine, and whatever they grab they say it is fate. Oh, I know, I have seen this lots of times, and the next one will be just as fond of him."

"Oh, Grandma, let poor Annie get cold before you think of the next one," said Mrs. Peters, reprovingly.

"All right, but I make my guess that he will be married in six months. Of course, you can't blame him, for there are the children to think of, and it takes a woman to look after them. And then there will be more children, and if their mother dies there will be another woman some place who will take the job of minding them and raising more. It is a great plan, and a great world for men."

Mrs. Peters looked at her neighbor in astonishment. "Grandma Brown," she said, "I never heard you talk that way before. It is a good thing the children are too young to understand, and I hope you won't talk that way before Hilda, for she is a wise little thing for twelve years old. Indeed, she knows too much. I didn't know what to say to her. I wouldn't for the world have her hear you. There is no use turning a child against her father."

Grandma Brown lowered her voice. "That's so," she said, "there is no use in making the child bitter. She will be that soon enough. So I'll be careful. And there is only a board wall between this room and the one she is in, and she's as sharp as a cat, I know."

In the next room, standing guard over her young pink sister, Hilda Berry, the eldest daughter of the house, heard every word that had been said, and in her heart there raged a bitter feeling of resentment. Her father was to blame in some way. She knew that sometimes her mother cried and was impatient with all of them; and once she said she wished she were dead and done with it all. But there was no one whom Hilda could ask. When she had tried to get Mrs. Peters to tell her on another occasion where she got all the babies she brought to people, Mrs. Peters had told her that was not a nice question for a little girl to think of. "God sends the babies, and it is not our business at all," she had said, and Hilda had tried to be satisfied with this meagre explanation; but she could not help thinking that when she had to mind them and wash for them, sleep with them and wean them, she had some right to be interested, or even consulted about their coming.

Ever since she could walk Hilda had had a baby dragging after her. Her earliest memory was of teaching her sister Mary to walk, and being soundly scolded by her father for letting her bump her head in the process. Never had she as much as gone to the stable to look for eggs without taking a baby by the hand, or with one in her arms; and scarcely a full night's sleep had she ever had with the incessant demands of a last year's baby. And to be told that God sent them did not increase her good opinion of the Almighty. Not one of them could she spare, for she loved them all with an almost fierce love; but she did wish no more would come until all of them were big enough to feed themselves and "tell." Her little arms were so tired some nights she could not sleep with the ache of them.

The sudden death of her mother had left Hilda stunned. It just could not be. In a vague way she held to the hope that Mrs. Peters would bring her back. Mrs. Peters could do wonderful things. The way she supplied babies all over the neighborhood was wonderful; and once she brought to life a boy who had been drowned; and Hilda knew she could make a flower grow from just a leaf, for they had one of these now in the kitchen window.

In the first outcry of her grief Mrs. Peters had told her she must not cry; she must be an extra good girl now, for if she wasn't she would never see her mother again. And knowing Mrs. Peters' powers, Hilda had held to the hope that by great goodness on her part she might have her mother given back to her. Mrs. Peters and God, who worked so well together in the matter of bringing babies to people who had not asked for them, might do a good turn in a pinch for the same people, and this seemed to be the time. Hilda knew that their Swedish neighbor surprised them all by what he did once. One of their cows had fallen into his well and been drowned. It had not been his fault, for the cow had no business to be in the field where the old well was. Her father admitted that he had no claim for damages, and when the Swedish neighbor had expressed his sorrow by saying it was "too damn bad," they thought the incident was closed. But two days afterwards they got a surprise. One of the Swede's cows had twin calves, and he brought over one of them for a present—the best one, as they found out afterwards—and everyone said it was real decent of him. It would be just like God to be decent at a time like this.

Following Mrs. Peters' suggestion that if she were not good she would never see her mother again, Hilda had worked with the strength of a full-grown woman, rising the first in the morning, and not quitting until the last thing was done at night. She would not give God or Mrs. Peters any excuse for not bringing her mother back.

But as the hour for the funeral drew near Hilda grew apprehensive. She tried not to be impatient, remembering that it would take time for God and Mrs. Peters to get everything arranged. Instinctively she knew that it would be harder to bring someone back than to shove a baby into even an unwilling family, and she kept warning herself that she had never known or heard of anyone who had been as dead as her mother who had come alive again; but perhaps it did happen and was not spoken of. There were things like that.

She looked out of the window and saw the fields all full of sunshine, with their new crops showing green and beautiful. Black shadows of the drifting clouds ran over the green, like twisting, creeping giant hands, which made her afraid, for they all seemed to be coming to the house with some evil intention. The sickening smell of wolf-willow blossoms came to her from the pastures. A meadowlark on the fence post sang straight at her. It was easy enough for him to sing. His mother wasn't dead, and he had no baby to mind, and, besides, any time he did not like the way things were going he could fly away and never come back. Hilda hated the meadowlark because his heart was so light, while hers was breaking, and she wished his song would choke him. She felt to him the way she felt to the light-hearted children at school on the few occasions she had been at school. She could not understand how they could be so care-free. When the other children, whose backs were not aching with the burden of little brothers and sisters, would propose a game, and dash into it with all the abandon of childhood, Hilda would sit stiff and unhappy, wishing that they would not do it. Somehow it hurt her.

The new baby slept quietly, undisturbed by the fact that her father had not yet looked at her. Hilda could have told her that his neglect would last until her successor arrived. Last year's baby was quite popular with Luke Berry—that is, when its behavior was beyond reproach—but he boasted his inability to do anything with a baby when it cried, and was emphatic in declaring that he would rather sleep in a snow-bank than in the house with a crying youngster.

The baby slept quietly, and Hilda felt free to go downstairs to see if there were any signs of her mother's return. The women in the parlor stopped talking when she came in, and many a sigh of sympathy fell on the silence when she tip-toed over to the coffin and looked eagerly into the cold, set face. She touched her mother's cheek, and wondered how it could be so cold and what made her lips so blue; but she did not ask the women, for she knew that all this was a great mystery to them as it was to her. Hope still burned in her heart. Maybe God would be "decent" like the Swedish neighbor. Maybe He was leaving it to the very last to let all the people come and see what would happen. Her grandmother, when she had visited them one summer, had told her lots of stories about God, and in every one of them God came out best. The one Hilda liked best was the one about the fire coming down from Heaven, and the man of God prayed for it. Hilda loved that one, though she couldn't help feeling a little sorry for the other men, who prayed so hard and did not get even a flicker out of their gods. That was very hard, especially after they had cut themselves with knives to show how bad they were feeling. Hilda would have been quite willing to slash herself now, but she knew it wouldn't do any good. The man of God had been very off-hand about it, her Grandmother had said, and even joked with the prophets of Baal, saying, "Your gods must be asleep, or off on a journey." She must not let on she was a bit afraid.

But Hilda's face was so white and her eyes so full of excitement that the women were afraid to speak to her. Their hearts were bleeding for her, but not one of them could frame a sentence of sympathy. Their wordlessness had driven them to the cleaning of the house. That was the out-let for their feelings, and Hilda did not misunderstand their silence. Neither did she resent all the scrubbing and tidying that had taken place, nor think that it was a reflection on her mother's housekeeping. Her mother worked all the time, and so did she. No one could work longer than that. The women knew that, and most of them did the same. But when anyone died the others let their own work go, even letting the cows go unmilked if necessary, to "do for" the family of the one who was gone. There was no criticism in these acts of neighborliness.

Hilda noted the new paper on the pantry shelves, the polished kitchen stove, the shining windows. Even the face of the clock had had the fly-stains removed, and Hilda's sharp eyes saw that part of the dome of St. Paul's had come off too. (Hilda did not know it was the dome of St. Paul then; she only knew that it was a great church somewhere in England, and that her mother had been careful to wipe it with a soft rag, breathing on it gently.) Every pot and pan was scoured and shining, the clothes-horse was full of freshly ironed clothes, and a great batch of bread filled the kitchen table, covered with her mother's clean apron to let it cool and not dry out. She listened for a minute to hear it crack and sing, and just for a fraction of a second in her delight she forgot the trouble of her heart. Her mother had often called her to listen to the bread and rejoice with her over another good baking. Her mother loved the smell of the clean clothes, too, when Hilda brought them in from the line all sweet with sunshine, and her delight in them had been Hilda's cure many a time for an aching back when the washing was all done, dried and brought in. She wished her mother could see the sparkling kitchen now, and then corrected herself by thinking she would soon see it. Hilda would not let her faith waver. Her grandmother had told her about Peter walking on the water, and doing fine, too, until he got afraid, and then down he went. So she must keep on believing!

But she felt the need of something. There was no one to turn to, and Hilda could not read the Bible which lay on the table in the parlor. She had tried, but it was not a bit like the reader at school, which had good big, shiny print, and pictures at the side to give a person a hint of what the word might be. She knew the Bible had a lot to say about God, and she often wished her mother had had time to read a little bit of it every night, the way her grandmother had done. Anyway, there was a motto her grandmother had left when she went away. It hung in the room where the baby was. It was very beautiful and looked like red velvet, though it was only paper when you got right up to it. And the words on it were in silver, cut deeply; and there were silver flowers on the side which came right over the words, a shower of them like little silver bells, and the words said, "Ask, and it shall be given you." She would say that over and over, and maybe that would do just as good as if she could read the Bible. If God knew as much as her grandmother thought He did, He would know she was doing the best she could. She thought it might help if she held the motto in her hands.

When the minister drove into the yard the men began to drift in from the stable, standing in groups around the door until Mrs. Peters, who always took the lead at funerals, got them persuaded to go right into the house and leave the space at the door for those who might come late. The blinds were drawn in the room but enough of the bright sunshine had stolen in to reveal the objects there. One bright ray of light, which came through a hole in the green Holland blind, fell caressingly on the enlarged picture of Hilda's mother in her wedding-dress of the year 1896, with its billowy sleeves and stiff *passementerie*. It was a crayon drawing which her mother had had made for her by a travelling salesman, who made a point of assuring his customers that they were "only paying for the frame." The frame was an elaborate one of fretted gold with an edge of oak.

To-day in the gloom of the silent room the young face of the bride gleamed and glowed in weird distinctness. It was the most living thing in this room of death, with its smiling eyes and speaking mouth and eager questionings. It was such a sweet, trusting, and confident young face, smiling into the future, and demanding an answer by its very expectancy to the question. What have you got for me, Big World? It seemed to urge with all the insistence of radiant youth, "Something glorious and wonderful, I know, but tell me . . . I am not afraid, whatever it is . . ."

Just below stood the coffin, its wooden rest standing on the black mat bordered with the Greek key pattern, gleaming white; the coffin sombre . . . black . . . and final!

The minister came in then, shaking hands with all the neighbors. He was deeply sympathetic, and tried his best to show it, but could not get away from the difficulties of his position. He held fast to his prayerbook, with the leaf turned down where begins the Burial of the Dead.

"A very sad occurrence, this; the saddest death there is, I always think, is when a young mother is taken away in the very flower of her womanhood. It is so very difficult for the husband and father. But we must be resigned to the will of God, and not question His goodness. I know the kind neighbors are showing their sympathy in a thousand practical ways." He included them all in his pleasant smile.

The Reverend Mr. Albright had come out from the City, ten miles away, to conduct the funeral. Mr. Berry had not seen him before, though he had often heard of him, and so had the neighbors, for he was quite a famous golfer, and his picture in his golfing costume had been in the papers on the occasions when he had won championships. When Mr. Berry had 'phoned to ask him to come out he had been very nice about it, and said he would be glad to come if the funeral could be early in the afternoon, for he was due at a Service Club dinner at six o'clock.

Mrs. Peters came upstairs to tell Hilda to come down, for the service was going to begin. The thin Mrs. Humphrey would stay with the baby. Hilda said she thought she had better stay. Always Hilda had had to stay back to care for a baby, and the habit was deeply ingrained; but Mrs. Peters would not hear of it this time. "You must be at the service, and go to the grave, too," she added, "no matter who has to stay behind. Mrs. Humphrey can manage the baby, and you must be at the service. Sometimes there's a lot of comfort in what the minister says. He will explain all about death, and show us why we should not grieve too much. My mother died when I was a little girl, and I'll never forget how the minister's words comforted me."

All the children were in the room, seated in a close row beside the coffin—all but the two-year-old baby, who had been taken to one of the neighbor's because she was too young to keep quiet. The others, hushed and awed, sat soberly through the service. Julia came to Hilda and held her hand.

Reverend Mr. Albright did not venture to stray from the words which were written in the book. Funerals always bothered him, for he felt embarrassed in the presence of grief. Human words seemed so utterly powerless. He wanted to comfort the forlorn row of little girls, especially the biggest one, whose eyes never left his face. But what could he say? Her mother had plainly died from overwork and childbearing. In his nervousness he did not even speak in a natural tone of voice, but hurried along, trusting that the beautiful words of the service would carry comfort without any help from him. Hilda wished he would talk to them and tell them what he thought, instead of just saying a piece. He looked so nice and friendly, and so sure that everything was all right, perhaps he could explain all she wanted to know. Hilda only remembered that he said, "Like as a father pitieth his children," and it made her heart still heavier. She had hoped that God was more like her mother, who one time cried over Hilda's sore hands when she had been out stooking wheat and had no gloves—not only cried, but found a pair of her own gloves that she had before she was married—and Hilda found out afterwards that they were her mother's only gloves, and she had to go bare-handed to town all summer and until the season came for woolen mittens.

Her father sat with his head in his hands, so deeply engrossed in his own grief that he had not a word nor a glance for any of the children. Hilda vaguely felt his displeasure—they were to blame someway for what had happened, mostly because there were too many of them! But she could not fix the blame on any particular one of the sad little group. She knew they all loved their mother just as she did, and would not hurt her if they knew—even the noisy one, who was absent because she was noisy, loved her in her own way. But, all the same, Hilda instinctively felt that her father considered that he had been badly treated by his family, and for her mother to slip away and leave him this way was downright shabby. Hilda wished she knew how to defend her mother.

"Ask, and it shall be given to you." She said it when she saw Mrs. Peters lifting the children one by one to look at their mother's white face. She would have cried then if she had not been saying over her promise and believing it so truly. Little Julia, having no promise to lean on, had to be carried out sobbing; and when she gave way, the whole family, except Hilda, broke into wild cries, which were only hushed when they were taken out and put into the buggies which were standing at the door, and where the prospect of a drive offered some consolation.

"I am asking God, and I am asking," Hilda repeated as she saw the men preparing to screw down the coffin-lid. She stood beside the coffin, wanting to be the first one to see her mother open her eyes . . . "Ask and it shall be given unto you." One screw had gone in, and the second one was being turned . . . "Ask and it shall be given unto you . . . Oh, God, hear me, I am asking; do it now, God—she'll smother if you don't! . . . Ask, and it shall be given unto you . . ."

Hilda had to stand aside to let the pallbearers get hold of the coffin. Grandma Brown had taken her by the hand and was patting it gently, and they were all moving out of the house. She had to follow.

Hilda did not take her eyes from the coffin all the way to the cemetery. It was in Mr. Peters' light wagon, and the buggy she rode in was directly behind. Sometimes when the horses trotted over the rough road the coffin was jolted. Hilda fancied she saw it move, and her heart almost stood still with expectancy. She could have screamed to the stolid driver, but she knew if God would keep His word He would do it handsomely, and bring her mother back strong and well. She was convinced now that it would happen right at the grave.

The funeral procession, like a slowly crawling black snake, wound its tedious way along the river-bank, sometimes dividing into sections as if the snake had suffered mortal injury; but these divisions no sooner occurred than they were healed, for the horse that had dropped behind would break into a trot of his own free will to regain his lost position, and those behind closed up. The road had many a tedious winding. Short-cuts there were through field and over summerfallow, but the unwritten law concerning funerals was well understood. The longest road must be taken. There must be no suspicion of hurry, nor any evidence of the worldly desire to save time. These things belong to life, not death. The last earthly journey of the deceased must be serenely slow, and free from all abbreviations.

The gleam of the afternoon sunshine fell dazzling on the growing fields. Away to the west the mountains stood in all their blue and silver majesty, silent, detached from worldly troubles, serene, and sure. They seemed to rest on the very foundations of the world. Hilda tried to look at them and get some of the comfort that her grandmother said she got when she lifted her eyes to the hills whence cometh help. There was no comfort in them for the little girl. They seemed to roll over her and crush her into a pitiful little handful of dust that the wind would drive away. Nothing mattered to them; they could not be sorry, no matter who died. What did they care for mothers? Secure in their dreadful permanence, they stood unmoved and uncaring. She went back to her text, and held to it with all the intensity of her devout little heart.

There was more comfort in the headlands and the road allowance, with their tender green grass, all blue-eyed and beautiful with the early crocuses, shading from foaming white through palest blue into deep cobalt and rich purple, and in the delicate embroideries of buttercups along the edge of the road, showing deeply golden against the black soil. Soft billowy breezes, scented with wolf-willow, lulled the air and carried the smoking dust away from the horses' feet.

Below them could be seen the placid valley, where the river wound itself through the evergreens and poplar, a twisted ribbon of silver which ran its full width when it ran straight, but folded itself at the turnings, and in one place made a row of shirring down the middle as it ran over the rocks. Saskatoon bushes showed deeply purple against the gosling green of the young poplars, and here and there a wild cherry tree in full blossom looked like a drift of snow that the sun had somehow overlooked!

The gate of the cemetery was open, and the procession moved slowly toward the open wound on the hillside with its swollen lips of lumpy yellow clay. The people alighted from their buggies and swarmed around the grave, where the coffin was already lying ready to be put into the rough box which was waiting. For once Hilda forgot to take charge of the younger children, but there were many eager hands ready to lift them down and take them to the grave. Hilda's teeth were chattering, and her legs seemed unwilling to carry her. God was far away, and the dreadful moment when her mother would be put in the grave was so near.

Hilda knew what happened when a person was buried. An Englishwoman, who officiated once at the annual event in the Berry family when Mrs. Peters was away, had told her. This lady's theology was as crude as her cooking, but in the absence of any other explanation Hilda had accepted it. "People are put in the ground when they die," said the lady from Brick lane, "and the worms eat them, and that's all there is of that." The question of life, death, and the judgement to come had arisen because that year's baby had died. It was with this thought in her mind that Hilda had carefully examined the coffin and tried to believe that no worm could get into it; but she knew that forever and ever is a long, long time, and she could not forget that wood, even the best wood, will rot, and under a rotten log there are always worms. Her first impulse was to stay beside the buggy, for a great physical nausea had come over her. But there was the text, "Ask and it shall be given unto you." She must do her part. She would ask—ask—ask right to the last moment. Then it was up to God.

The women who stood around the grave noticed how deathly pale she was, and marvelled at her lack of tears. It did not seem natural for a girl of twelve to stand at her mother's grave with eyes that glittered in their dryness, and they were more than ever convinced that Hilda Berry was a "queer little stick," and when they saw her lips moving they were confirmed in that opinion. The grave had a poplar tree at its head, and in the choking silence before the minister began to read the service, Hilda held to the green trunk of the tree, dimly conscious of the gentle whisper of the wind through its leaves. The little leaves, not yet full grown, were turning over and over, glittering like little coins, and the shadows made a moving tapestry on the side of the open grave, which somehow softened the horror of it. Laying her cheek against the smooth, cool bark of the bole of the tree, Hilda found a comfort which in some way saved her heart from breaking.

The sweet words of consolation were hurried through. Then the men put on their hats, and some turned away.

Luke Berry stood stricken with grief, and the women in the black clothes wept profoundly. Grandma Brown, sustained by a peppermint which she drew from a deep pocket in her full black skirt, whispered to Mrs. Peters, to whom she handed a duplicate: "I am not going to cry for poor Annie. This will be the first night's sleep she has had for ten years. I hope she will have sense enough to tell them in Heaven not to call her early, and just let her sleep it off; but I am not so sure that she won't be jumping up every ten minutes, thinking she hears the baby cry."

When they began to shovel the earth down into the grave Mrs. Peters took Hilda by the hand, and would have led her away, for all the people were going, but she held to the poplar and shook off the hand roughly. Her eyes were closed and her lips were trembling. Vaguely frightened, Mrs. Peters stood beside her.

The buggies were winding out of the gate. Her father had gone, and so had all the children save little Julia, who ran back to Hilda and stood holding her skirt. When the last shovelful of earth had been put in place, and the grave patted down smooth like a hill of potatoes, Hilda loosened her hold on the tree and, turning to Mrs. Peters, said, "I am ready now." Her voice was steady, but the eyes that looked into Mrs. Peters' were not the eyes of a child, but two great pools of darkness.

When they reached home Hilda went upstairs before she took off her coat and tam o'shanter. There was something she wanted to do. In the room upstairs, where the thin Mrs. Humphrey was trying to comfort the wailing infant, Hilda went to the wall and, taking the motto, richly red and silver, in her hands, she broke it across the middle. She stood for a moment or two irresolute, with the two pieces in her hands, then, going downstairs to the kitchen stove, she took off the lid and dropped the pieces on the coals.

Then it was that something broke in her, and when Mrs. Peters came into the kitchen she found Hilda on the floor sobbing the dry, killing sobs of those who find themselves without hope and without God in the world.

II

Life has a way of going on, no matter who dies. Even the slipping out of a mother cannot stay the pitiless course of time, which in Hilda's little world was made up of never-ending occurrences—cows to be milked; children fed; dishes washed; the baby changed and fed; bottles washed and filled—work without end, a dizzy round, bewildering and numbing because there was no end, no hope of achievement—ceasing only when utter exhaustion shut it all away from her with a kind black wall of sleep, so thick and sound-proof that it excluded even the baby's cry.

Always the wakening came slowly, tormentingly, and in this fashion: In her dream she was doing something pleasant, bringing up the cows to the bars, or playing with the dog in the pasture, or picking berries on the river-bank. Suddenly came the baby's cry—piercing, insistent, and full of terror. She turned at once to rush to its relief, only to find her feet would not move; they were heavy as lead. Still the cries! Still the lagging feet! She struggled frantically, and strove to cry for help, but her lips were frozen, too . . . After what seemed a long period of frantic effort and horror, the cry that was in her heart worked its way smotheringly to her lips and thus brought deliverance.

So began Hilda's days.

Nothing was the same, even outside! The river had a cruel gleam in its steely blue waters. She had no joy in the wild roses or columbine, for there was no one to exclaim with delight over them. The garden she and her mother had planted was a maze of weeds, forgotten by everyone but herself. The mountains, even on the brightest days, wore the frown they had on the day of the funeral, forbidding and scornful. While her mother lived Hilda had been able to picture great sunny rooms in the mountains, where green plush carpets on golden stairs, held in place by golden rods, led to other rooms where hung huge chandeliers of sparkling lights, fringed with glittering icicles, making glowing rainbows on the polished floors beneath; where white wicker furniture had bright chintz cushions on which green and blue birds, with scarlet breasts, sat on trees all white with blossoms.

Her mother had woven for her many gay fancies as they worked together through the long days, grieved as she was to see her faithful little helper so harassed and burdened with household cares.

"Never mind, Hilda," her mother would say, "these children will grow up sometime, and will be useful, and then you and I will have nothing to do. You will have breakfast in bed every morning. You will press a button. A timid knock will sound on our door. 'Come in' you will say. Enter Mary in a smoke-blue dress, white apron, and cap.

" 'Did you ring, Miss Berry?' she will ask you.

" 'My breakfast, Mary,' you will say; 'oatmeal and cream, poached eggs, not broken, buttered toast, peach marmalade, coffee—and hurry.'

" 'Will she do it,' you ask. Indeed she will, and she had better. I will remind her that you carried barrels of water to wash her clothes, and fed her tons of bread and milk with a spoon. Certainly she will do it."

"And one for you, too, Mother; a tray for you?" Hilda had asked.

"I think I'll have Julia for my servant, very smart in a gray and silver uniform," her mother had replied.

Many hard places were passed pleasantly by these happy fancies of good days ahead, days of comfort and ease and reward.

But now everything was changed. Her mother was dead. Her God had gone on a journey. She had no hope of help from anyone. This was her fight, and hers alone. There was no one to care now whether she was tired or not. There was no escape, no turning back. She would carry on the work her mother left, expecting no help, no mercy. Life was like that, she thought, brokenly.

Hilda was awake early the first morning after the funeral, attending to the baby, and sat with the little thing in her arms watching the dawn that streaked the sky with rose and gold. She was thinking of her mother's last words to her, running them over in her mind as a devout worshipper would count her beads.

It was the day the doctor had come, and, hearing her mother moan, Hilda had run into the room. Mrs. Peters had gone out of the room with the doctor, and for a few minutes Hilda and her mother were alone.

"Is it another baby, Mother?" Hilda had asked in alarm.

Her mother had nodded wearily. "And we didn't need another, did we, Hilda? But maybe it will die, like the one last year."

Hilda had seen her mother's lips quiver as she said it, and knew it was not from pain of body only, but of heart as well.

"Oh, no, Mother," she had said quickly, "we mustn't let this one die. We'll raise it, and be glad of it. I don't mind another one, really I don't. I'll mind it and be glad."

It was a brave lie, and Hilda was glad now that she had told it, for it brought a wan little smile to her mother's eyes.

For a while she had not spoken, and then, drawing Hilda close, she had said hurriedly, as one who is pressed for time: "Listen, dear, and try to remember what I say. You are young, but you'll remember if I ask you very particularly, won't you?"

Hilda had nodded wonderingly.

"Learn to speak out, Hilda," the mother had continued, "when you feel something ought to be said. All your life, I mean. Don't let anyone make you so frightened that you cannot speak. I have been like that, and it is no good. I often wanted to say things to your father, but I couldn't; I let the time pass when I should have spoken. You should have been in school. I wanted you to go every day, but I was not brave enough to make a row about it. I just took the easiest way, and it was wrong."

"Don't worry, Mother," Hilda had said, alarmed at her mother's burning hands and the finger tips so cold, like little balls of ice.

"Your father is not a bad man—see how good he is to his horses—but he didn't understand, and I didn't make him. His mother spoiled him first; then I sat still, too patient. It isn't patience, it's cowardice. And now we're gone, both of us, two grown women, and leaving you, a poor little girl twelve years old, to do what we hadn't the courage to do. It's a heavy inheritance. And I'm sorry, Hilda!"

Her mind had wandered then. "He was foot-loose . . . he would walk out if I said a word . . . and I was tired . . . always a baby in my arms, and one coming . . . You won't be hard on me, Hilda . . . I was so sick . . ."

Hilda had put her arms around her and begged her not to worry over anything, but just get better.

"Your father is not a poor man . . . he could hire help for us. I knew, but he wouldn't talk . . . he just went dumb." Then she roused herself for one great effort. "Peace can cost too much, Hilda. It has cost me too much. Don't do it . . . don't be patient. Speak out. They can only kill you—and it would be best to die fighting . . . not like me, dying because I was too dumb . . . You will be good to them, I know. I'm leaving you a woman's job, and you a child."

The old dog, black-and-white Jake, had come into the room and stood beside the bed, sensing that something was wrong.

The sick woman had put her hand on his head. "Jake will help you—won't you, Jake? Do your best, Jake, when I'm gone. A little girl and a dog . . . and maybe God will help . . . Anyway, I can't help it now . . . I am too sick."

The nurse had called Hilda to come away. And that was the last. Hilda had been sent with the children to one of the neighbor's to keep the house quiet.

All that seemed a long, long time ago!

In a month the new housekeeper came. Mr. Berry brought her in one day, saying, "This is Mrs. Mauvers, Hilda. She is going to look after things. I hope you will be a good girl and help her all you can." Hilda shook hands with her gravely. She was a tall woman, with dead brown eyes set in a creamy face, and a queer smile that came slowly and went quickly leaving her lips apart, and rather ghastly in their lack of mirth. She was showily dressed in an embroidered suit, with a heavily beaded blouse, and exuded a strange cloying perfume that filled the room and hung about even after she had gone upstairs.

It did not take her long to re-arrange the sleeping accommodation. Hilda and the baby had occupied the front bedroom since the funeral, the best room that looked out upon the river, and this she quietly appropriated, asking Hilda to remove her things at once. Her manner was one of authority, and Hilda obeyed, but not without a sense of injustice.

The second day she made another change. "No children at the table—your father's health, my dear," she said to Hilda. "It is our first consideration, is it not? He must have quiet at his meals; no gentleman should be annoyed by children."

It was at the slack period of farm work, when Luke Berry had let his men go, and so he and Mrs. Mauvers had their meals alone in the dining-room. So keen was she for undisturbed mealtimes that she sent the children to the river-bank, giving them a cold lunch of bread and butter and jam.

"The bane of the New World," she said to Hilda, "is impertinent children, too well fed, too much noticed. Children should always be kept in the background—always. I have been in this country long enough to see homes ruined by indulgent parents and impossible children. When I get the house in order I'll put the baby on a system. You are giving her too much care. Remember, a baby should cry a certain amount each day."

"She is not three months old yet," said Hilda quickly. "It's dangerous to let a little baby cry."

Mrs. Mauvers smiled her slow-coming smile while Hilda spoke, then in a flash it vanished, leaving the little girl looking into clay-cold eyes. Hilda wished she would go away, for her presence lay like a blight on everything. When the children came in they spoke in whispers, and walked about on tip-toe, shrinking away if she looked at them. There was something about her that seemed to possess the whole house. Hilda felt it was no longer a home for any of them.

It was no wonder, Hilda thought, that she could keep the house clean. She had no interruptions in her work, for the children made no demands on her. When little Marion fell into disgrace she was put back to bed without her breakfast, and all the sympathizers were driven from the house. However, they assembled in the backyard and carried on a sign-conversation with the small culprit, who stood on a chair to see out of the window. The conversation seemed to deal largely with reprisals, but when Mrs. Mauvers opened the door the sympathizers scampered away like frightened rabbits, and little Marion was left to meditate on her sins.

Mrs. Mauvers' voice was coldly authoritative when she spoke to the children or poor old Jake, who had tried to be friends with her. It was not like any voice the children had ever heard. Hilda and Julia and Mary had a guessing contest about it. Hilda said it was like walking on spilled white sugar; Mary said it was like a grass cut; but little Julia, after long deliberation, said it was just like a button on a duster. Her voice changed entirely when Mr. Berry came in. It became soft, and purring, even playful, when she, in her crisp house dress and boudoir cap, sat at the head of the table, beaming with good-humor.

From the room above the dining-room, where Hilda kept the baby at mealtimes, she could look down through the stovepipe hole upon them as they sat at meals. Fragments of the conversation floated up to her.

"I only want a home now; I am not a business woman, I am a homemaker . . . and when I read your ad, I said, "There I may be able to scatter a little sunshine and thereby comfort my own sad heart . . . I love the country with its healing balm and silence—and—and—I hope I can please you, Mr. Berry."

Hilda couldn't hear what her father said, but she noticed that he sat long over his dinner.

When dinner was over Mrs. Mauvers retired to her room for two hours while Hilda washed the dishes and swept up the kitchen. It was in this interval that Mary, Julie, Edith, and little Marion stole back to supplement their frugal meal. But when Mrs. Mauvers found that this was being done she made a firm ruling—indiscriminate eating was not to be tolerated.

One night the baby cried, and Hilda's ministrations were powerless to restore peace to her little mind. Mrs. Mauvers, in a bright-red gown embroidered with black and gold birds, was upon the scene in a few moments with a bottle in her hand.

"This must stop," she said, with the rasp in her voice, "your father must have his rest. No gentleman can bear a crying child."

She took the baby from Hilda and laid her on the bed. "I will give her something to soothe her," she said.

"No! no!" cried Hilda. "I can quiet her soon. It's just a little colic. All babies cry sometimes; you say it's good for them. We never give our children anything."

Mrs. Mauvers poured the spoon half full and gave it to the baby before the half-awakened Hilda knew what had happened.

"Your father's rest is our first thought," she said.

"He could go to the granary," Hilda said, indignantly. "I don't like this; I'll ask Mrs. Peters."

Mrs. Mauvers laughed her short mirthless laugh. "You will do nothing of the sort. You will go to sleep like a good little girl, and be very thankful little sister has been given something to cure her little pains and make her sleep so soundly. See, I'm leaving you the bottle. It won't hurt her."

The baby slept soundly, not waking until ten o'clock the next day.

When Hilda complained to her father in the field next day he cut short her story. "Do as you are told, Hilda," he said, "never mind what Mother used to do. Mrs. Mauvers knows her business. It would have been well for your mother if she had had as much sense about managing things."

There was something about Hilda's manner and the way she looked at him that annoyed him. Mrs. Mauvers was right about youngsters having too much notice taken of them.

Mr. Berry was ploughing down the weeds in the summerfallow and could see, as he worked, the long valley gleaming in the strong July sunshine. Away to the west stood the mountains, mistily blue, with their snowy summits glistening white. Luke Berry loved his farm and loved his work. The feel of the new furrow under his feet was comforting to him. He could not remember the time that he was not glad to be out in the fields at work. It was all he craved. And often of late years the fields had been his solace when increasing family cares had begun to embarrass him—so many children; the littered kitchen; his wife ailing, distracted, overworked. He was glad to get out of the house, and was driven back to it only by hunger.

Poor Annie, how soon she had faded and lost her good looks! He had been ashamed sometimes to find himself so glad to get away, especially when another baby was on the way, but he excused himself by thinking she had the telephone, and neighbors, and the doctor, too. Poor Annie, dragging around half dead, surely there should be some way . . . well, life was certainly hard on women. He would rather be dead than tied to a kitchen and a pack of kids; but, of course, women had always done it, and maybe they did not mind. Their brains were different from men's . . . but still it didn't seem right!

An oriole darted between the horses' heads and rose into the air with a burst of song and a flash of gold and red. Luke watched it, fascinated. That was the life, free as the air, going where he liked! That's what made birds so happy—they were free. But, he reflected, there are birds in cages that sing and live their lives contentedly because they know no better. There it is—men and women! And in that moment Luke was supremely happy in the sex allotted to him.

Life in the Berry household settled down into a dreary routine for Hilda and the other children. Mrs. Mauvers tolerated them only when they were doing something. Julie kept the lamps clean. Mary prepared all the vegetables. Hilda, in addition to the entire care of the baby, washed the dishes. There was no fun, no stories in the big kitchen now. An atmosphere of gloomy silence was on the children's spirits, noticed and commented upon by the neighbors.

"That black witch sure has put a spell on Luke when he can't see that she's starving his kids," said Bob Walters, the auctioneer, as he drove home with his brother Dan. "It was a tough sight to see Hilda sneakin' out to the granary with some grub for them the other day. They say she feeds him like a prince and lets the kids eat turnips, or anything they can rustle. I wonder some of the women don't go over and see him. Luke wouldn't like to hear what the neighbors are sayin' about him! No, I don't consider it's my business— it seems more like a woman's job. It's sort of small business for a man to be carryin' tales."

"If Grandma Brown were home," broke in Dan Walters, "she would be the one to tell Luke off, and the black one, too. The old lady's not tongue-tied. It's a damn shame, that's what it is! Luke seems sort of mesmerized. He buys the bread in town now, and sends the clothes to the laundry—and the other day I met him bringin' home a phonograph. If he had treated Annie that well he might have her still."

Hilda stoically performed her heavy share of the work, hoping against all appearances that she would be allowed to go to school when it opened. Rainbow Valley had only a summer school, beginning the first of July and continuing to the end of the year. She tried to introduce the matter to Mrs. Mauvers, but the deadline was hard to cross. Some people have an easy approach—a smiling, sunshiny path which leads straight into their soul. But not so Mrs. Mauvers. A moated grange, a dark tunnel, terrifying and mysterious, kept the world, at least the juvenile portion of it, at bay. When Hilda tried to approach her she found the sort of welcome a hungry traveller gets from an iron gate that is bolted and barred.

Sometimes Hilda almost hated the baby that had come to them so unwelcome, costing their mother's life, and now keeping her a prisoner night and day, shut off from every pleasure. It was going to burden her forever, it seemed, with no release in sight—for the years are long to a child, and without mercy. Why should she be tied to the baby forever? Her father cared nothing for it. Mrs. Mauvers had often said it would be a mercy if the little thing would follow its mother. And her mother had said that night that maybe it would die like the one before. And yet, when it cried, Hilda never failed to give it the best care her young hands could provide.

The morning of the Saturday before school started, Hilda had taken the baby in the little wagon that did service for a baby carriage over to the friendly straw-stack, where the children spent their happiest hours. Thither came Katrina Anderson, the daughter of their Swedish neighbor, bringing with her a dozen of her mother's sticky buns, still hot, and filled with butter that dripped lusciously from the paper bag. Hilda, with the little tin pail she had brought for the purpose, sought the cows under the shelter of a hill and milked the pail full, and quite a successful picnic was held on the side of the stack farthest from the house.

Old Jake, like the fine gentleman he was, did not press his claim on the buns, for he knew Hilda would seek the help of the cows to supplement his scanty rations, too, when the children had been fed. Miss Anderson, having provided the major portion of the meal, courteously refrained from the feast, though urged to do so, in order to leave more for the others. Miss Anderson did not for one moment let any-one think she was refraining for that reason. "Them buns!" cried she, "I eat so many of them buns to-day I scarce could see! No—thank you. I never wish I could see a bun again. My mother say, 'Katrina, you well should grow if you don't bust'."

When the meal was over Miss Anderson drew attention to her new dress, fearing that Hilda was not going to speak of it. "I don't like this old dress at all," she began. "We got it on the catalogue, and it ain't so good, but still for school it will do for hard scuffin'! It looked so good in picture Mamma says to Pa, 'Oh, let the kid have it—what's a few dollars?' And Pa says, in fun like, 'You wimmin make a poor man of me, with binder twine to buy, and the bottom gone from pigs, and bills for thresh, and all.' It don't look so awful good to me, maybe, like it did in catalogue. The girl there was taller, maybe." Miss Anderson twisted her bulky form critically, and looked as far around the back of her dress as nature would permit.

Hilda interposed politely. "It's just lovely, Katrina. The color and all suits you fine. You're not too stout; you're just a splendid straight-up-and-down figure."

Katrina, thoroughly appeased, passed on to the next order of business. "A new teacher's comin' to our school, oh, swell! Her father is a wealthy blacksmith, and she is no need to teach one little bit, but just she likes. Mamma says we'll let her see Rainbow Valley is not so worse, and have her out for visit at our place, with spare ribs and cardimum bread. Has your black lady got your clothes for school? Gee! I bet she'll hate to mind the baby. She never washed a stitch yet, has she? But say, your pa sure is sweet on her, ain't it? I guess it will be soon a weddin', and your poor ma not already dead so long. But they might as well get married as live in sin! Ain't it the truth?"

"What's that?" Hilda asked, flushing under her coat of tan.

"Oh, I'da know; that's what they say!" Katrina threw out her hands with a fine gesture, disclaiming all responsibility.

"I don't believe it," said Hilda, loyally. "My dad is a good man. See how kind he is to his horses." She remembered her mother's appraisal of him.

"Well, anyways," said Katrina, "you ought be gettin' on with school. Comes a few years and you will be big girl in grades and should be in High. Here is our Rosie now going to City to Normal her second this winter."

"What's that?" Hilda asked. Here was another mystery.

"I'da know," Katrina confessed; "only it's done in cities, and it's not everyone as can, and our Rosie is one of them. But Ma says it's rotten shame for you to be tied to a kid all your life, and maybe this one ain't never goin' to be strong, perhaps."

"She's a good kid," Hilda exclaimed hotly; "takes her bottles, and sleeps, and everything. She is not big, but that's nothing."

Katrina drew near, and her voice breathed secrecy. "Hilda, say, I'll cross my heart and spit on a stone never to tell—does she give the kid dope every night so it will sleep and not be disturbin' them. They say she does, Hilda."

"Certainly not!" Hilda replied warmly. "People shouldn't say such things. I mind the baby, and she has nothing to do with it."

"Well, anyways, Ma says dope like that makes kids' heads big to swell, and when they grow up maybe they try to walk—like this—and they goes over." Katrina showed how easily it could happen, even with a child that had never been given the offending medicine, by nearly falling on the sleeping infant in the wagon. Restored to her feet by Hilda, she resumed: "Ma says it would be pretty bad for you, and would make you feel mean, if you found, after all your troubles, you had raised a crazy kid. But I must go. I just came to tell you about the teacher and how well she is. She is going to make a fine concert, all so 'stelig,' for Christmas. Maybe I'll sing—Oh, I'd be too scared." Miss Anderson held herself rigid in a trance of nervous but delicious anticipation. "I just wish I could make a sing like you, Hilda. Then my mamma would buy me the best dress on catalogue, I guess, maybe. Goodbye, Hilda."

From a considerable distance on her homeward way Katrina shouted back, "Ain't it grand your pa is gettin' a car on the City! Yaw, sure! Didn't you know, I'll bet you did.

Gee, don't it seem queer? Your poor ma never got nothings like this. Wouldn't she be sore if she knew? I guess she don't, though. And what she don't now won't hurt her! Come over again soon—I can't go to your house no more!"

Hilda, disconsolate, drew the little wagon home, the other children choosing to remain. There was no inducement for them to go home, and the straw-stack was on the way to Mrs. Peters'. Katrina's words had found a lodgement in Hilda's heart, and the approaching opening of the school in the Valley was agitating her. She determined to make a bold venture and ask her father. She would put her fortunes to the test.

When she entered the kitchen with the baby in her arms and began to prepare a bottle for the needs of her young sister, she could hear the murmur of voices in the dining-room. Mrs. Mauvers' voice was falling soft as goosedown.

Mr. Berry had evidently asked where the children were.

"I gave them their lunch as usual, a good wholesome lunch, and I expect they are gone for the day. They quite enjoy their jolly little picnics, and Hilda has gone with them. I am just a little afraid she meets that rather awful Katrina when she is out. She came here once, quite boldly, to the door, and asked for Hilda, and told me her mother was going to come to see me. Fancy! I told her I was quite busy, and not at all lonely; and I don't think Katrina will come again. I think it is much better for us to keep Hilda quite by herself."

Hilda waited breathlessly for the reply.

"What's wrong with Katrina?" her father asked carelessly.

"Oh, Mr. Berry, what a question! She is a frightfully common little girl, with a sensual mouth, unusually large ears, indicating morbid curiosity—a frightfully common child."

Mr. Berry laughed, and Hilda could tell his mouth was full.

"The kid has to have some company, you know; minding a baby night and day must get pretty tiresome," he said. "Anyway, my wife never objected to Katrina. She and Hilda have always been friends." Mrs. Mauvers sighed meaningly. "Children in this country are given great liberty, I see. Indeed, it seems there is no discipline at all. I am trying my best to bring order to your household; but, of course, if I cannot have your support I cannot go on. The father's word must be law. He is master in his own house." Her voice trailed away into a minor key.

Mrs. Mauvers had chosen the moment well. Luke Berry had just tasted his generous slice of custard pie. "Oh, I'm not interfering," he said hastily; "I think you are doing all right. You are certainly a good cook, and you seem to manage the children easier than Mrs. Berry did. It seemed her work was never done."

"Some women are poor managers; she probably lacked system." Mrs. Mauvers began, stopping in amazement as Hilda burst into the room with hot words on her tongue.

"My mother's work was never done because she did her work!" Hilda cried impulsively. "She took care of her children. She did not turn them out and let them rove about like lost turkeys. This woman, Dad, does nothing but get the meals and keep the house looking tidy . . . all to please you! Everything is done for one purpose, to stand well with you."

"Hilda!" commanded Mrs. Mauvers, rising to her feet, "leave the room at once!"

Hilda did not hear her. She was addressing her father. "She never touches the baby; I mind it, and wash for it. And you would let her criticize mother! Mother never bought her bread nor sent out her washing. Mother did everything—and now—and now—"

Luke Berry looked on helplessly. "Hold your tongue, Hilda," he said, "that's no way for you to talk. Mrs. Mauvers is doing very well."

Mrs. Mauvers left the table and with handkerchief to her eyes sought the window, sniffling convulsively. She had been mending a strap belonging to the single harness, and had left it on the sewing-machine. She took it in her hand now.

"Look what you've done, Hilda," her father said meekly. Darn it all! How he hated getting mixed up in women's quarrels!

"Let her sniff!" cried Hilda. "But she's not going to criticize my mother, I can tell you, nor you either."

"Hilda! Hilda, have you forgotten that you are speaking to your father?" Mrs. Mauvers cried dramatically, coming back to the table. Then she turned to Luke. "Are you going to allow a chit of a girl to insult me," she cried tearfully, "when I am doing my best to make a home for you? If I had spoken to my father like that he would have beaten me to death, but he was a man of authority, respected by all. He demanded respect from us. If Hilda were my child I know what I would do."

Hilda paid no attention to her. "Dad, are you going to marry her? Katrina says you are, and that you're getting a car. Mother worked herself to death and got nothing. She never had anything!"

Whereupon Mrs. Mauvers began to scream, and in the excitement Luke Berry, with quite a show of temper, shook Hilda, though not roughly, and told her to go to her room until she learned to curb her tongue.

Hilda wriggled out of his grasp and faced him. "We might as well have it out, Dad, while we are at it," said she. "If I go to my room who'll mind the baby? I couldn't leave her with Mrs. Mauvers. She'll give it dope to make it sleep, and that is very bad for babies, Mrs. Peters says . . ."

"I will not stay to be insulted," interrupted Mrs. Mauvers, in her regal manner. "Hilda has been listening to evil gossip. I told you, Mr. Berry, I told you! Now it's for you to say. I am going—I will not stay to be insulted." She gave the impression of leaving the room, of sweeping majestically from the place where she had been so cruelly maligned, but managed to remain near enough to hear and see.

The baby began to cry, roused by the uproar, and that sound, always distasteful to Luke Berry, reminded him of the discomfort and disorder of his life—the dismal home-comings, the broken nights. Fiercely, now, unreasonably, his anger blazed against Hilda. He never knew how he found the harness strap in his hand. "You'd talk to me like that, would you?" he shouted. "I'll teach you who's boss in this house. Just when we've got someone who can run things you'd make a row, would you?"

She was a slim little wisp of a girl, and she did not resist his fury. She remembered her mother's words and threw them at him defiantly. "You can't do more than kill me, Dad," she said.

Cruelly, cruelly the strap bit into Hilda's tender flesh. But even in her pain and rage she did not forget her little charge. They made a picture of misery as they went up the stairs.

"She has been getting quite beyond herself," Mrs. Mauvers said, as the door closed above, "and has been very rude to me several times, but I did not wish to be a tale-bearer. I had hoped to win her over. Now, come and finish your pie, Mr. Berry, and try not to be upset. One must maintain discipline." There was a gleam of triumph in her cold eyes, but her voice was of honeyed sweetness.

To this Luke Berry made no reply. Pulling his hat down, he left the house.

For once Luke Berry got no comfort from the sunshine and the mountains and the feel for the kind old earth. Hilda's eyes, so like her mother's but for the gleam of defiance, smote him with a vague fear. There was something back of it all, something he could not understand.

Luke Berry was not given to analysis of his thoughts, but he was dimly conscious now that Hilda had a weight of woe on her heart, and that her outburst of rage indicated a long smouldering. "Poor little kid," he said, "I am sorry I struck her. I wish I had talked to her quietly; but I couldn't with that woman there. Damn her and her father! Who cares about either of them? I wonder where that strap came from?"

Looking across the creek to his house, Luke was struck by the deserted appearance it bore. Not a child to be seen about the place, not a movement of life. He wondered where the children were. He so rarely saw them now. It was all very fine to have his meals in peace, but these children were his—he had some responsibility. This woman was overdoing the thing.

At five o'clock Mr. Berry unhitched his team and went home. It looked like rain. It had been a miserable afternoon. He even jerked his horses and yelled at them, thinking grimly, even while he was doing it, that he had fired men for doing the same thing.

No, Mrs. Mauvers had not seen the children since morning, but they often stayed away all day. There was no cause for alarm—their stomachs would bring them home. She had given them a "basket."

"What about Hilda? Has she come down?" he asked anxiously.

"No," Mrs. Mauvers replied; "I thought it well to leave her alone until she professed sorrow for her rudeness."

Luke Berry, more uncomfortable than he liked to confess, made the rounds of the neighborhood, and in answer to his inquiries learned that his children had come to Mrs. Peters, at three o'clock, been fed, and had left about four. The youngest one, Marion, who was not feeling very well, had been put to bed after Mrs. Peters had administered medical treatment, and was now asleep. But Julie, Edith, and Mary had gone home, she thought.

"They don't seem to be very welcome at home any more, Luke," said Mrs. Peters, "so you can't blame the little things for wandering. Your housekeeper wants them to keep out of your sight. What's wrong with a man when he can't bear the sight of his own children?"

"I didn't know it until to-day, Mrs. Peters," Luke stammered humbly. "I don't want my children fed by the neighbors. I didn't know this was going on, but I thank you for doing it—you know that."

"I would do more than that for Annie's children," Mrs. Peters said, gravely. "I would have been over often, Luke, but that duchess of a housekeeper of yours gave me to understand I wasn't wanted; and as you knew where to find me I didn't like to butt in. I wasn't sure how things were. Hilda is so loyal to you she won't say a word."

"You're always welcome, Mrs. Peters," he said, and hurried away.

A drizzling rain began to fall, and the gray night was closing in early. It was quite dark when Luke found the children. The barking of the dog guided him to the spot. They were asleep in one of the pigs' holes in the straw-stack, solemnly guarded by Jake. In Julie's grubby hand was a half-eaten turnip.

Luke Berry was a plain man, of few emotions, but the sight of his three little girls, ragged, barefooted, and dirty, sleeping in a straw-stack where pigs had burrowed, guarded by the dog, more faithful and tender than he had been himself, stirred him to a great repentance.

The physical needs of his children, their clothing, food, and shelter, were something definite and plain. He understood and acknowledged his duty there. Starved mentally and spiritually they might be, and he would feel no pang of conscience; but this—this was a deep and bitter disgrace. He had been shamed, too, in the eyes of his neighbors. Awakening the children tenderly, and with many a kind word, he brought them home.

Mrs. Mauvers, serene and smiling, gave them all a very friendly greeting. "And did you have a lovely day, children?" she said. "Your papa was quite worried about you, but I knew you would be safe." Then, quite as an afterthought, "But where is dear little Marion?"

Luke explained briefly. "Set places for the girls, Mrs. Mauvers, after you have washed them," he said. "The girls will eat with me after this. And will you please call Hilda and ask her if she will come down."

Mrs. Mauvers' face darkened. "Oh, she has been down," she said. "She is in much the same mood, and was quite impertinent with me again. She took up a fresh bottle for the baby. I think it very unwise to disturb them."

When the meal was over and the children had gone to bed Luke Berry went at once to his room, where he stood for a long time looking out into the drizzling night. Every shred of self-esteem had been stripped away from him. His mouth was filled with gravel of remorse. What a selfish brute he had been to these poor little children! What must Hilda think of him? Faithful, hard-working little Hilda! He tried to think of how old she was, and was ashamed to find he did not know . . . Well, he would make amends. Hilda must go to school. He would get Mrs. Peters to take the baby until she was a year old, anyway. Mrs. Mauvers would have to go—he could no longer bear the sight of her. Poor Hilda! She had never had the freedom a child should have. But he would make it all up with her to-morrow.

To-morrow! A whole eternity can lie between to-day and to-morrow.

The dawn was graying the window in Hilda's room when she awakened the next morning, and for one thrilling moment she forgot all the trouble of the day before that had torn her heart with rage and pain; forgot that she and her father had quarrelled, and that he had definitely decided against her; forgot everything in a delicious dream, the glamor of which was still upon her.

In the dream she was getting ready for school. A new dress, shoes, and coat were lying on her bed—brown shoes, smelling deliciously; a lovely dress, nicer than Katrina's—blue, with touches of red—and a leather school-bag. Then with waking came remembrance! The sting of her sore shoulders brought it all back with a choke of tears—the quarrel—her father's rage and heavy blows—Katrina's words, "Crazy kid, even after all your trouble, not able to walk!"

"Don't be too patient, Hilda; it's no good," came back her mother's words. "Don't give in. Always remember what I am saying" . . . and she had been doing it all summer, and she could go on and on! . . . "Too old for grades. Should be in High." The days were going. All the children were getting ready for school, not one of them shackled and tied. It was not fair. There was no one to help her.

Thoughts of God came to her, sitting on His throne, watching her, maybe. Not He! What did He care? Did He care for her mother? She had been patient and loving, and had trusted Him. What did she get? A grave of yellow clay! Her children neglected, hungry, fed by the neighbors. That woman downstairs, the black-hearted devil, in her place. She would have a car to ride in, be praised and admired, for she took time to keep herself nicely dressed. She had no baby to tire her out! Hilda hated her in that hour with a murderous hate.

The first glow of dawn was shining in the window, making a luminous patch on the wall. It caught the small bottle of sleeping medicine that had stood untouched on the stand since the first night. Hilda sat up in bed and watched it, fascinated. She could not withdraw her eyes from it.

A horrible thought! Hilda caught her breath with a sob—no, no that would be wicked! But the thought persisted. Then she would have time to mind the other four. She couldn't mind the five. She could take them all to school with her if she hadn't the baby. It wouldn't be wrong—just a long sleep, with no pain, no struggle. Her mother had hoped that night that it would die . . . Her mother wouldn't blame her. No one else mattered. Her mother would know there was no other way . . . no one to help her.

Terrible thoughts for a child—black and bitter thoughts; but this was a child with a woman's burden and only the heart of a child to bear it.

Hilda got out of bed just as a yellow wave of sunlight smote the wall above the stand. The floor creaked under her feet like the breaking of timbers. The potent liquid in the bottle glowed like topaz. She poured out a brimming teaspoonful, so full she could not raise her eyes from it. As she carried it toward the bed, the baby began to stir uneasily, beating the air with her little hands. It was hard to carry the spoon steadily, her heart was beating so.

Though her eyes were on the liquid in the spoon, Hilda knew the door was slowly opening. Through the gloom of the room something low and bulky was coming toward her with a slow motion. She stopped, trembling, cold with fear. It was coming nearer . . . nearer. The spoon fell with a clang on the bare floor. The moving bulk took shape—blessed, familiar shape—as Jake's cold nose was shoved caressingly into her hand.

Here was someone, warm, loving, real, who had come to her when her soul was crumbling under its burden of woe. Jake, who knew the best of her—Jake, the deliverer! She fell on her knees beside him, and, burying her face in his soft fur, burst into a passion of weeping.

"Oh, Jake! Oh, Jake!" she sobbed, not caring who heard her, "you saved me! Oh! I was going to . . . oh, no . . . I wouldn't! I forgot, but you didn't. You didn't forget what mother asked you to do . . . 'A little girl and a dog,' she said. Good dog, Jake! How did you know? Who sent you? Was it God? Oh, I hope it was God! I hope He cares about us! I want to have God again! It's hard to do without God, Jake. But how did you know? How did you get in? But you came to me . . . you came . . . in time." She took the dog's face in her hands and searched his eyes for an explanation, asking him again and again how he knew to come. But all she could read in their amber depths was a love, unquestioning, unfathomable—a love so deep that it went far beyond the limitations of a dumb brute's intelligence—a love so perfect and unselfish that it could easily become a channel for the love of God.

The baby was waking happily on the bed, gurgling softly to herself. Hilda took her in her arms and rained kisses on the little face, while her own tears flowed freely, bringing marvellous relief to her burdened heart.

"My baby! Hilda's little precious pet! Hilda wouldn't hurt the little darling! Isn't she sweet, Jakie? Crazy kid, indeed! She's the best baby we ever had. And we'll never leave her, will we, Jakie?"

In enthusiastic assent Jake wagged his tail, brushing the brown bottle to the floor, where the contents oozed harmlessly away.

Hilda washed her face and brushed her hair carefully at the stand. The pain in her shoulders was gone, and her heart was strangely light. Looking at herself in the glass, she saw a face illumined, rested, glad. The events of the day before seemed trifles to her now, things that could be as easily forgotten as a dream.

The rain of the night had ceased at dawn. A bright sun was flinging fingers of flame into the sky. Hilda's room faced north, but the whole sky was glowing with the promise of a new day; and the last trace of the rain, a thick plank of a cloud, lying low in the sky, had a piping of rose on its eastern edge.

Hilda dressed herself with particular care. There was plenty of time; no one was stirring. The baby was now sleeping soundly again, her regular breathing making the sweetest music Hilda's ears had ever heard.

It was clear to Hilda now. God had not been able to send her mother back, but He hadn't forgotten her. When her sorrows were about to go over her head He had spoken to her the only way He could. He had cared for her soul; He had not left her. He had not let her . . . oh, no, no, she couldn't say it! No one would ever know. God had done a greater thing than sending back to earth again a tired woman to work and suffer. He had saved a soul from sin, and He would help her now with her father . . . "Luke is not a hard man—see how good he is to his horses." She had misunderstood God, but now she knew. It is "souls" He cared for. He couldn't keep the strap from cutting into her shoulders, but He had healed the hurt of it now by flooding her soul with light. There was no more hate in her heart. Behind her, around her, was a new presence, a comfort, a strength, and understanding.

She would tell her father; she would make him understand. She felt it would be easy to make him understand, for it was all so clear to her.

The sun from the eastern window was flooding the kitchen when Hilda went downstairs. Her father was waiting for her with new words on his tongue. He had thought of what he would say, but when he saw her radiant face his words deserted him. He didn't need them. He just held out his arms.

"Carried Forward" was published in *All We Like Sheep, and Other Stories* (Toronto: Thomas Allen, 1926), 184–234.

THE GRIM FACT OF SISTERHOOD

W/hen Mrs. E. P. Smith, late of Prince Edward Island, came to live in Northern Alberta, in a "foreign" community, she was horrified to discover that her neighbors did not wash on Monday! She was still more horrified to find that they were not particular whether they washed at all or not, and had a way of hanging out their dirty clothes on the barb-wire fences which enclosed their houses, letting the rain and the sun go as far as they liked with them.

When Mrs. E. P. Smith realized that this was their way of washing—their substitute for soap and water—her contempt for such shiftlessness was unbounded. She wrote home about it.

There were still further discoveries for Mrs. Smith. When the teacher, who was also from "The Island," came over to have tea with her, she told her that in many of the houses, hens roosted on the foot of the bed and the pig came in at meal time to file his claim of the left-overs.

Mrs. Smith wanted her husband to sell out at once, and go back to Charlottetown, but he was doing too big a cash business to contemplate selling out, and he thought with a shudder of the dribbling and anaemic trade which Charlottetown had given him in the five years he had endeavored to supply them with "General Merchandise at Lowest Prices consistent with Best Quality."

"Go out and show them how to keep house!" he said to his wife. "You are tidy enough for four or five women, and know enough about housekeeping to run the whole town."

"Oh, won't you come!" cried the teacher eagerly, "I am trying to organize a mother's class on Saturday, and I do need help so badly."

Mrs. Smith refused, with spirit.

"Indeed I will not," she said, "I intend to have nothing to do with these women. If I must live here, I will live here, but I shall keep to myself. It is impossible to teach these people—they are too dirty—too ignorant—too foreign, and I do not intend to go near them!"

Mrs. Smith was a woman of strong personality. Everyone felt it. The Ruthenian women felt it when they came to the store and saw her, on the rare occasions when she was there. They looked wistfully at her well-groomed figure, and well-dressed hair. To them she looked like a beautiful but unfriendly goddess. Unfriendly she certainly was, and intended to remain, for she said, "I will begin with them as I intend to end. I want nothing to do with them. We are here to make money and get away as soon as possible to a civilized place."

Twice a year she went to Edmonton, and spent a week at one of the hotels, she and Aileen, her eight-year-old daughter, and when they returned, with their city-cut clothes, the curiosity of the little village ran high. But Aileen, like her mother, kept aloof from the Ruthenian children, and resented their friendly advances. When little Rosie Lelge, braver than the others, reached out one grimy little hand to smooth Aileen's gray squirrel muff, Aileen drew back in pained surprise, and pierced the offending Rosie with a haughty glance.

Little Rosie's mother was present when this happened, and the incident sank into her heart, although her weather-beaten face lost none of its stolidity; but when she arrived at the teacher's house on Saturday afternoon for the lesson on breadmaking, and delivered her ultimatum, it was evident that she had been deeply stirred.

"Teacher," she said, "you good—you nice—you learn us things, but Mrs. Smith—at big house—she not like us—bah! she think we just—dirt—I not come back—I like old way best—I not learn Canadian—Canadian—not like us—we not like them."

It was in vain that the teacher protested. Rosie's mother was a leader in the village, and when she voted to strike, the others followed.

The teacher, in despair, appealed again to Mrs. Smith.

"They feel it—that you do not like them," she told her. "They are sensitive and easily hurt, and now they won't learn Canadian ways, and I was getting along so well. Mrs. Bowkski had done one washing our way, and had stopped giving her baby coffee, and now she will go back to her old ways, unless you come out to our meetings and be friendly with them. Don't you see how much depends on you?"

Mrs. Smith held firm. "It is a physical impossibility, Miss Taylor," she said coldly. "I never could go near people unless they were clean and nice. Perhaps you do not understand it, but all my family are just the same, and Aileen is like me exactly. I simply can't—do it—and if these women are hurt, I am sorry, but I cannot help it. They will have to be hurt, and that is all there is to it. I am simply putting in time here."

"But, Mrs. Smith"—the teacher had grown bolder—"don't you see what an opportunity you have? You could do so much for them, and you are doing nothing, or worse."

"Why should I do anything?" Mrs. Smith asked in surprise. "I keep my own house, and my own little girl. I look after my own affairs. Why should I be expected to do more?"

Miss Taylor got up to leave. Argument did not come naturally to her.

"Mrs. Smith, there is no such thing in life as 'our own affairs.' It is a false phrase. What concerns one, concerns all. I can't argue, but I know you are making a terrible mistake. You are keeping back the progress of these women, and we will all suffer for it, someway. There is a law which cannot be broken by any one: the Bible speaks of it."

"Now don't begin to preach," cried Mrs. Smith, "for I can't bear preachy people. I simply will not be preached to. I will live my own life, as I see it."

Miss Taylor left the school soon after that, for in spite of all her efforts, she failed to get the women to come to her Saturday classes, and she went into another district, where her work was unhindered.

The new teacher did not concern herself about the home life of her pupils, but spent her time in fancy work and other ladylike pursuits. She and Mrs. Smith were very congenial.

In October of that year, scarlet fever broke out in this community. The first case was in Mrs. Bowkski's family. When the doctor was hastily summoned, and pronounced it scarlet fever, he said to Mr. Smith that he often wondered that there were not more of these "dirt diseases," for the manner of living, in this particular community, was so unsanitary! "It is a pity," he said, "that little Taylor girl did not stay here, for she seemed to be getting hold of the women, and teaching them something, but she suddenly quit and went over to Saskatchewan. I wonder what happened? Since then, they seem to be worse than ever! Better send your own little girl into the city. This is a bad form of the disease, and will spread. And in a few days the town may be under quarantine."

Mrs. Smith, who had come into the store, heard what the doctor said. She rushed home in a frenzy of fear. Scarlet Fever! Her heart was cold with dread. She had but one thought. Where was Aileen? She found her peacefully playing with her dolls in the nursery, calm and happy, but to the mother's fevered imagination, the child seemed heavy and flushed. Hastily she made preparations to leave the place which had become so hateful and so fraught with terror, but there was no train until the following day.

When she and Aileen stood on the platform waiting for the train, she found to her horror, that the quarantine had been placed on the little town, and no passengers could get on or off trains. Her indignation knew no bounds, and the whole Canadian Northern Railway System was brought under the withering breath of her displeasure; but the train moved quietly out, leaving her more angry than ever. There is a finality about the rear end of a departing train!

Then followed for her long, anxious days. The disease spread rapidly, and soon almost every house in the community was affected.

A public nurse was sent out by the Department, and the teacher was pressed into service. In vain they appealed to

Mrs. Smith to help. Terrified beyond control, she shut herself and Aileen away from any communication with any person. She urged her husband to close the store, but he refused to do anything so shortsighted and un-neighborly, but agreed to have his meals at the restaurant.

For three weeks the epidemic raged, but there were no deaths and at the end of that time, the nurse went back to the city. The day after she left, Aileen took it, and sank rapidly. Poisoned by fear as she was, she had no power of resistance. On the seventh day, she died.

Mrs. Smith has gone back to the Island, a very sad, and very bitter woman. She cannot see why her little girl should have been taken, when she was so careful to avoid contact with any of the people of the village.

She remembers sometimes what the teacher said about a Law which binds us all together, either for good or evil, and her heart rebels against it; but the Law remains, and it cannot be entreated or gainsaid, ignored, revoked or evaded, and there are no exemptions!

∽

"The Grim Fact of Sisterhood," publication information unknown, is taken from an undated typescript of the McClung Papers, vol. 24(3), located at the Provincial Archives of British Columbia.

O, CANADA!

Mr. Felix Martin opened the door and bade us enter. "You will have to take us as you find us," he said grandly. "We are rather rough and ready; but I told my wife when we came to Canada that she must adopt Canadian ways and forget the formality of Maida Vale."

It seemed to us that she had forgotten more than that, as we looked about us at the incredible confusion. The chairs were all full of garments, cooking utensils, and papers; but Mrs. Martin arose with the baby in her arms, and evicted a flock of children from an old couch that had been serving as a teeter. Mrs. Burton sat on the high arm and I found a place on the listing end of it. Between us stretched a no-man's land, where the cover was broken by an outcropping of iron springs, twisted and rusty, from which the stuffing oozed dustily.

"Yes," said Mr. Martin, pulling out a chair from under its miscellaneous load. "We are typical Canadians now and are glad to do our part in building up this great empire within the empire. We came here but seven short years ago and already five little olive branches have come to bless our union."

The evidence was there, eighty per cent of it, behind the stove watching us with bright eyes, gleaming under their tangled locks, and the remainder on Mrs. Martin's knee asleep.

"Five little olive branches," he said, indicating them proudly, with his yellow fingers outspread, "and I can say it to you, ladies, without offence, in my wife's presence, the gods are about to bless us again."

We knew it. We knew it when we got his letter at the Institute meeting asking us to come to see them.

Mrs. Burton, President of the Women's Institute, who had been sitting gingerly on the high end of the couch, now sat down heavily in her excitement, with the result that I was thrown upward, causing a slight interruption; but Mr. Martin's monologue went on.

STORIES SUBVERSIVE

"Five little native-born Canadians, steeped in British traditions, and loving the old flag . . . and another on its way to this land of opportunity . . . And now, ladies, I will tell you why I asked you to come . . . Your society has been helpful to us, and we are grateful. Gratitude has ever been one of the attributes of my family and in some degree an attitude of my wife's family."

We knew what was coming. We'd heard this before. Gratitude in Mr. Felix Martin's heart was a lively sense of favors yet to come.

"Our circumstances have changed somewhat since the last time we asked you for help, and you so kindly rendered it. Do you think, my dear Edith, you had better send the three eldest children out to play? They could have a happy time in the ladies' car."

"My car is locked," said Mrs. Burton quickly.

"No, no, we won't go. We want to stay. Let's stay," came from behind the stove.

"Very well, then, you must be very quiet and not interrupt papa and mamma.

"As I said, we are in different circumstances this time . . . happier circumstances."

"Not happier, Felix," corrected his wife gently. She was a faded little thing, with blue lips, and stringy, greasy hair, which I longed to wash in rain water and plenty of white castile soap.

"We cannot stay the hand of death," he said to her reproachfully. "We would not if we could."

"I am sure we are not wishing dear Auntie away . . . We will be very grieved when we hear she is gone. You know you will, Felix, too. You have said so."

He motioned for silence.

"My aunt is now an aged woman, and her end draws near . . . She has always promised that my brother and I shall be her heirs. She named me Felix, because her lover, who was drowned, bore that name. She is now nearing the shore . . . Yesterday a letter came, from my brother, which has changed our outlook on life."

He opened his coat, and produced a letter and read:

"Dear Felix: I have just come from Aunt Cynthia and think you should know that a change is coming. She talked rather strangely and does not seem quite herself. The curate goes to see her every day, and it seems like the end. She said she was sending you fifty pounds, and expressed a wish to see you and your five children. I hope everything is all right. I thought I had better write you.

Your loving brother, Cyril."

Mr. Martin replaced the letter and looked at us with a little gleam of triumph.

"I have not boasted of my expectations," he said modestly. "I deemed it best to walk among my companions here as one of them, a breadwinner and a worker, even as they are. But now I want you and your admirable members to know that your kindness will be repaid, every cent and more. You notice my dear aunt expressed a desire to see me and my family. That, of course, is impossible. But Mrs. Martin and I have decided that I should go. My dear auntie's dying wish is sacred. But how to leave Mrs. Martin, in her delicate state, is a matter that wrings my heart."

Mrs. Burton interrupted.

"Have you received the fifty pounds?"

"Not yet," he said just a trifle irritably, "but what is a paltry fifty pounds?"

"It's nearly two hundred and fifty dollars," she said, "and, if applied to your debts, would be very welcome to the people who have supplied you with meat and groceries and clothing for the past years. I should think that would be your first duty."

Mr. Martin drew himself up stiffly, but the President of the Institute refused to quail.

"All in good time," he said, "they will get their money . . . I will cable it to them."

"A bank draft is cheaper," I ventured.

"Enough of this," said Mr. Martin, feeling that the meeting was getting out of hand. "I called you in, ladies, to tell you our plans and ask for your endorsement.

"My duty is by my aunt's bedside! That is plain. But my wife and little ones. Let no one say I have not provided for them . . . I could have gone to other societies, but the Women's Institute is my choice: I have had some little experience with service clubs . . . Before little Tottie was born I asked one of the clubs here to help us. I attended one of their luncheons at considerable inconvenience to myself, and listened to their ghastly songs about gray mares and hard-boiled eggs . . . and they sent us books of bread and milk tickets; and to my wife an invitation to come to their clinic. But what we needed was ready cash . . . I was working for the city at that time, but at a miserable pittance. I was really in need. And when I went to another society here, which shall be nameless, the president told me to my face, it was a crime to bring children into the world like rabbits—those were her words!"

He lifted Winky on his knee and wiped her little sore nose with a piece of newspaper—"Bad lady to call my Winky a rabbit."

"What I want you to do for me now, for I am a direct man, and do not believe in beating about the bush . . . I want you to come with me to the bank and get me a loan sufficient for my needs on the journey. And then take Mrs. Martin and the children away from this depressing little house while certain repairs are being made. We made a plan of it last night. It is a good chance to get it done while I am away. I am anxious to be off, every day is precious . . . You helped me when we had nothing . . . So now when I can repay you handsomely I have chosen you from all the societies in this city! I am not the sort of man who would forget his friends."

Mrs. Martin smiled at us in turn, making a pretty little bow, a sweet little congratulatory smile. She was glad for our sakes.

"No bank will give you a loan," said Mrs. Burton, "Your aunt is not dead, and you have nothing to show that you have any money coming to you."

"I am amazed at you, Mrs. Burton," he said, "and you a banker's wife! Must I go over all this again? You don't understand . . . I am not a pauper to be spoken to this way."

Mrs. Martin dabbed her eyes with a very dirty handkerchief: "Don't chew the lady's handbag, Winky," she said wearily. "The color may run and poison you."

The tension was broken by the arrival of the postman who threw in a letter.

The children came at the sound and scrambled for it. The baby wakened and cried lumpily. Tottie darted under my feet to get the comforter, which Mrs. Martin licked and put in the baby's mouth. While this was in progress, Mr. Martin secured the letter from Winky.

Mrs. Burton and I rose to go.

"Stay," commanded Mr. Martin. "This letter may settle the matter and quiet every doubting voice. You shall know all."

He opened it with a flourish and began to read. His eyes grew wild with some emotion, and the letter shook in his hands. Then he sat down suddenly and moaned, and the baby, losing its comforter, joined its wails with his.

"My curses on her, perfidious woman," he hissed, "and on that damnable villain!"

"Felix, Felix! the children!" expostulated the wife, dancing the crying baby on her knee.

The letter had fallen to the floor at my feet. I handed it to Mrs. Martin, but she, busy with the baby, motioned me to read it. I read:

> "My Dear Nephew: You will be surprised to hear I have married the Curate, who has been so very kind to me in my recent illness. By a curious coincidence his name is Felix. Happiness has quite restored me and I know I shall live a very long time. But I am sending you fifty pounds

with my love. Tell darling Edith to send me a photo of those precious lambs.

Lovingly, Aunt Cynthia

P.S.—I will send you a clipping from the *Post* re wedding."

We took a hurried farewell of Mrs. Martin, a noisy farewell, for the comforter was lost again, and the four children were wildly searching, and seemed to think we were concealing it.

When we were at the door Mr. Martin raised his head and placed his hand on it as if in blessing. "I am not beaten," he said, tapping his head, "bloody, but unbowed. Mrs. Martin, I will provide for you—my marriage vows shall hold. I have a plan, my dear. These filthy tradesmen shall not see a penny of this money. Not a penny. My wife and babes come first. I will lay it on the races, I have always been lucky in horses. Darling, dry your eyes; trust me. We can do without their help. Tell the wretched banks to keep their loans. Tottie, come and kiss papa."

The family's fortunes were rising; the comforter had been found. It seemed a good time to withdraw.

~

"O, Canada!" was published in *Star Weekly* (9 May 1931), *Time and Tide: The [British] Review With Independent Views* XII (12 September 1931): 1059–1060, and *Flowers For the Living* (Toronto: Thomas Allen, 1931), 206–212.

The Canadian Short Story Library Series

The Canadian Short Story Library series undertakes to publish fiction of importance to a fuller appreciation of Canadian literary history and the developing Canadian tradition. Work by major writers that has fallen into obscurity is restored to canonical significance, and short stories by writers of lapsed renown are gathered in collections or appropriate anthologies.

John Moss
General Editor

Selected Stories of Robert Barr
Edited by John Parr

Selected Stories of Isabella Valancy Crawford
Edited by Penny Petrone

Selected Stories of Mazo de la Roche
Edited by Douglas Daymond

Selected Stories of Norman Duncan
Edited by John Coldwell Adams

Voyages: Short Narratives of Susanna Moodie
Edited by John Thurston

Short Stories by Thomas Murtha
Edited by William Murtha

Waken, Lords and Ladies Gay: Selected Stories of
Desmond Pacey
Edited by Frank M. Tierney

The Race and Other Stories by Sinclair Ross
Edited by Lorraine McMullen

Selected Stories of Duncan Campbell Scott
Edited by Glenn Clever

Selected Stories of Ernest Thompson Seton
Edited by Patricia Morley

The Lady and the Travelling Salesman:
Stories by Leo Simpson
Edited by Henry Imbleau

Many Mansions: Selected Stories of Douglas O. Spettigue
Edited by Leo Simpson

Selected Stories of E. W. Thomson
Edited by Lorraine McMullen

Forest and Other Gleanings: The Fugitive Writings of
Catharine Parr Traill
Edited by Michael A. Peterman and Carl Ballstadt

Pioneering Women: Short Stories by Canadian Women,
Beginnings to 1880
Edited by Lorraine McMullen and Sandra Campbell

Aspiring Women: Short Stories by Canadian Women,
1880–1900
Edited by Lorraine McMullen and Sandra Campbell

New Women: Short Stories by Canadian Women,
1900–1920
Edited by Sandra Campbell and Lorraine McMullen

The Quebec Anthology: 1830–1990
Edited by Matt Cohen and Wayne Grady

The paper used in this publication meets the minimum requirements
of American National Standard for Information Sciences –
Permanence of Paper for Printed Library Materials, ANSI Z39.48-1992.

Printed in November 1996 by

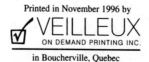

in Boucherville, Quebec